T0119673

DREAM LIVES OF
bUTTERFLIES
STORIES

DREAM LIVES OF
bUTTERFLIES
STORIES

JAIMEE WRISTON COLBERT

BkMk Press
University of Missouri-Kansas City

Copyright © 2007 by Jaimee Wriston Colbert

BkMk Press
University of Missouri-Kansas City
5101 Rockhill Road
Kansas City, Missouri 64110
(816) 235-2558 (voice)
(816) 235-2611 (fax)
www.umkc.edu/bkmk

This project is supported in part by an award from the National Endowment for the Arts. Financial assistance for this project has been provided by the Missouri Arts Council, a state agency.

NATIONAL ENDOWMENT FOR THE ARTS
A great nation deserves great art.

MAC
MISSOURI ARTS COUNCIL

Cover art & design: Mark A. Gatson
Interior book design: Susan L. Schurman
Managing Editor: Ben Furnish
Author photo: Marisa Wriston

BkMk Press wishes to thank Teresa Collins, Emily Iorg, Chelsea Seguin, Sandra Meyer. Special thanks to Karen I. Johnson

Library of Congress Cataloging-in-Publication Data

Colbert, Jaimee Wriston,
    Dream lives of butterflies / Jaimee Wriston Colbert.
        p. cm.
    Summary: "21 linked short stories set in 20th and 21st century St. Louis, Missouri, Hawai'i, and Illinois. Characters include a lepidopterist and her mother with dementia; a pregnant teenager; a bipolar man and the homeless, aspiring model he shelters; a middle-aged woman stalking her estranged husband responding to Jesus; and an agoraphobic Hawai'ian psychic searching for her drug-addicted son"--Provided by publisher.
        ISBN 978-1-886157-59-0 (pbk. : alk. paper) 1. United States--Social life and customs--20th century--Fiction. 2. United States--Social life and customs--21st century--Fiction. I. Title.

    PS3553.04384D74 2007
    813'.54--dc22

                                                    2007029458

In memory of my brother
Arthur James Wriston III (Jimmy)
1955-2004

Acknowledgments

The author wishes to thank Shawn Shiflett and Mary Troy for manuscript reading and consultation; Mary Troy and the MFA Program at the University of Missouri-St. Louis for support and inspiration, and Randy Albers and the Fiction Writing Department at Columbia College Chicago for support and friendship during the initial writing of this book. For writerly encouragement and advice: Joy Passanante, Jack Driscoll, Cathy Hardy, Mike Steinberg, Wesley Brown, Shawn Shiflett and Cheryl Drake Harris, and to Madison Smartt Bell for his ongoing generosity. For their wonderful endorsements: Kim Barnes, Diana Abu-Jaber, Madison Smartt Bell and Jack Driscoll. With special thanks to my colleagues at Binghamton University for their unremitting support, and to my family, always. I also want to thank BkMk Press for believing in this book and for being such fantastic people to work with!

These stories from *Dream Lives of Butterflies* have appeared in the following journals (in order of appearance):

"Girl Dreaming" (latest version) *The Boston Fiction Annual Review*; selected for the Boston Fiction Festival.

"Just Watching For Jesus" *Green Mountains Review*, Vol. XVIII

"The Manager's Son" *Prairie Schooner*.

"Dream Lives of Butterflies" *Louisiana Literature*.

"And Another Thing" *Connecticut Review*.

"Fly Me To The Moon" *Natural Bridge*.

"Haole Girl" *F Magazine* and *Harpur Palate*

"Pablo, Pickles, A Song For The Prairie" (as "Song For The Prairie") *Natural Bridge*.

"Girl Dreaming" (as "Bug Dreaming" earlier version) *Incliner,* Tenth Anniversary Issue.

"If Lucy Ran" *Long Shot*, Tenth Anniversary Issue.

DREAM LIVES OF
bUTTERFLIES
STORIES

PART ONE: GIRL, DREAMING

PART TWO: AND THE RICH GET RICHER, AND THE POOR HAVE CHILDREN

PART THREE: METAMORPHOSE

PART ONE: GIRL, DREAMING

"One morning I'll leave home and never find my way back—
My story and I will disappear together, just like this."
                                    —Charles Wright, *Appalachia*

PROLOGUE

Where it begins is when I first see him, God, coming back to me most often now in the memory of a scent, my father's Sunday hair cream, fine and sweet as the tropical breeze, as a hummingbird's tongue. My own marriage will not give me this contentment, the comfort of a routine fragrance. And is it God behind the altar, white light steaming through like the pathway to heaven itself, not some hollow, hot church in the heart of Honolulu? Is it he who stands there, tall as, well, God, face a craggy mountain, fluid and brown as a mud slide, eyes are light itself? God behind the altar, *Love Never Faileth* inscribed in bold, dark letters. I am still too young to understand, to have learned, that this isn't necessarily true. Love does fail. Fragile as bone it can break; bendable as rubber you can twist it this way, that way, into something barely resembling its original shape; and like the disappearing ink in those detective novels my father was so fond of, love really can just fade away. If you're not careful. If you let it. Or even if you don't. But here, in the memory of my church, he is God, and not to be questioned.

I am Caroline, pronounced *line* as in *mine*, not *in*. Eventually I become Carol, just Carol, like the songs. When I first see him

I am a child still, born in the brown and gold hills of California, growing up on the blue-green island of O'ahu. I see the world in its colors then. I have good eyes and a voice like a songbird, I'm told. Feathers in it, curls and lilts of elation. My voice is my asset, I must use my assets I'm told. As many of us girls are, the shoulders then the heels of World War II (my father, a U.S. Marines captain, fought in this war and lived to tell about it, though he wouldn't—is this where my habit of silence begins?), I am being molded for my future as a wife to someone who will provide for me, mother of his children. By then I will have mostly lost my voice, but I can't know this yet either. He will be my prince, my savior, my ever-handsome, correctly featured Ken doll—which is not from my own childhood but moving now into our daughters'. One will play with Ken and Barbie. The other favors a microscope. One will love me because I'm there, the other will never forgive her father when he isn't. *Love can faileth.*

But I don't know these things as a child, and I grumble when I'm made to iron my own father's handkerchiefs as part of this training, steamy-glowing Hawai'ian morning, air thick, as luscious, as yellow as yolk; my mother in her pink checkered housedress, its full sweep of skirt, her voice a winch, a vice, reaming out the multiplication tables at me: 12 times 12 is...? Who knows what she might rather have been doing? Who knows if *she* knew what she'd rather be doing? Later I am soothed in my failures at math, my mother telling me in the end I won't need algebra when I find this provider, this *king*. I am before the calculator.

After I see God behind the altar of the church, things start to become different. Years later when the stories you are about to hear unfold, another mother tells another daughter she won't need algebra. How do I know this? God? A dream? Such are the echoing of our stories. How many choices do we have?

Here is what happens: It is 1950, it is Hawai'i, I am twenty. It is night, moon white and stars grainy, the blackness of infinity. Though even stars, I have learned, like stories, must someday end. Even stars fail. I am with a girlfriend and two boys, all of us college age though these boys were not students. Where did we meet them? Memory fails, but these weren't the kind of boys you bring home to your parents, they were the ones you snuck out with, their arms wrapped casually, possessively (you wanted to imagine) about your shoulders. You breathed in their scents so gratefully, these strange and unpredictable *princes*, smoke on their breaths, their washed, white shirts, cigarette packs rolled into the sleeves of these shirts, ball-like muscles pronounced and proud. You felt proud. It is you, after all, daring to be part of the shadows they make, as if these could be yours, your own making, boys of the radio songs, the ones always breaking someone else's heart.

Makapu'u Beach. I learned to bodysurf there. I learned how to be a child there and then, briefly, to be GOD.

Waves pounding and roiling and whistling up onto the sand, smell of the night, deep and poignant, a tang of sour. We are drinking something the boys brought, tart with a hard, slow burn, makes me want to do things, be someone I haven't been; makes me feel desperate and nervy, warm and cold all at once. I feel a part of this blue-green world in a way I have never felt before, its blood, its tissue, the bones of its land, what it needs to thump and beat, to breathe, be alive. Could this be GOD?

We take off our clothes, which is something I haven't done in front of a boy, under-the-bra gropings in their cars, suffocating wet kisses…, but GOD comes naked to the water, GOD is the body, moving into this sea that is HIS creation. Warm, small waves become silky, dark arms beckoning, sky a steep, black lake above us. It is then that I feel the loss of something, though I'm not sure what, pushing me under, holding me down. Inside the heart of the ocean is like salt jelly, cool and squiggly, and one of the boys moves between my legs where only GOD should be allowed, but if I *am* GOD how can this make a difference? Something hot opens up in me, volcano erupting, rips between my legs like a sword plunging up from inside this ocean, primal beginnings. It's the oldest of songs, ancient as the shark, that perfect beast, rising out of the waves, hurtling ever upward.

1998

HAOLE GIRL BLUE

I'm a white girl, *haole girl* they call me in my neighborhood. It's not like it's a choice. If I were given a choice about this I'd look like my best friend Nalani, who's half Hawai'ian. This means she's got more rights to Hawai'i than me, Nalani says, when she's mad at me. Which isn't so much. Like I said, we're best friends. Nalani's skin is the stripy tan of buttered toast.

We live in Punalu'u, Hawai'i, where the air is pink and wet, and the mynah birds chatter up such a storm every morning, crack of dawn, you think you'd get *lōlō* from lack of sleep. *Lōlō* means stupid, which I am not. A little slow sometimes, my mama says—But you'll get married, and then you won't need algebra ever again, she says.

My mama's hope is that I'm married before she dies. She wants to know I'll have someone in this world besides her, she says, so then she can rest in peace. Not that marriage is the *be-all-and-end-all*, she reminds me; only if it's to the right guy. The right guy, Mama says, is the one who stays.

She says it could be anytime, her dying, but she's been telling me this about as long as I've known her, which is all of my life of course. She's got this disease called Marfan's, where she's really long and skinny in her fingers and toes, and her heart's too fragile, her doctor says, to pump to all that needs pumping. Abraham Lincoln had it, but he didn't die from it. She's got arthritis in her hands, fingers twisty and gnarly as twigs, and she wears five copper bracelets that jangle when she moves. It's what the Egyptians did, she told me, wore copper for arthritis. My mama knows things like this because she reads. Reads, reads, reads, all of the time. It's about all there is left for her to do, she says.

Me, I'd rather paint, and not houses like Mama thinks when I tell her this. I just can't understand a thing like algebra, and I don't see much use for it either, I tell her. I can't get *vested* (that's a Mama-reading word, so sometimes if I ream these words back at her she's impressed enough to actually listen) in what X equals, or what Y equals, or whether, in fact (that's my algebra teacher, Mr. Soto's way of talking), X equals Y. I mean, who cares? It's not like they're even real. No Ys strutting their stuff in low-slung pants, no Xs in short dresses, some unspeakable need to be part of Y.

I tell Mama I just want to paint walls, and she reminds me we're living in Uncle Ray's house, who's only an uncle by *someone else's marriage*. It's not even our house, she says, Why on earth would you paint it? I doubt he'd pay you, and besides, she says, Uncle Ray keeps threatening to take his house back. He's already got one, he doesn't need *this* house, but people who have money can behave this way and there's not a damn thing the rest of us can do about it, Mama says.

I let her go through all that since it's rude to interrupt, then I tell her I don't mean painting houses. I mean painting *walls*, I say, tunnel walls, construction-site walls, the outsides of old buildings, seawalls that keep the ocean from washing up onto the road, those sorts of walls. Pretty much anything but houses. I'm a tagger, or anyways I'm *aspiring* (another Mama word) to be one, a graffiti artist. Nalani already is one. Her tag is a giant cursive A, for *akamai*, which means smart. Nalani's so smart they skipped her a grade in school, put her in my grade, and still she's the smartest in our class. When we graduate she'll probably be the one to do that aloha-it's-been-wonderful-be-the-best-we-can-be kind of speech. Nobody gives her any *huhū* about being smart, not Nalani. I figure if the guys let me be one too, a tagger, then my tag will be a giant C, for Creamy. It's what they call me, my nickname, Creamy, since I'm a white girl. That's when Nalani's around, and they like her around, so they let me be too. Otherwise they call me haole girl—Get the fuck outahere, haole girl! Tagging is mostly a guy thing.

They don't mean anything by it though. We're identified by what we are in my neighborhood. You're a *hapa-haole* if you're at least part Hawai'ian and part something else too, like Chinese; you're a local if you're a lot Hawai'ian and some other things too, but not haole; maybe you're a *benny*, a Filipino; maybe you're a *moke*, which is a big male Samoan and the *tita* is the big female Samoan. At the bottom of all this is me, pure haole, a white girl. The way I see it, if I could be a tagger I wouldn't have to be *just* a haole girl. I'd be Creamy with a huge, shining, True Blue (blue's my favorite color) C. I'd be somebody.

My mama though is *horrified*, that's what she says. I'm horrified you'd even consider such a thing, Lucy! Public buildings aren't really for the public, she says, You ought to know that, you can bet someone owns them. There's people who own and people who don't. We're the don't type, she adds, that bitter look in her eyes, her mouth squinched down. But that doesn't mean you just go out and deface what people do own. It's illegal, she says. It's not art, it's vandalism.

Nalani does, I whine. I know this is immature, *Nalani does*, but everyone generally admires what Nalani does. And I can pretty well tell that mentioning how beautiful graffiti art is, all those shapes and letters and colors looping and swirling and blending together, the way it changes a dull plain wall into *something*, wouldn't do it for Mama.

If Nalani jumped off the Pali, would you? Mama asks. It's the old "if somebody jumps" question that's supposed to make you feel *lōlō* for letting another person lead you around, for not *standing up on your own two feet*, which is the other way my mama puts it.

But honestly, if Nalani jumped off the Pali I'd have to believe there's a pretty good reason for it, or that there's something there to catch her, like a big old sloping banyan on the side of the mountain the rest of us can't see, bending its gnarly branches, its airborne roots just for Nalani. She's that way. But I don't say this. I just give Mama a sour look that lets her know how I feel but doesn't get her red faced or coughing, or something that might *tax* her heart. She's told me about the things that could tax her heart, and most of these have me in a starring role. My mama returns to her reading, as if the subject is all *pau*.

But the subject is not pau, not finished, not for me. Nalani gives me one of her old paint brushes, says she's into spraying now anyway, that *real* taggers spray, and I take that brush, a bucket of water and some blue food coloring I nab from Mama's spice cabinet, I take these down to the Punulu'u sea wall. This is not the kind of lava wall that jets into the ocean, the kind you walk out on, spray from the waves shivering each breath, blue sea, blue sky, and you in the center of it, like being in the heartbeat of the world. This one's a concrete wall keeps the ocean from rolling up onto the rich people's lawns. I'm not so lōlō to think food coloring and water's going to make anything lasting on this wall. That's the truth of tagging; you make your mark, often by sneaking out into the night or the early morning so no one can see, then it stays there for everyone to see. If they don't want your mark they have to sandblast it. But I can practice, until the day I save up enough money for my own paints, my own True Blue. Then I'll be real. A big, beautiful C.

How I got that name, Creamy, comes from a long time ago. We were little kids, Nalani and me, and our other, almost best friend, Cherise. Cherise would rather be Nalani's best friend than mine, but she likes me OK. One day, like I said, we were kids, we were trying out some coffee Cherise's mama left hot in the pot before she tore off to work. Her mama works in the bank, and that's an important kind of work. Important enough to leave almost a whole pot of coffee so as not to be late.

Waste not, want not, my own mama would say. We're pouring it into thin little cups with these roses painted on, Cherise calls them *demitasse* or some such word, sipping it down with globs of cream and sugar because we're trying to *like* this coffee. We're pretending we're important too.

Cherise is black, but she isn't really, not like black paint or a night without a moon. She *says* she's black, her mama is black, and we're supposed to call her *a* Black. It's a pride thing, she says. On this day the suns reams down on Cherise's *lānai,* a wavery pattern of it through the monkey pod growing beside, doves are doing their dove sounds, the air's that sharp, sweet trade-wind air, not the muggy Kona kind—jewel-like is the way my mama describes this air—I think she got it from some book. It's a really *good* morning, and Nalani tells Cherise her skin looks like the coffee we're drinking.

That's the color, she says, dark not black.

And she gets away with it, mostly because she's Nalani, but also because it's a good morning.

Cherise says to Nalani, Well your skin *is* coffee, with the sugar dumped in! And she giggles and Nalani does too. Everyone likes Nalani, that's why she gets to be sugar.

Nalani stares at me, says I must be the cream then since I'm a haole girl, and we all laugh like it's the most hilarious thing in the world.

That's how it started, Creamy. It's a better name than Lucy, I think, and since I've got that hopeless haole kind of skin anyway, not really like cream, more splotchy and freckly and all kinds of weird marks on it that announce to the world—Hey look, haole skin! I kind of like it OK. When you're kids you can talk this way. We didn't care. We were friends.

These days Cherise is not interested in tagging and she isn't interested in me, either. The guys are all interested in Cherise though, they say she's *hot.* She tries to get Nalani to go places with her where the guys are, older guys, not the geeky ones at our school, she says. She tries to get Nalani to go into town with her, Waikīkī, where *real* guys hang out, mainland ones and surfers, and some that go to the university. Even *graduate* students, Cherise tells us outside the Hau'ula IGA, the afternoon sun blasting down, and she's standing with her hands plastered on her hips, light blazing through her hair she's let snake out all wild-like, like some dangerous Medusa. That's what Mama called her, said—That girl's up to no good these days, you watch, one *dangerous Medusa*.

Cherise turns to me, Creamy! she says, only she pronounces it in a way that doesn't make it sound like such a good name, *Creeeeemeeee...*, I bet you don't even know what a graduate student is!

I tell her, I do too! But I don't and they both know it. Cherise laughs and then Nalani laughs too, but not like it's really so hilarious; mean this time, a different sounding Nalani, more of a Cherise-sounding Nalani who's laughing at me. And I get this kind of tight, burning feeling in my throat like I swallowed lit coal. It hurts enough to cry, only I'm not going to let them see me do that. Instead, I grab Nalani's *lauhala* paint bag that's leaning against the side of the IGA, it's the closest thing to me so I don't even think about it, and I yank out a can of yellow spray paint—Marigold Yellow, not even my favorite color—and I spray her feet, with her blue slippers on. Blue *is* my favorite color, but I wish to God Nalani wasn't wearing it.

She doesn't grab the can away from me, doesn't even call me *bitch* and spray me back, which I would've preferred. Even in the face, I would've preferred being sprayed in the face to what she does instead, because what she does instead makes me the loneliest person in the world, standing there in the broiling Hawai'ian sun, in front of the IGA.

Nalani thrusts her bag at me, says, Here! Take them, baby! I'm not into tagging anymore, anyway. She stares coldly at me, a hollow, nothing kind of a stare, like someone who doesn't even know me, wouldn't want to know me, then she seizes the bag back again. On second thought, she says, You don't deserve to be a tagger. You're not smart enough. Then Cherise and Nalani loop their arms together, coffee and coffee with sugar, but no cream, and off they go.

꿹꿹

There was this time a couple years back, when I asked my mama about my dad. I never asked before because with her head always stuck in a book and her heart so *sensitive*, you don't want to alarm or surprise Mama with any conversation out of the ordinary. What's-for-dinner? kind of conversation is mostly what she can take. But I had been bursting with being curious about it for so long, ever since Nalani, who's got a dad that actually lives in her house, asked me about mine. When I told Nalani I didn't have one, she said, shaking her head at me, that wise, tolerating look she gets, Of course you do, you have to. Whether he lives with you or not, somebody had to get your mom *hāpai*, and that person's your dad. Ask her! Nalani said.

Mama said she never married him so it didn't really count. She said if they had been married then maybe they would've tried harder. But as it was, she said, he had the kind of manic depression that became more and more just a constant depression, and my mama couldn't be with him that way, she said, it was too hard. When he was manic he got it in his head he could be somebody else, and when he was depressed you kept wishing he *was* somebody else. It was like living with somebody waiting to die, she told me.

When I think about this now, it's pretty strange that she said that. Because sometimes I feel like *I'm* waiting for my mother's death, not wanting it to come, but figuring it's going to anyway, just reach out and grab her one day. I'll come home from school and her books will be there, alphabetically in her bookshelves the way she likes them, but Mama will be gone.

When I asked her where my dad is, she said he left her and me when I was just a baby, and he moved to an apartment in St. Louis. Because he thought St. Louis was in the middle of the country, she said, and that the middle was the place to get lost from the rest. That's what he told her anyhow, my mama said, and she didn't care enough at that point to wonder if it was true. It's what he wanted, she said, to get lost. Hawai'i was too small and set apart, so he probably figured a city that announced itself as the Gateway to the West would do it; it wasn't east and it wasn't west, just somewhere in between.

The thing is, my mama told me, one day she was reading a book about Lewis and Clark that had a map of the USA in it, and she noticed that St. Louis wasn't in the middle at all, it was really almost a good two-thirds of the way east. And furthermore, she said, that whole Westward Expansion business, which is what the Gateway Arch monument was about, meant stealing native people's lands to do it. Think of it like this, Lucy, Mama said, It's as if they were *renting* and you could just take the land back. Only they weren't. It was theirs to begin with.

I called my father a month after asking my mother about him. It took me a while to get up my courage and a while after that to find his number. Some apartment in St. Louis, I told Information. I tried the three numbers they gave me, of guys who had his same name, then I knew I got him on the third try.

I said, kind of weak-voiced, my heart hammering up through my throat, but I was trying to sound casual, Hey, this is Lucy.

And he said, Lucy!

Just like that. I figured he must have thought I was someone else. He didn't even hesitate when he heard my name, like this was a name he hadn't heard for a while, or even that this was a name he wasn't sure he *wanted* to hear. And he was the one who named me. After *I Love Lucy*, my mama said, the one person who could make him laugh. Insisted on watching her every day, sprawled out on the couch like a slug on a sidewalk, laughing at a stupid TV show.

He was just too cheerful sounding on the phone, I decided, for a depressed person waiting to die. So I hung up. Anyhow, he left before I could walk, so chances are he doesn't remember me at all. It's ironical, Mama said, one of her reading words and she sounded pretty satisfied about it too, that he walked out before *I* could walk.

But these days I'm wondering if my dad had stayed around, if he could've taught me about guys, about the way they are, about how to *be* with a guy. Then maybe Nalani and Cherise would be friends with me again. The only guy I sort of like even close to the way Cherise and Nalani seem to like guys, is Brandon Nakamoto. I feel a kind of fluttery thing inside me when I'm near him, like a moth got stuck in my stomach, batting my insides the way they whack against a lightbulb on a hot summer night, slamming it again and again.

It's a strange kind of feeling that has to do with Brandon, I know this much. Because I feel it even when I stare at the back of him sometimes, his skinny neck and his arm muscles rolling and pumping, kind of jittery but sweet-like, tagging something with his can of spray, concentrating on it like nothing else in the world matters. Brandon is nice to me when the other taggers aren't around, but when they show up he says, Get the fuck outahere, haole girl! so they won't think he was being nice to me.

If I knew more about guys, then maybe I could be with Nalani again, spend the night at her house, talk about the kinds of things girls who like guys talk about, our hair maybe, makeup, which I don't wear but I would if it could help things; it would be like tagging, only on my eyes and lips instead of a wall. I could talk with her about *doing the thing*, which are Cherise's words for *getting laid*—and these are the words I heard Nalani use, whispering to Cherise on the bus yesterday, her hand cupped around Cherise's ear. I heard though, I was right behind them. Even though they pretended I wasn't.

❧❧

As it turns out, it isn't my mother who suddenly dies. She's the one who tells me about the accident on Monday afternoon, I'm just getting home from school and the only thing on my mind is a snack because I didn't get lunch. I don't go into the cafeteria anymore. I figure Cherise and Nalani will be there, and that's a lonely thing, seeing them eating together, and the guys, the taggers saying, Get the fuck outahere, haole girl! How would I have known that today Cherise and Nalani weren't even there?

It came over the news, Mama says, about a half hour ago. She's got the TV on like she does when she isn't reading, when she's resting her brain; That's what TV's good for, she says, letting it all go empty. I'm sucking in the salt smell of the sea blowing through our screens, big nose-fulls of it even though we're a couple streets back from the beach, only rich people get to live right by the beach. And then I think I'm hearing it, the rumble and rush of the waves, the in-and-out breath of the sea, because I don't want to listen to what my mother is telling me.

She's gone, Mama says, passed away, *make*. Didn't even make it to the hospital. Thrown from the car, and someone else was too, some university student. Not the one driving, Mama says, he's going to make it OK and so will Cherise. I'm sorry, Mama sighs, picking up her book again, flicking the remote to turn off the TV, I know you and Nalani were friends.

It seems like all of Punalu'u comes out for her funeral, and they're making those speeches about her inside the small, modern church—One of those reborn Protestant places, my mother said, You're supposed to feel like you can't get to God without stopping there first—wood and glass and cramped and hot. Speeches about how smart and how beautiful she was; what a good citizen and student and friend and daughter and granddaughter and child of God she was; how we may think it is tragic that this life with all its potential was taken away, but the Lord works in mysterious ways, and maybe he wanted one as precious as her for a reason we cannot, are not meant to, understand. Was she saved? the preacher howled, Do not doubt this! Nalani will go on to her greater glory. Those kinds of speeches.

I steal a glance over at Cherise who's sitting with her mother. She's got a sling on one arm and a stiff, medical-type collar about her neck. Her face is scratched and puffed up like a blowfish; I can't tell from the accident or her crying. I know Cherise liked Nalani too, maybe she even liked her as much as I liked her. Lots of people are crying, but not me. I can't seem to, even tried to make myself cry by thinking about really awful things, run-over mongoose, their guts strewn about Kamehameha Highway, or drowned kittens washing up on the beach. I wanted a kitten, something to hold on to, that would love me without having to consider first if I'm worth it, but Mama said chasing around after a kitten would tax her heart. Imagining one drowning, even this isn't making me cry.

Cherise doesn't look at me. Nobody looks at me, not even when they talk about how much Nalani's friends will miss her. They look at Cherise, but Cherise just stares straight ahead at the empty space over the preacher's head where there's a high, angular window, a stab of dusty light poking through, tears tumbling down her cheeks like Sacred Falls. We swam at Sacred Falls, Nalani and I, but nobody here knows that. And I'm beginning to wonder if maybe, just maybe, they're not looking at me because *I'm* not really here. Maybe I can't cry, can't really *feel* anything about Nalani's dying because I'm dead myself. I'm just some *hologram*, a Mama-reading word, an image of me who's not really me at all.

When I'm back home again Mama, who didn't go to the funeral because she felt too tired, slaps down her book on the scratched mahogany end table beside the sofa, says sternly, Lucy, you have to accept that Nalani's in a better place.

My mother's not religious, but she believes in an afterlife, she calls it, a heaven-like place that's not necessarily up in the sky, but more like a prairie, she thinks, grassy and free like the prairies used to be. Before people destroyed the prairies, and now they have to cultivate them and re-seed them and import nursery-born butterflies to pollinate them, she said, to make them wild again. The way Mama sees it, death is a kind of going back to the way things were.

I listen to her like I always do, it would be impolite not to, and anyway I wouldn't want to upset her and then maybe her heart gets *taxed*, and suddenly she's out on that prairie with Nalani and I have nobody. That's the way I would usually think. But, though I start out thinking like this, listening politely to my mama, this time I don't really feel these things behind her words. I don't feel the threat of her dying, coming apart every minute she's on this earth, as Mama once put it; Marfan's is a connective-tissue disease, she explained, everything slowly disconnecting. But I don't feel anything.

I'm going to go paint! I announce, surprising myself about as much as Mama.

She says, For heaven's sake, Lucy, at a time like this? Is it the rebel you want to be, is that it? You can rebel in ways that don't destroy other people's property, you know. For instance, you can tell me you're never going to get married, since you know that's what I want for you. Now there's a nondestructive form of rebellion.

I'm never going to get married, I tell her, *and* I'm going to go paint. It's not about destruction, I add. It occurs to me that sounded pretty smart, like something Nalani might have said.

I still don't have the money to buy my own paint though, and this is a problem. Because the urge is firing up inside me so strong now I can feel that True Blue C catapulting through my blood, my muscles, my bones, my organs, *connecting* to my heart like life itself. Like I *am* alive, if I can do this. For a minute I consider going to Nalani's house and asking her folks if I can have her lauhala bag. Probably they wouldn't want it, and maybe she still has her paints in it. But I couldn't do that, not while they're grieving so fresh. Maybe they don't believe she's on a prairie somewhere. Maybe they don't even believe their own preacher's version, that God had a reason for taking her to his better place. Maybe they can't accept she's in her greater glory. Maybe they're afraid she's just plain gone.

The burning inside me is too strong and I run into my room, which isn't really my room—Mama always sets me straight on this, it's Uncle Ray's room because he can take his house back at any moment—and I grab up Nalani's old brush she gave me from under my bed where I stuck it, as if I have to hide it, as if I have any real paint for it, and I race back out of the house.

I'm not sure where I'm headed, the most visible wall I can find, I'm thinking; if you make your mark on something visible, then you are visible too. I run up Kamehameha Highway, the ocean roaring on one side, the traffic roaring and honking in the street, and I feel like I'm hearing all of this in a dream. Because I pay absolutely no attention to it, not even to the car full of locals that swerves almost up on the grass beside me, pretending like they're going to hit me: Hey, haole girl, you like run from me! I pay them no mind.

Suddenly I know where I'm going, and I head off the road at the Crouching Lion Restaurant, toward the rocky path at the side of the hill, leading up the bold, bare face of the mountain behind. Nalani said folks should never go up into the Ko'olaus at this place; It's where the Night Marchers come down, she said, Hawai'ian ghosts, the army of the dead. She said I didn't know this because I'm not Hawai'ian, not even a small part Hawai'ian. But now it's Nalani who is dead. And going to places you shouldn't is what tagging is about, at least that's what Brandon Nakamoto said. None of this matters anymore.

I kick off my slippers and begin the climb up the stark rocks, feeling their heat and roughness beneath my bare feet, breathing the ocean, the red smell of the iron earth, and somewhere back in the mountains where it's green, the ripeness of this island, guavas, mangoes, papayas, 'ākala and 'ōhelo berries that stain your teeth when you bite into them, sour as old rain. I tug my brush out of the back pocket of my shorts where I jammed it, up on the highest ledge that faces the sea, where the rocks are giant and become a form—a lion, how the restaurant got its name.

Here it is like a wall, a place where everyone can see. I take my brush without any paint, and I move it across the face of the rock in a big, swooping motion, a semicircle, a half of something that's not quite whole, but it's a half that says *something*. For me, C, for Creamy. I feel the motion of the brush under my hand, dipping and swooping, back and forth, becoming its own movement, spinning over the surface of the sun-warmed rock like the world spinning under my feet, real as that. It could be an *L*, for Lucy, I realize, it makes no difference what the letter is named. I'm thinking *blue*, a fine, new blue, not Cerulean Blue or Midnight Blue or even True Blue. My blue. And above the blue sky, below the blue sea, and here, on this mountain, me.

JUST WATCHING FOR JESUS

First there is the tap, tap, tapping, then the scritching and the scratching on my bedroom screen, the blackest middle of the night. I know who it is, who else can it be? I'm on the fourth floor of this apartment building, brick, built snug and flat as my husband's girlfriend's little *bee*hind. It's not like there's a ladder coming up to my window, this isn't exactly a fire drill. I roll over on my back, grab my pillow and try to plug up my ears, smooshing it over my face.

Marybeth? Marybeth, you in there?

Go away! I whisper, but not so he'd hear me.

It's Jesus, Marybeth.

Jesus, Jesus! I mutter into my pillow. You about scare the bejesus out of me when you do this!

No, Marybeth. I am. The Word is. I don't *be* Jesus.

Oh Lord, I'm thinking, this is just what I need, some linguistically retentive savior at my bedroom window in the middle of the night.

Marybeth, I have a message for you, a directive. There is something you must do.

Jesus, I say, The last time you came here and told me what to do, I did what you said and I almost got arrested for stalking my own husband! It's what they called it, *stalking*, can you believe that? The man's got a girlfriend who's thirteen if she's a day and they want to arrest *me* for stalking. What a world.

I scrunch the pillow down harder over my face, my ears, though if it's Jesus, he has ways of being heard, of course. I think longingly of my wine in the fridge, burgundy, my favorite, color of blood, that promise in my throat.

Marybeth? Are you listening to me?

I sigh, stamp my leg out a little on the bed, like loosening up a charley-horse cramp, a gesture my daughter Sandra has always done when she's irritated, and now her little brat daughter Cassandra does it too; *Cas*sandra, who is a Sandra of a different name.

How can I not listen to you, Jesus? You're bellowing into my window, if you don't mind me saying it. Is being holy the same as being loud?

Watch for me, Marybeth, search me out in the most unholy of places, and there you will find me.

Oh good God! I'm thinking, He's doing it again. The most unholy of places, that I know of anyway, has got to be Toby Manza's new place, living with that undernourished teen queen, two brand-new, fancy-ass cars and a house in South County, one of those gated neighborhoods. Keeps people like Marybeth out, Toby Manza said—to our own daughter Sandra, that we made together in the back of his pickup!

Except it didn't keep me out. I stood in his yard, the house beyond like a monolith or a pyramid, some kind of tomb it's got to be, I was thinking—'cause otherwise how could you justify just two folks living there, and one of them pint-sized, when a whole piss-poor town could yank up its roots and move comfortably inside? The lawn under my feet was as green as an inchworm and every bit as slithery, like stepping on something made to *look* real, but nature wouldn't grow it that way because it's just too perfect. And suddenly this water comes out from nowhere, rising off the grass toward heaven like Jesus himself.

So of course I started screeching, sky clear as a baby's cheeks over my head, and there's water whirling and swirling and storming all around.   Miracles don't happen much to people like me. Underground sprinkling system, Toby Manza told the police when he signed the restraining order.   Just keep her the hell off my property, he said.

A restraining order? I asked the police.

It's for protection, one of them said, sizing me up, smirking. You're not supposed to be out there harassing your ex.

We're still married, I said, And just what the hell is he protecting anyway, his lawn?   Now Jesus is sending me back.

How Toby Manza got his money is the way most folks who don't have money get it, they win the lottery, which is not so likely, or somebody dies.   Toby's parents died in a plane crash before he ever really got to know them, he said, so he was raised by his Grandpa Manza in New York for a while, and then when things got too much for Grandpa Manza he sent Toby to a relation in Shady Tree, where I'm from.   Toby doesn't look Italian despite his last name, so he fit right in.   Shady Tree has mostly people from Northern European descent, light-eyed, doughy-skin types, easy enough laughter for things that aren't so funny, like if it's going to rain for the next five years, but try to tell them some kind of a real joke, one where the punch line ends in sex maybe, and their brows twist into this sort of looped- down, puzzled expression.

Then Grandpa Manza dies, a few years back, and the lawyer fellow who was taking care of the Manza money calls up Toby, says, Why don't you put the funds into a good investment and make them multiply?

So Toby Manza does this, buys into a few stocks and such, whatever the lawyer suggests, and damned if that lawyer wasn't right about this, the loaves and the fishes—the original Manza money begets more money, and this money has baby monies, and before Toby can even learn to spell the word *investment*! he is a person who has money.   People with money don't have to live in cramped city apartments, they don't have to live with their middle-aged wife, their stubborn daughter, and their daughter's stubborn daughter. So Toby Manza moved out.

I explained all of this to Jesus the next time he visited. I was weeping and chugging and sucking and weeping—the two of them kind of go together at times, cheap wine and sour tears. I had hunkered down on my bed doing these things, then the tap, tap, tapping, the scritching and the scratching at my screen.

You're a tree branch! I shouted at first, Go away. Maybe that cat, that big-eyed, big-eared one that's always hanging around, shimmied up to the top of the branch and is trying to get in, I was thinking, maybe a cat.

Well, any semi-sober fool knows there are few trees big enough in St. Louis city to reach my fourth-story window; there are no trees even big enough in Shady Tree, Illinois, where if there *had* been trees that big, despite the name they'd have mowed them down to make room for more soybeans and corn. Rock Falls, Paw Paw, Earlville, Shady Tree, all of them just different names for the corn and the soybeans.

We moved to St. Louis because there's opportunities. That's what Toby Manza said, I told Jesus. And wouldn't you know it, Jesus, I said, damned if Toby didn't find one, if you'll pardon me saying so (it occurred to me maybe Jesus didn't think about these kinds of things, being holy and all, and maybe he didn't like to hear *damn*, though my father said damn's OK in a pinch so long as you don't put *God* in front); she's a snug little opportunity, recent graduate of the training bra.

That's when Jesus said, once again, Watch for me, Marybeth, in the unholiest of places. For I will make my presence known.

During my next visit to the Manza compound I'm trying hard not to make *my* presence known on Toby's lawn. I step gingerly about like there's land mines in this earth, but it's only buried sprinklers, I remind myself. This time it's night, following Jesus' example; what kind of damned fools show themselves where they're not supposed to be in the day? I'm hoping Jesus will make his presence known soon, in this unholiest of places, before the sprinklers shoot up and I'm soaking wet again. It's October and there's a nip in the night air. The sky is the color of purple chalk, like somebody scribbled it up there, a stretch of scraggly clouds, too much city light to see any stars. Back home in Shady Tree we would've had the killing frost by now. Back home I would still have a husband in my bed, for whatever that's worth. There's not too many anorexic pre-adults parading about in razor-cut hair and jeans so tight you'd have to peel her out of them like a banana, after the likes of Toby Manza in Shady Tree. And maybe I'd have a grown-up daughter who doesn't run around with a motorcycle gang, claiming *Love is a thing invented by Hallmark to sell greeting cards.*

Well what about Cassandra? I asked Sandra, when she said this to me. What about your own child, huh? *Cas*sandra, who is a Sandra of a different name, sat snarling on the kitchen counter, where she's not supposed to be—though it was stained and gnarly before we ever moved in—dangling and kicking her bony little legs. There's things you're supposed to teach children, like how to sit on chairs.

That's different, Sandra said, She's just a kid. Sandra yawned and sighed, said, I need a nap.

My daughter naps a lot lately; unless she's with one of her motorcycle men, she claims she has no more energy, so then it's me who's got to muster the what-it-takes to pull that *Cas*sandra, the Sandra of a different name, down from all the places she climbs up to. Cassandra is a five-and-a-half-year-old mountain goat, the product of my daughter's relation with some leather- tongued he-goat, before she was barely old enough to grow her own little horns in, so to speak. Sometimes I think my granddaughter is trying to climb herself up and out of this world.

This time I manage to make it to Toby Manza's window without getting sprayed, crawling on my belly practically, trying to avoid the automatic spotlight that senses your presence, beams down on you like the light of truth. Through the partly opened mini-blinds I can ferret out two shapes, Toby's and the sub-sized one. I crunch down low, which is pretty hard to do given the overall size of the window, almost to the ground itself. I guess when you have something to look at, like a soccer field pretending it's a backyard, you build a big window so you can stare out at it and convince yourself you deserve it.

From down here the ground smells musty and ill used, probably chemicals they put on the lawn to make it that green, the color of an overripe lime. It sounds like Toby and his girlfriend are having one of those confidential conversations you have just before sex, he's telling you all the things he likes about you, and you're nodding, sighing, letting his hands mosey down upon all of those things. As I lean closer to get a hint of exactly what they're saying, crack! my forehead comes up hard against that damn glass.

Inside Toby Manza doesn't miss a beat. That you, Marybeth? he shouts. I'm betting it is, and you've got to the count of ten to get off my property before I call the cops and they arrest you for real this time, goddamnit!

On the bus back to my own neighborhood my forehead is smarting. I'm going to have a bruise there the color of a plum and the size of a toddler's fist. I'm pretty irritated at Jesus about now, but I'm whispering it, since I'm in a public place, just in case he is listening like God is supposed to, always listening, always there. I'm not sure if this applies to Jesus, but maybe God will give him the message that I'm pretty unhappy here.

I just can't keep watching for you in my husband's unholy place anymore! I whisper, Because it's getting me in a helluva lot of trouble. I turn my head away and press my throbbing face against the cold night window.

Tell him that, OK, God? Tell your son what I said.

Back inside the apartment I see Cassandra perched high up on the unpainted living-room shelves. Toby built them and was going to paint them, but he never got around to it before Miss mini-flanks got around to him. Cassandra makes a sour face, uncombed curls springing off the top of her head, every which way like the kid pasted them there, then sticks out her tongue.

You little orangutan, get the heck down from there! I command her.

Sandra comes wheeling out from their bedroom, coughing and sputtering, one of the leather-coated motorcyclists in tow, head-to-foot brown, looks like an oversized chocolate-covered almond.

Jesus Christ, Mom, don't always be yelling at her!

And don't you say Jesus Christ! I tell her, because you never know when he might be listening. Teach this child not to climb on things, teach her *something*, for God's sake, children need discipline.

Discipline is a thing invented by the powerful to keep the powerless from realizing how miserable they are, Sandra announces smugly. Where you been anyway? You look like hell.

I stare down at my clothes, my sweatshirt covered with bits of dead leaves and twiggy things, from the bush beside Toby Manza's window; the knees of my khaki slacks are as brown as the earth. I rub my aching forehead carefully. Sandra starts coughing again, a dry, hardened sort of hacking.

When you going to see a doctor about that cough? I ask her, annoyed, but at what I'm not sure—there's a lot to be annoyed at these days.

When hell freezes over, she says. Doctors don't deserve the money they make, and they damn sure aren't getting the money *I* make. So? Where you been?

I been watching for Jesus, I tell her.

In bed later I wait for him to come. I brought in the burgundy and an extra tumbler, figuring I'd offer him some, be hospitable and all that. In the meantime I can satisfy my own driving thirst. And I do this.

I'm thinking about my name, how it was the same as his mother's, only different. We were maybe the only Catholic family in Shady Tree, so we didn't go to Mass much needless to say, since there wasn't one, and we were pretty quiet about the fact we were Catholics.

My father said, I am a farmer and this, by God, is my farm. The Father in Heaven will understand.

But I wasn't too sure *my* father would understand, about Toby Manza. When I first introduced him, my father frowned at the Manza part. Not because he was thinking, Oh, Italian! the way some in Shady Tree might. What he figured was that despite his efforts to conceal our religion, like had found like. And now everyone would know.

Toby Manza was never a Catholic, I assured him.

Toby Manza never had any religious beliefs to speak of, though I didn't tell my father that. Which is why I am pretty sure that Toby is in what Jesus means about the unholiest of places. I mean, what else would I know? It's not like my life has any unused time in it, after work and taking care of the Sandras, to go hanging around in unholy places.

My father used to call me Mary, and my mother called me my full name, Mary Elizabeth. Mother of God! my father would howl when I did something he didn't like. You're named after the Holy Mother, and you behave like this?

It was Toby Manza who suggested Marybeth for my name, running my two names together sort of, and this after I told Toby, crying and on my knees, that my father could never find out about my being pregnant. I was sixteen years old.

I'm named Mary, after the Holy Mother! I moaned. Don't you get it? Mother of God! I can't let my father know! Making a baby in a pickup is not exactly immaculate.

That's when it happened, the thing that changed everything. After Toby renamed me Marybeth, after we tried to make the pregnancy go away ourselves, by natural means since I was a Catholic, practicing or not, and could never, I told Toby, get an abortion. Not that we'd find one so easily in Shady Tree. But if we did, then maybe I'd burn in hell. And I'm not a person who's even especially fond of hot weather.

Toby said, Jump around a lot. If you shake things up, maybe it'll loosen something.

I jumped around a lot, off the barn roof and into the haystack, out of his Ford pickup when it was barely moving;

Toby Manza taught me how to drop on my shoulder and roll. It didn't work. The baby kept growing, and I kept growing with it. Toby gave me his oversized shirts to hide my shape, and my father said, Mother of God, you're born a girl yet you dress like a boy!

One night it came out of me anyway. Too early, but still it felt like salad tongs were squeezing my insides, like I'm a giant beefsteak tomato. I stuffed a wash rag in my mouth and reminded myself I deserved the hurt. The baby slid out a fully human being—except for one thing. She was born blue as the hand towel I laid her on when I cut her away from me, my mother's coupon snipping scissors. I was alone in my little upstairs bathroom, my parents downstairs, Toby Manza home at his house.

And I was holding this dead little baby, not much bigger than my own hand, her hands about the size of a cashew nut. A terrible fear shot through me at what I done, this baby, that never breathed a breath of this life. I must have jumped this baby right out of me, after all! She knew what kind of chances she'd have, living in this world with me and Toby Manza, and she decided not to breathe.

I guess I went a little out of my head that night, because when Toby finally came over and my parents were in bed, he mopped the blood up off the bathroom floor, and then he took the dead little baby from me—I let him do this—took her like something we had to throw away. He wrapped her in a plastic Hefty bag, covering his own hands in plastic baggies first so he would never touch her body, then wiping her tiny body with his plastic-covered hands, so there wouldn't be any of my prints on her either, he said.

Nobody will know it was ours, he said.

And Toby Manza took the bag outside, and he laid it under a bush in a neighbor's field whose land abutted the highway. Maybe he thought, looking like garbage and all, that the neighbor, Mr. Tucker, would just assume someone driving by threw the bag out of their car and he'd put it in his garbage can without ever opening it. The garbage men would take it away, and that would be that.

I didn't know what Toby Manza was thinking, and I still don't, because he's never let me talk about it with him. Far as I can remember I had no thoughts at all, my mind was this big numb blurry thing inside my head, my eyes were still looking out of my head, but what they were seeing at that point and for the rest of my life, was a different world.

The next day Mr. Tucker found the bag and reported it to the police. It was all over the paper like some cataclysmic event, like the Four Horsemen of the Apocalypse themselves had laid that baby down on the frozen land. Shady Tree would not believe the baby came from one of them, assuming some outsider had veered off the highway and dropped her—Thrown her out into the freezing night, they said. They even named her, or somebody did. Angel Rose, because Mr. Tucker claimed the bag landed under his favorite rose bush. It's a name I would never have chosen. I'd have named her something like Kathleen, or Tina, functional names, names you can live with.

Don't tell! Toby Manza hissed. Don't you ever breathe a word of this to anyone.

On her little gravestone was inscribed: *Here lies a newborn, Angel Rose, who never had a chance. Help us learn to accept the mystery of her death in a holy way.*

Toby Manza and I managed to finish high school before I got pregnant again. This time I married him and gave birth to Sandra, enough months later so that if the folks in Shady Tree who speculate about these sorts of things talked about this at all, they kept it to themselves. And we went about setting up a life together, the three of us.

Only for me it was the four of us. For me there was also the one missing, always present. There are the things you cannot forget. They haunt you, wear you ragged like a piece of clothing you will never get rid of, all of your life. I figure this is the reason Jesus has caught up with me. I did a bad thing, tried to hide what I did. So maybe he's ready to forgive me now, watching for him in the unholiest of places. Or maybe he just wants us to scare the bejesus out of Toby Manza, who has shown no remorse—aren't you at least supposed to fret a little over the bad things you do?—and who doesn't believe in him anyway.

I'm working for Sandra's boss these days, this place she calls The Corporation. Most of the time Sandra doesn't feel up to going to work, she says, so I'm doing her job. She's the color of an eggshell and almost as thin. Maybe hanging out with those motorcycle folks at night, down at Joe's Rig—that's a bar—has stolen her get-up-and-go for the day. I do data entry, which is about the most useless thing in the world, far as I can see, punching the numbers Sandra's boss gives me into the computer so the computer can "assimilate" them, then it coughs up some other numbers on its own. These other numbers, Sandra explained, are what The Corporation is about.

Recently Sandra told me she didn't think she could go back to work at all anymore. She's slipping away more and more from *this world*, she calls it, hanging with her motorcycle men, where she can be herself, she says. She says she isn't feeling so hot, and when I look at her closely, I see this is true. But I don't know what I can do. I tell her to see a doctor, and she says, Hah! And Cassandra says this too, right after Sandra. She's the color of a bad day, coughing most of the time now; unless those leather-men are around, Sandra hasn't much use for anything else. She lies on our beat-up sofa, its stuffing leaking out around her head like a halo or a pillow, like it's supposed to do that. Cassandra is stretched out above her on the top of the sofa, the two of them taking in the soaps or the talk shows, the sorts of things children shouldn't watch. My daughter looks like a bag of bones someone has not-so-painstakingly assembled into a human being.

Which leaves me alone with her boss. Who one day writes on my calendar a date for him to take me to dinner. When I tell Sandra about this the night before she says I should go.

Why is your male boss inviting *me* out to dinner? I ask.

It's a corporate handshake, Sandra says. A way of being friendly to his employees.

Yeah, sneers Cassandra, Sandra of a different name. For a crazed second I feel like sticking my tongue out at my granddaughter, who has climbed up on the back of my ancient recliner chair, squatting there on her little haunches like a duck. But I stop myself. Someone's got to be the adult around here.

I did it when I first got hired, Sandra says. She shrugs. Could've been worse, I got a raise just for listening to the stories of his sad life.

He goes home to a house that has more glass in its windows than all of Shady Tree (I happen to know Sandra's boss lives in Toby Manza's *community*, they call it out there), and he's got a sad life? I say. So why can't we just shake hands for real?

A corporate handshake! I'm thinking. The things you can get away with when you've got *investments,* numbers begetting numbers. And they call *me* a stalker.

I take my wine bottle to bed, leaving Sandra and Cassandra to clean up the dinner dishes, which they won't, but it's a gesture on my part that they should anyway. I'm too tired, Sandra says, Leave them to morning. Like morning's a person besides myself who's going to wash them.

I'm not all that bad looking, I'm thinking, slurping down my burgundy, propped up by my five favorite pillows and lolling about under my bedcovers with the window over my head wide open, even though the late October night has teeth and a wind sucking at the screen. I'm from a place where the words corn and *soybean* appear in people's conversations more often than should be considered normal, so I suppose I'm not particularly sophisticated. But I'm a natural redhead still, I used to be fashion-model thin without even having to throw up and I'm not exactly a pork loin now. Far as I can see, Toby Manza picked an unripened version of what he already had.

Before Jesus started coming regularly to my window, it occurred to me what I should do was make Toby Manza jealous. Make him wish he didn't give me up, that maybe the younger, newer version of the same thing doesn't necessarily make it a better thing. Maybe there's even kinks in the new thing, like his floor-length leather coat he bought after his money came in, to have the look of someone who has money, when his woolen one was perfectly good; then the damn beast was so heavy he hardly ever wore it, like schlepping around two cows. Some look, hanging in the closet, taking up the space of three normal jackets, appearing stiff enough to march out of there on its own. Though instead of the coat walking out, Toby did.

But how to do that, make him jealous, when he stopped noticing me even before he left? I got out of the habit of dating long ago, and anyway, dating in Shady Tree where there was nowhere to go, generally meant sitting in a guy's pickup in some farmer's dark field, middle of the night, doing the stuff that puts a kink in any future dating, makes you a mother instead. That was my life. And then Angel Rose, and that changed my life.

So when the kid in the shoe store started flirting with me, at first I didn't even realize he was flirting, slipping the new pumps on my feet, running his hand up my ankle like my ankle is part of my foot, telling me I have *great feet*, that sort of thing. I'm not a shoe-store kind of person, generally getting my shoes at Payless or Wal-Mart, places where you ferret out the box that has your size, drag it down off the shelves, slapping what's inside on your feet in front of God and every other shopping person. But Sandra convinced me to go to this shoe store in the Union-Station-turned-yuppie shopping mall, to get *really good shoes like Dad would*, cause my feet had started this thing where they ached all the time, cramping up at night, and I was throwing my legs about like Sandra and Cassandra do when they're irritated. I probably froze up the circulation in them, just sitting at that Corporation computer eight hours a day, punching those numbers in. You can't imagine how worn a body can get, when you don't even move. It's a kind of *diapause*, which is a word I learned back in school when I was interested in things like biology, when I still believed things like that could make a difference. It has to do with the resting state of a butterfly, places like the Arctic when the world around them is too cold, so they just quietly survive inside themselves.
This young man comes out with about every high heel ever made in my size, stilettos, he calls them, to show off my *great legs*, he said. Well, I didn't come in there for high heels and I told him this, that I came in for a pair of *really good* shoes so my feet would stop hurting, real leather, no doubt expensive. Like tiptoeing around in butter, Sandra assured me. She knows

everything there is to know about leather, from hanging out with those motorcycle men.

So then what he does is, he takes me out to lunch! Of course, I'm thinking, Boy, the service they have in these pricey shoe stores! trying to delude myself and all, since fact of the matter, I *was* a bit hungry, and maybe more than a little flattered he would ask me. Which is why I'm hesitant, you might say, about Sandra's boss taking me somewhere for a meal. In Shady Tree going out to a meal meant the Tasty Freeze. In St. Louis it seems to mean a glass of wine, and when can I ever stop with just one glass of wine? That's just wetting your taste buds till they're squirming and wriggling and doing back-flips down your tongue, begging for more.

After a couple or so glasses of wine, this young shoe salesman, who told me his name was Tim but only after I must have asked him fifty times (it's my policy when a man takes you out for a meal you should at least be familiar with his name), swept up my hands in his, gazed moon-eyed into my face and asked me to spend the night with him. At this point I was pretty positive he was flirting with me, and that I should be trying to figure out a way of getting him and me to wherever Toby Manza was, so I could make Toby Manza jealous.

Tim said, I can do you all night. I can make you so sore you won't be able to walk out of my room the next morning.

And I said, This is supposed to be something like an attractive offer?

That night Jesus came to my window. Marybeth, he said, don't you go looking for love in the wrong places. Which I think is a country song, but who am I to question Jesus' words? Look for me, he said once again, in the unholiest of places.

Thinking about this now, guzzling the last of my bottle of red, I decide I won't do that corporate handshake with Sandra's boss tomorrow after all, even if it means Sandra and I lose her job, cause any place he takes me has got to be the wrong place. I'm going to go to Toby Manza's, in broad daylight even. There's no doubt his is the unholiest of places, but it's not the wrong place. I can't help it if I still have feelings for the man. He's my husband. I don't know if it's love or just a kind of longing, but there's something unfinished about my life without him in it, that nagging inside like you've forgotten something, climbing into an empty bed that's always a shade too cold. No restraining order, unless it's signed by God himself, can restrain me from watching for Jesus there.

But the next morning happens earlier than I expected, with Cassandra shaking my shoulder, tugging my hand, Come, Grandma, come!

Now Cassandra doesn't call me Grandma much, doesn't talk to me much at all, except *Yeah!* to whatever her mother says. I pop up into a sitting position, still numbed from the wine, and confused. Jesus? I whisper.

She's yanking and pulling at me, and when I flip on the lamp beside my bed she's got this wild-animal look in the little beads of her eyes, deep and driving and scared.

Lord's sake, Cassandra, what's the matter? What time is it? Why on earth you up?

Mommy's not breathing right!

I practically fall out of bed, my head spinning, throbbing, the wine hasn't settled down inside my blood yet, and I follow her toward their bedroom. She's moving like a snake, slithering and slipping down the dark hallway, fast for someone who usually just climbs onto something and sits glaring out at the world.

I hear my daughter before I'm even inside their room, the rasping harshness of her breath rattling in and out of her, like those dry hacky coughs all got stuck inside her throat, one piling up onto the other. I race in, ahead of Cassandra now. The light hanging over her bed is on, and below it Sandra's face is the color of her sheets, a terrible cinder grey.

Call 911! I order Cassandra, and she does this without my having to repeat it.

I lean down close to Sandra's face, her breath is sour, worse than mine even from all that burgundy. I won't touch it again! I plead, to God, to Jesus, to the Holy Mother, to whichever one of them will hear me and make my daughter all right.

We're taking you to the hospital, I whisper to her, stroking her cheeks, burning under my fingers. And when she doesn't protest, doesn't say something about hospitals being setups for quack insurance companies and the rich who keep them in business, that sort of thing, that's when I know how sick my Sandra is.

At almost noon a distracted young doctor, baby-faced and finely combed, looking like a poster boy for a high school graduation shot, strides into the little room where they've left Cassandra and me—Cassandra's on top of the magazine table, I don't even try to make her get down. He motions me over, where she can't hear.

Your daughter's very sick, he says.

Well, duh! I'm thinking, tell me something else I don't know.

We've got her on intravenous and oxygen, but I have to tell you, the prognosis isn't good. She's got Pneumocystis carinii pneumonia. Her T-cell count is very low.

I must have looked at him like a cow might, drifting up from a swallow of grass, a nobody's-home sort of look. Like he spoke to me in Arabic maybe, a language I could never know.

He sighs, PCP, AIDS pneumonia? Were you not aware she's HIV-positive? There are medicines that might have prevented her getting PCP, you know. If she has a father or any other family it would be a good idea to call them. I'm sorry, he adds, We'll do the best we can.

For a moment I feel like shouting acronyms in this doctor's face, *Didn't you know she was PCP, HIV?* Acronyms like FUCK-U! There are no words that come out of my mouth though, I can barely taste any language for this on my tongue at all. Jesus! I whisper inside my own head, my head, which suddenly feels like it's been severed from my neck and is drifting like a balloon a few inches above.

I call Toby Manza at work and at first he refuses to talk to me, he's about to hang up—Marybeth, goddamnit, don't you get what a restraining order means? It means zero contact!

Then I blurt it out to him, about Sandra being in the hospital. She's very, very, very sick, I say, and I'm praying he can hear how sick she is underneath all those *verys*, because I can't say the other word, I can't believe in it, though they let me go in and see her, made me put on a surgical mask so that suddenly I looked like one of them, all eyes and sterility. My hand kept flying up near my mouth under the mask where my breath came through, just checking that I was me.

She's like an octopus, hooked up to tubes all around her, inside a plastic oxygen mask that fits over her mouth and nose so she can't soak up more germs, I tell Toby.

What I don't tell him is that I don't really know if this is true or not, or if they're just trying to keep her breathing. I was afraid to ask. Even I could see this plastic getup was just a transparent little window to a world that is not the one I'm in.

How could this happen? Toby whispers. His bright green eyes look stricken, blinking owlishly in their tinted contacts, over the gauzy mask a nurse helped him put on. He's staring at me accusingly, like I am the one who made it happen, or somehow should have been able to stop it.

We're standing in Sandra's room, but back from the bed a ways, so that under the plastic and attached to the tubes she looks even smaller, more gone from the way she used to look, a strappy, gangly sort of young woman with a heart big enough to understand the wrongs of the world, just not enough will to do something about them. She's perfectly still, sleeping I have to believe, a thick, drug-induced sleep. I'm remembering there was this interim period, where she was starting to look less and less like the Sandra I thought I knew, but what was to be done about it? I suppose inside me I knew something was wrong, a mother must know, musn't she? What could I have done?

I thought PCP was the name of a drug! Toby says, louder this time. I jump a little, heart hammering.

Angel dust, horse tranquilizers or something, huh? he asks.

It's pneumonia, I whisper.

Toby shakes his head, which oddly enough I notice has lost more of its hair, even since the last time I saw him. No, he says. It's AIDS, he says.

In the small waiting room outside Sandra's room Cassandra has climbed up onto the window ledge, a slab of fake marble under a high, long window that looks down on the hospital parking lot. Toby stares at her like she's a stranger, which I guess she is. Should Sandra's kid be up there? he asks me.

Cassandra…, I start to tell her to get down, but then I don't. Maybe that's not the sort of thing a child needs to hear, after all.

Toby Manza says he's going down to the cafeteria, do we want anything? I shake my head and Cassandra shakes her head too.

Don't be long, I tell him, Sandra might need us.

She doesn't even know we're here, he says.

She doesn't know *you* are here, I say.

I know right away this was a mean thing to say and I'm sorry I said it; I know Toby isn't such a bad person, I know he loves his daughter, but I can't take it back. I can't take anything back, I realize, and I never could. I stare at Toby and he stares at me, and between us is all we have lost.

I'm going down, he says. Then, like it's an afterthought he adds, I'm not sure I can bear this, Marybeth. How does someone bear this? He gazes at me, bewildered, his hands hanging red and raw at his sides look about as helpless as any pair of hands I have ever seen. Then Toby Manza turns away, then he turns back again for a second, as if he's about to say something. But there's nothing else to say. My husband closes the door after himself.

I look up to where Cassandra is, but she's not looking at me. On an impulse I climb onto the window ledge beside her, and I feel a moment of satisfaction that I can fit there, that I'm not so much heftier than that runt girlfriend of Toby's after all.

I dangle my legs down, slap my aching feet softly against the concrete wall under me, like Cassandra is doing, both of us keeping a sort of light rhythmic beat, turned a little sideways, staring out.

If someone walks in here they're not going to approve, I say. I wonder if I can get arrested for climbing? I've nearly been arrested for stalking, sounds like they could be from the same family of arrests, climbing, stalking. I'm mumbling these things, sort of half to myself in a nervous kind of way, but when I look again at Cassandra she's staring at me, intently, like she's really listening.

You're like your mother, I say, listening to the wrong kinds of things.

I want to go home, she says. I want Mommy and I want to go home. Her forehead wrinkles up like she's about to cry.

I nod, Yeah, me too. Well, but then who's going to watch for Jesus? Someone's got to wait at this window, watching for Jesus.

She frowns, scrunching those dark little eyes like little stones, the eyes of her father I'm guessing, that none of us will ever know. It's where Cassandra is not a Sandra. Sandra's eyes are wide and pale, like mine.

There's no Santa, she announces, and there's no Jesus. Mommy said so. She said they were invented to make people believe there's hope.

Cassandra kicks the wall harder, her bare leg bumping against mine. Both of us tugged on shorts before the ambulance came, neither of us thinking about it being almost November. I feel her bony warmness, my granddaughter's skin, thin as a bruise. I stare at her feet, her small toes curled up like new leaves in the sandals I bought her. From Tim, the young shoe salesman who couldn't sell me a pair of pumps, after all. I felt a small triumph that Cassandra wears them often. And I almost smile, for a moment. Because I heard Sandra's voice, another kind of Cassandra, coming out of her.

Well, but it was Jesus who told me to watch for him, I say. In the unholiest of places.

Where's that? Cassandra scowls.

What I'd like to tell her is that I'm not so sure anymore, that maybe, in fact, it's this whole damn world where things like this happen. Daughters are lost, husbands find someone else, and people who have done terrible things go to bed every night with what they have done, guzzling wine, praying for someone to love them. I gaze out the window, and I see Toby Manza climb into one of his sleek new cars. It's some sort of sports car and he's left the top down, as if maybe at one point he had thought, if only the day would get warmer! As if there really had been this possibility, this hope, and he could've taken off down some eternally flat stretch of road, a hard, blue sky his roof, warm breeze playing through. Toby Manza sits inside for a couple seconds and I imagine him staring up at us, on the other side of this window, just as I tried to stare inside *his* windows, wondering at the world he had built for himself without me in it.

I slide my arm around Cassandra's small shoulders, tentatively pulling her closer. She lets me. I watch as Toby Manza drives out of the parking lot. Cassandra is looking at something else, her expression glazed, far beyond this window, away from here. Maybe there's a reason she's always climbing, I'm thinking. So I follow her, down the horn-blaring city streets, the concrete parade of buildings, even the arch, I imagine, its giant curved steel glinting in the afternoon sun like a silver rainbow; past the mud-colored Mississippi River to where the land opens up again, wide and flat and slow, where the prairies were and the prairies are, the cornfields, soybeans; where babies who never lived are buried under false names, and people who could not live true to themselves are forgiven anyway. Where life, tainted and unholy as it gets, just needs to go on.

1999

PABLO, PICKLES,
A SONG FOR THE PRAIRIE

First thing Pablo needs you to know about himself is he's not the Spanish kind of Pablo, he'll tell you, he's the Irish type who should've been named Patrick or Peter or Jerry, or even Franklin, that's his brother. See, his mother had those gotta-get-him-or-I'll-die hots real bad for this man named Michael, which is more your Irish kind of a name, only it turns out he's Spanish, with ancestors in Barcelona, Spain, even. Should've called him Miguel, Pablo says, pronouncing it, *goo-el*. Then she discovers Michael's been doing this other lady at the same time he's doing Pablo's mother, telling them both how he's madly in love with them. Pablo's mother isn't sure how much she loves Michael, whether what she's feeling is love-lust, or just your basic gotta-get-him-or-I'll-die lust, but she's going to make him suffer for pretending to love her, or maybe he loves her some but he loves the other lady just as much; however the die was cast, Pablo's mother told Pablo, it wasn't rolling any closer to the altar. And her biological clock, she told him, wasn't simply ticking, it was firing off its alarm. So she marries Pablo's Irish father, the very next man she meets who doesn't make her want to puke, she told Pablo, just to spite Michael. Immediately she gets pregnant with Pablo, and that's what she names him. Pablo. A Spanish, spite kind of a name.

So Pablo, who's as tangerine haired and that freckly sort of skin as any guy sucking down Guinness in the Dublin Pub and Grill, feels he's got to constantly explain about his name. To make matters worse Pablo's father, the Irish one, disappeared long ago, before Pablo's brother Franklin was even fully born. Now Pablo doesn't know who he should spite, his runaway Irish father, or the namesake Spanish one, who didn't have a Spanish name and wasn't his real father anyhow.

The way Pablo tells it, Franklin had his little foot stuck out of their mother, a breech birth and the doctor's trying to turn him back around, his mother groaning and wailing, going at it for just short of an entire day. It seems Pablo's father was just too tenderhearted to bear his wife's agony a moment longer. He takes off his mask and his gown, the ones they give the fathers so they can be with their wives, folding them up neatly beside Pablo's mother, her legs caught up in those stirrups so she could hardly come whaling after him like she would've done otherwise. The nurses and doctors are hollering, Don't take that mask and gown off, you'll cause contamination! What Pablo's father says is, I'm sorry, but I just can't go through with it. Then out he strides, never to be seen again. No one was sure what Pablo's father meant by not being able to go through with it, the birth, which any fool knows has got to be worse on the mother, or the long-ass haul of eighteen-plus years after that.

Here's where I come in. I'm Neville, Pablo's girl. I'm the first girlfriend he's had who's got a boy's name, and I'm the first girl he's done that he actually likes, he tells me, a lot. He can't use the other L word, he says, because as any idiot can see his family's busted up. And what do you think caused that? I'm supposed to answer the L word, Love. Doesn't do nobody any kind of good, Pablo says, shooting me that scowling squinty-eyed look of his. Do I want to challenge it? this look asks, because he'll be goddamn ready with the proof.

We live in St. Louis, but I'm not from St. Louis and I haven't been in St. Louis long enough, I guess, to entirely appreciate it. I'm from the prairie, and Pablo says the name of the town I lost my baby teeth in, learned to ride a bike in, sold Girl Scout cookies door-to-door in, these sorts of standard issue, middle-class, wannabe-American things, he calls them, is not important. It's all the same out there, he says, What's in a name? Strip malls, cornfields, more strip malls, Burger King, Arby's, Dunkin' Donuts and McDonald's, soybean fields, roads like flattened slugs and the open places, he says, Nothing but acres of goddamn weeds; open places waiting to be filled. He dismisses my family for being standard issue. You got a mother and a father, right? he shrugs.

My mother was taking the Greyhound into St. Louis five days a week for as many years cleaning other people's houses, and my father finally said, Ella, we can't have you doing this. Taking the bus he meant, so we moved here. Last week my high school biology class went to some Midwestern environmental exhibit, and they had this picket fence with a fancy nameplate on it surrounding a scruffy grassy area they had labeled *Prairie Garden in Progress*. Like if my mom didn't bother to plant our garden back home with peas and lettuce and pole beans, just let it grow wild, trading the wire-mesh deer fence for something useless but pretty—what deer in its right mind wants a mouthful of bluestem?—then that's what she could've called it, her Prairie Garden. It's the thing for low-maintenance landscaping, we were told, once you get it started and it takes hold.

Pablo and Franklin and their mother live in the same apartment complex we do, so that's how I met him. We're in the rent-controlled buildings, part of a cluster of apartment buildings, not all of them low rent, some of them regular rent —Like they-steal-half-your-paycheck-just-to-live-under-their-goddamn-roof rent! my father snarls, north side of the city. The area around it is coming up, the manager told my mother, which means for a couple blocks further north of us there are boarded-up buildings and empty lots with shattered glass, then your normal-type neighborhood behind us, boxy houses, mostly brick, the wooden ones all painted beige or brown or tan, and on the block south of this you can get espresso coffee in fifteen flavors, buy old books that cost more than brand new ones and shop in a store selling international cooking spices with unpronounceable names.

That's what coming up is, my father said, Salt that curls your teeth and you got to speak a different language just to buy it. They'll probably raise the rent over it, he growled, Salt that costs more than the foods that need it. My father doesn't read the Bible, probably has never read it, but there are stories he remembers hearing that made him think about things. Lot's wife being changed into a pillar of salt was one. Because she looked back, he said, No more reason than that.

Pablo and me, we like to sit outside at night on the steps to my apartment building, eyeballing the little slice of steamy sky you can see between the other buildings, and smoke cigarettes. The sky's not so dark here, I've noticed, kind of a wounded gray. You can't see many stars, like the sky isn't sure if it wants to be night over St. Louis or not. I mentioned this to Pablo once and he told me to let go of the choke hold I've got on my past. Get into it, Neville, you're not a prairie chick no more. Just because where I lived before had a bigger, brighter sky doesn't make it a better sky, he said, Just more empty.

Pablo first started doing me under the back metal stairs that lead up to my unit. That's what they call the apartments, units, and my mother hates that word. It's like we don't have any real kind of a home, she says, Like we live in something measured. She says things like this, then she sighs, shrugs, and goes to bed. My mom sleeps deeply since she takes the kind of pills that make sure this happens, but my dad just sits and watches TV all night, real loud because he doesn't like the sounds of other people living in the units around us. So this is why Pablo figured under my stairs was the safest place to do it, nobody would hear us.

Even before we moved to St. Louis pretty much what my father did day and night was watch TV, just not so loud. He's got that post-traumatic-stress thing from the Vietnam War, but he takes the kind of pills that don't make you sleep, because if he sleeps too soundly he gets these terrible dreams and he wakes up shouting and sobbing and swearing he's going to kill someone who's not even here.

Under my stairs or not, it wasn't safe enough for everything, turns out. Turns out I should've had Pablo use the kind of rubber condoms they used to call safes. *Safe* is just not a word I gave much thought to. I didn't get the blood last month and my insides have been feeling sort of jumpy; like the shadows we watch when we're lying beneath the steps after we've done it, poking out our heads, sucking down a shared cigarette, the two of us. It's my favorite part, my head tilted back against Pablo's chest, smelling that spicy-sweat smell of him, breathing the same smoke, listening to the ba-boom ba-boom of his heart, noise of the city muffled and distant until it disappears, easy as something you can forget. The shadows are from two scraggly honey locust trees on either side of the concrete path that weaves through the complex; they play on the sides of our buildings at night, Pablo's and mine, sort of stretching and bumping and lacing themselves together in patterns from the outside lights, but in the daytime these trees don't even touch. That's how my insides have been feeling. First they were alone, and now maybe they're not.

I plan how to tell Pablo so he won't say to me, the way guys often do, that he'll be there for me, that he'll drive me to the place where they vacuum it out, that he'll even pay for half. These kinds of considerations I don't need. Then when they're done he's gone and you're left emptier than the prairie sky. I think about, what if it's a boy? I think about telling him this, that it's a boy, and if Pablo runs out on us then he's doing the same thing to his own son that his Irish dad did to him. The Spanish one, too, in a way, even though Michael wasn't really Pablo's dad. But he could have been. Of course girls need fathers, too, but I just wonder if Pablo thought it was a boy, then maybe he'd see some kind of pattern here, fathers and sons and the fathers who run out on their sons.

So the next night he pulls me from the top of the steps where we're sucking off a cigarette, to underneath them, starts tugging down his pants; then he asks me how come I'm not taking off mine? We don't do it like they do in the movies, unbuttoning each other's buttons, kissing each other's necks and throats, our hands easing down to the more tender parts, romantic like. I guess St. Louis isn't such a romantic place as Hollywood. Maybe having giant, waving palm trees instead of the scrubby honey locusts that make the shadows helps.

Well, I tell him, because it might hurt your son.

What the fu…?

My meaning hits him before he even gets the word out. Pablo's no dummy. He's a senior at our high school, where a lot of the other guys we hang with have long since dropped out. He talks about going to college. Maybe, he says.

Pablo studies my belly, real quiet, his eyes moving up and down, to the sides where my hipbones used to jut out like sugar bowl handles, but not so much anymore, then back to my middle. We're still standing, but you can't really stand up under these steps, you have to kind of lean and stoop, and I'm trying to thrust out my belly, make it look bigger to prove the point, which is pretty hard when you're leaned over and stooped.

How do you know it's a boy? he asks finally.

Now I'm a little surprised at this, because he skipped the first part of the question. Everyone knows you're supposed to ask the girl how does she know she's pregnant. That's the question I was prepared to answer. So I don't think about the medical tests they have now that can tell you the sex; I mean, if you're going to lie, lie with a bit of the truth backing you up. Instead, I give him the dumbest answer possible, the thing my best friend's aunt from back home told her, and her aunt's best friend before that, and so on. I tell him about the pickle test.

If you crave pickles more than any food in the world, and you put one on the top of your belly and it doesn't roll off, it's a girl, I tell Pablo. If the thought of a pickle makes you want to puke but you hunger for weird things, banana pancakes at midnight, Taco Bell enchiladas or an entire can of baked beans, it's a boy. If you put a pickle on your belly and you've got a boy in there, it rolls away from you far as it can get.

So, I shrug, my face flaming but thank God he can't see it in this milky darkness; I'd rather blow a car's tailpipe than eat a pickle.

You want a baby? Pablo asks.

This also takes me back, because when I planned it out I saw myself convincing Pablo he wants a baby. My wanting a baby is not something I've let myself think about much. It's a bigger problem thinking how I'm going to tell my folks that maybe I'm going to have a baby, since it will just add to their miseries and they'll be sure to let me know this.

I shrug again, I don't know. But Pablo, the thing is—I'm real direct here, trying to force a toughness I don't particularly feel—The thing is, we got one.

I make sure to say *we*, because in these kinds of matters you got to make sure the guy knows the baby is every bit as much his as yours, that just because it happens to be growing in you doesn't make it only your problem. That's what those pamphlets from the school nurse's office said anyway. Probably I should've read some of them sooner than I did.

I realize I said that word, *problem*, not out loud to him, to myself. I lower my eyes and stare at what I can see of the packed dirt we're standing on, the ground we lie on when we're doing it. Missouri hasn't had much rain to speak of, and the earth is cracked and cakey, what you can see of it in St. Louis that's not concrete or somebody's yellow yard. Probably in the daylight there are cigarette butts here, most of them ours, and bugs, and all the veiny, grainy stuff dirt is, so that afterwards, if Pablo thinks about it, he swipes his hand down my tailbone and the backs of my legs, wiping it off so my folks won't see. In Hollywood they don't do it in the dirt, that's for sure. I can't think of a single movie where they're not on some nice fluffed-up bed, except if the girl gets raped, then maybe she's shoved up against the hood of a car. Rape is not any kind of love.

I gaze at Pablo again but he's not looking at me. Do you love me, Pablo, at all? I whisper. I can't be sure if he's heard me or not, or if he's just ignoring me because I said the L word. He's pinched out another cigarette from the remains of the pack, and now he crouches down to light it, peering out at the night. The tip of the cigarette sparks and glows a small orange, like a firefly, darting back and forth to his mouth then into the space between us. Kneeling down beside him I hear the soft throaty sounds of his inhales, his exhales. But not too close. For some reason I don't feel like being too close to Pablo. I think about my father and my mother upstairs in our unit. They're not sleeping together, but they're not apart either. My father gets his crazies, my mother calls them, and he can be real nasty when these come on. But he doesn't mean it, she says, Not in the long run anyways.

Well, I ask Pablo, could you want a baby?

He doesn't answer at first, just stares into the shadows the trees make, and under one of them a long-eared cat slinking across the concrete path. I've seen it before, a homeless cat, small and sour and sad looking, but he's got an attitude, too, you can tell; he wants it understood that he's not so cool about just anyone, either. Like if they offered him a home, he'd have to inspect it first.

Pablo makes a cluttery sound in his throat, clearing it as if he's about to make a speech, then in a voice that's flat and hard and suddenly very grown up, like he's already gone to college, had a work life and come out of it all on some other side, far away from this St. Louis, under these low-rent stairs, he says: The way I see it, in this life you're either a deserter or the one who gets deserted. He swivels full around and stares at me straight. So the thing is, Neville, I guess I don't know yet which I am.

Later I have the strangest dream. I'm in this prairie garden, long, wavering grasses, switchgrass, Indian grass, big bluestem, purple prairie clover and black and yellow butterflies, the air shimmery hot; but it's somebody's design, grown in a deliberate arrangement, not the way it would really grow, wild and reedy and free, and not the way it is where I come from, corn and bean fields mostly, even strip malls like Pablo says, but some prairie too, grass and sunflowers and stiff goldenrod, and a slowness to it all you can taste on your tongue, sucking it in, whistling it out, clean and light as wind. The dream turns dark, a starless dark, a big, empty dark, and I'm suddenly so alone in the garden of someone else's making that I wake up crying, hollowed out like I don't have a thing inside me, not even my own bones, empty as something that's not even real. I squeeze my hands against my stomach, my chest, feeling for the slow rise of my breath, just to make sure I'm still me.

I think about going into the front room where my father is slumped on the sofa staring at the TV, and asking him for one of those pills that make the dreams stop. But I know this about being pregnant, I read it in the pamphlets: whatever you eat your baby does, too, so that this baby, even though I haven't thought enough about whether I want him or her—this baby would also eat the pill and might never, ever dream.

Instead I grab my too-big nylon jacket that used to be Pablo's, even though it's September and it's pretty hot around here, and I head outside. I can smell Pablo in the fabric's wrinkly shape; when I pull it on it's his skin settling lightly over me. I don't sit on the back steps though. I head over to the side of our building, our units, where a fire escape is. Once I tried to get Pablo to climb up this with me but he said he didn't like heights, that he preferred his feet pretty flat on the ground, that way he always knew where he stood. It's only five stories, but that's just high enough, turns out, as I shimmy up on the roof, to see the sky. The whole sky, above St. Louis where the downtown lights make it lighter, but also the part heading in the direction I come from, past the Mississippi River. This part is darker and as my eyes adjust, more and more stars glimmer out of the black.

It reminds me of the way notes pop out on a music page, back home in the days before my father lost his job, when I begged them to send me to piano lessons, and they did. I wanted to make something beautiful. Two years of tortured scales and notes cringing off the page, wishing I could magically knit these together and out would flow the waves of music I heard in my head. I imagined myself becoming part of this music, fingers floating over the keyboard, the silvery ease of water.

But here, on this night, the page becomes the darkness and the notes are the stars, the song. I start humming this dumb little tune they play on the radio, not the cool music Pablo tries to get me to listen to, alternative he calls it. I feel suddenly happy and I can't imagine why. I'm probably pregnant and I haven't even finished high school. I'll never be a piano player or anything else I might have dreamed of, a movie star, a scientist, not even a person who builds Midwestern environmental exhibits—Prairie Restoration Projects they're calling these. I'm a person who comes from the prairie and never even understood we were disappearing. Pablo may or may not become like his fathers before him and also disappear. But I suppose I don't love him, so why would it matter? I reach under the jacket, lift up my T-shirt and lightly rub my belly. It's warm, still mostly flat, not pointing out anyways. Who knows, maybe I'll get the blood tomorrow and it turns out the whole thing was a dream, like in one of my father's dreams, where his ghosts are alive, and then they aren't.

They're gone, my mother whispers to my father, sitting near him on our worn-out sofa, stroking his spidery hair, pressing his head against her breast; as if it's my father who is her child, my father that she needs to nurse into this world. The war is over, she says, They're all gone. Then they hold each other and they rock, back and forth, they rock, they sway, eyes shut, grasping on to each other, as if they are the ones who've been left.

GIRL DREAMING

I can barely remember what it's like, Neecie says, calling me for the umpteenth time this month. Maine, she sighs, deep drag off her cigarette, Where you can't see the air.

I cluck my tongue into the phone, loudly I hope, in her ear. Poor Neecie, I chirp, You know, I was just noticing the Maine air this morning, and I do believe it's got this mauve thing going. Dressed for the fall, but subtle you know, the Calvin Klein of seasons. Calvin's the only designer's name I can think of offhand to razz Neecie with; we don't exactly live the designer life, this part of Maine.

Neecie sniffles, clears her throat. Well you just poke all the fun you want, Cindra, at my expense, but a land that's flatter than flat with a layer of visible air hunkered on top like it's pretending to be some sort of actual terrain is not my cup of you-know-what.

That's what she's been harping on lately when she calls, how she sees the air in St. Louis. It's that muggy, she says, A sickly, shivery sort of haze. Especially you can see it at night, she tells me, hovering under the garish streetlamps. Neecie reams out words like this whenever she learns one, as if she's always known it, like she's been born into the kind of life where these sorts of words are actually spoken. Looks like air you can bite, she says, You'd take in a mouthful, lumpy and grainy as old bread.

Yeah well, I remind her, It's not like it doesn't get humid in Maine. Especially in the woods where you lived, remember? Hope, Maine, come summer and you used to say you hoped for any other bloody season. That air can be seen too sometimes, just hanging out between the pines.

Neecie doesn't miss a beat. There's no woods here, she says, No woods in St. Louis city. You got to go to a special place to even see a clump of pine trees, like the arboretum, somewhere like that. They call it a pinery, if you can imagine. Putting trees on display like they're zoo animals. I'm telling you, Cindra, I look up into all my neighbors' windows, folks I don't even know, and every night I see them individual TV sets, flickery blue lights through window blinds that are all the same. They're watching something, Neecie says, and I'm just sitting outside in the dark, all by my lonesome, smoking my smokes. (Neecie's sure to let me hear this too, her loneliness; she wants me to pity her, as in maybe I should ring her up on the phone once in a while.) What kind of a community is it, I ask you, Cindra, divides itself into who watches what on TV? There's this little cat with big ears comes by, making his rounds. Won't sit near me though, just squats under the elderberry sometimes, where he can keep an eye on me. Nobody wants to be with him neither. Probably never even had a mother, I'll bet.

That's impossible, Neecie, I say, Don't you remember your biology? Fact of life, he was born from a female cat so she's his mother, whether he lives where she does or not. But I know what Neecie's getting at. She's my adopted mother-in-law, so to speak, and right now I got more problems in this world than I don't call her Mom. That's what she wants more than anything it seems, except maybe if she could move back to Maine, for me to call her Mom, not Neecie. It's not about any kind of love. It's about winning. She'll think she's won if I call her Mom. And besides, sighs Neecie, your sort doesn't go in for designer clothes, do you?

Our sort, I snarl, but under my breath, she won't hear it. Neecie moved to St. Louis three months ago, two years and four months after her daughter and I got committed (which is to say our commitment ceremony, but it's feeling more like the other these days, for me anyway). Since then she's sent me four cotton-polyester shirts, one's got the arch embroidered on it, and cards and pamphlets about westward expansion, which means elbowing your way into places you may not be needed or welcome, far as I can tell. What difference can it make that a president builds a monument to honor this? The shirts are size small, Neecie likes to think of me as small, but the truth is I'm as medium as it gets. So how do I tell her that her daughter, her Baby Girl she calls her, has done her own kind of expansion back here in good old Hope, moving from our bed to another woman's in Rock Harbor? She wanted me to gather up her belongings, so I told her, Sure thing, Baby Girl, mosey into our yard you never got around to mowing this summer (that was her job, the yard), and I hucked all her things out onto it.

So what do I tell Neecie when she next calls, wanting to talk to her? Sorry, your fucked-up daughter isn't here anymore, she's living with another woman? Or maybe, your daughter doesn't live here anymore, she's out fucking another woman! Either way I'm the one looks like the loser, can't keep Baby Girl home. That's what she'll think, Neecie will, though what she'll say is, Oh, honey, I'm so sorry for you! and she'll send me another too-small shirt.

Because of course she's expected it, and Neecie loves to be right. Loves to see her expectations come to their natural fruition, she'd say, like some damned fruit that needed to ripen, another word she's picked up; it's a way of winning, after all. I was the mousy girl from the Midwest (Cleveland if you're wondering, but it's all the same to Neecie) her Baby Girl fell in with. Could've had anyone in Hope, but of course she chose me, lucky me. I'm certain Neecie believes her own daughter wouldn't even be that sort if it wasn't for me, though she's sure to let me know it's OK I'm not normal; Neecie, Christian martyr that she is, will accept me anyway. And now in the way life has of playing its twisted little jokes, Neecie's new husband has dragged her out to St. Louis, the Midwest! Just so he could make a living.

Two days later Neecie calls again, says, You know what? They got cricket-type creatures in St. Louis the size of bats. And the noise they make!—steep pull off her cigarette, I can almost feel the exhale in my ear, the heat of it, smell the stink of it—Don't know how anyone sleeps around here, just thinking about them bugs is enough to keep me checking my window screens, big as bats I tell you, scrunching their legs together or however they do to get that ungodly sound. I bet they're grinning when they do it; it's almost obscene, she adds. My Baby Girl around?

No, Neecie, I sigh, and suddenly I'm sick of this whole damn business, partners that walk out without a word for what's possible, no hint of what you did or didn't do, or would do if you had known... God knows what? That life between your own two legs had become old hat? comfortless? or maybe too much comfort, lulled to sleep every night, same old sounds, same wind through the same trees outside the same bedroom window, knowing this sameness when you wake. The new woman in Rock Harbor is a carpenter; perhaps Baby Girl gets her wrists nailed to the bedposts every night, she did have those crucifixion tendencies! And then there's the irritating adopted mother-in-law that calls and calls and calls. Consider me your adopted mother-in-law, Neecie said last year, surprising even herself with her own magnanimity, her generosity of spirit, deciding maybe, just maybe I wasn't going away.

You want the truth? I ask her, my voice breaking. Truth of the matter, she's not been here for a couple weeks. Do you want to know why? She's shacking up with a slut in overalls, that's why, turns a screw easy as stepping out of her steel-toed boots! I blurt this out, and then I feel like toking off a cigarette, too, even though I've never smoked, not the legal stuff anyway, sucking it down hot into my lungs, feeling it swirl around, letting it invade me—it's for damn sure there's nothing else getting into me these days. When you think about it, Neecie, I add, voice lower, flatter, swallowing back hysteria, a lump of sickness down my throat, Your baby girl's found someone pretty handy, blowtorch, blow job, she's got it covered.

Another woman, Neecie states flatly, quietly, not a question but I take it that way.

Duh! I say.

Then she's silent, not quite the sugary, oh-so-sorry I expected, or maybe I thought she'd hang up on me, hoped for it, those words blow job in her ear. Maybe she doesn't know what a blow job is. I get an image of my mother-in-law, her satiny lipsticked mouth pursed into an *O*, blowing on her husband, actually blowing, like she's trying to cool it down. How might she imagine this, or would she even let herself try, between her daughter and another woman? I'm waiting for the other shoe to fall.

Well then, Neecie says finally, Fact is, Arnold's not around much neither. He works out at the airport you know, Lambert Field, and when he finally does come home, darned if he can hear a single word I say unless I scream it. He drives around a little golf cart half the day, chasing birds so they don't fly into the jets' engines. It's not much of a life for me you know, Cindra, the neighbors don't talk to me, except this lady next door, tells me she's a psychic, lets me call her on the phone if I want a prediction. Do you think she invites me into her home though? Phones, computers, television, what would these people do with a life that doesn't unplug or recharge? But I'll be doggoned if I'm going to carry on a conversation at the top of my lungs with a husband whose ears are full of jet noise. Why he won't keep them ear-muffler thingies on they're supposed to wear, I don't get it. It's a silent life for me here in St. Louis, I'll tell you.

Neecie! I'd like to shout at her, was this about you? For once it wasn't about you. But I don't. What's the use? She'd even turn that into something about her; how come you're always yelling at me, Cindra? she'd say. So why'd you marry him then? I mutter, You knew he'd be working at some airport, it's what he does.

You wouldn't understand, Cindra, you're a young woman still. I'm too old to be alone, she sighs. Our society is not exactly charitable for an older woman alone, you know. Then your screws fall out entirely and you become like the psychic lady who I've never seen leave her apartment, not once. Maybe she knows something the rest of us don't.

I peer around my empty house, not even my house, certainly not our house, just this place in the woods we rented and now she expects me to foot the whole damn bill since she's not living here anymore, she's pointed out, so why should she help pay? And how do I manage this on a part-time waitress's earnings?

I'll probably have to cocktail, I hiss into the phone at my mother-in-law, push alcoholic beverages to mashers and drunks, just to make ends meet.

Is it some baby business, you suppose? Neecie asks. You suppose that could've been why she left? I know Baby Girl used to talk about wanting a child of her own someday. Do you think if you'd been able to give her a baby?

Neecie! This time I do shout it, How you think babies get here, anyway? I can't exactly go down to the Wal-Mart, buy one and wrap it up for her, you know? Babies are not part of their seasonal displays. She's got a role in this, too, if you get what I'm saying!

Now, Cindra, don't get huffy with me, all I'm meaning here is your lifestyle has some limitations. You know I'm not one for being prejudiced, I'm just pointing this out.

I wheeze out about as polite a *goodbye* as I can manage, clunk the receiver down then run into the hall, not much of a hall. just two dingy walls and the empty space between, to our bedroom. Which is my bedroom now I suppose, my double bed that we just got a new mattress for, not new but not so used either—dragged it home from a church rummage sale, the kind of church that attracts the kind of people who can afford to get rid of a barely used mattress, cause they're buying up in beds to the next, queen size. The kind of people who go to church maybe, because they feel guilty they got it so good, pray out their thanks to make sure they don't end up like the rest of us, living in someone else's house, sleeping in someone else's bed, alone.

I fling myself down on that mattress, bounce around for a moment or two—it's all mine now, I can pummel the hell out of the thing like it's a trampoline if I want to—and I try to imagine the others doing me, making love to me, Tom Cruise maybe, or even the kid that sells the deli meats down at the Shaws. I've seen his hands, gloved and sleek, squeezing up that rump of bologna. He's got a good face, a face you could come home to and it would be there. But it's not his face I would memorize in the daylight, play back in my dreams, sure set of a chin, those thick lashes like fringes of velcro, every blemish, each particular skin cell, DNA proclaiming this, the one I love; it's hers.

I got a good face, too, and I need to remember this. It's Neecie who called me mousy, I overheard her after she first met me, after her daughter told her about us. She didn't even like my name, said it didn't sound American to her, not even for somebody from Ohio. Cindra is my parents' names combined, Cindy and Ray. Why should I have to defend my own name?

Baby Girl loved my face, or so she said, running her fingers over it back when we were—she was—in love. Then there was this period of time, weeks, a month or two? when she wanted me to change it, but nothing too dramatic—to make what was good even better, was the way she described it; just a little something, she would say, maybe some lipstick to set off my almost straight teeth, or a diet to carve those cheekbones. Bring out the woman in you.

I slide my own fingers down my face now, the bridge of my nose that isn't too big, my cheekbones that really are there, my lips, not even chapped. I touch my collarbone, shoulder blades, bones fine and sharp as fins. I didn't get fat and there wasn't enough time to get old. I figured out how she liked to be touched, not ever letting her know she didn't know this about me. None of these were enough.

I stare at my hands, smooth and ropey and unmarked; waitressing is, after all, relatively clean work, you feel it more in the legs than the arms, and your jaw muscles, the smile frozen in place. A carpenter? Though at least she builds things, something in the world where there was nothing before, a spec, a space, someone's dream. I only fill these spaces, move inside; sometimes I can barely see my way back out of them.

Neecie calls the next week, I'm about to turn in, my feet are raw and cramped from the heels I wore cocktailing the Breakwater Lounge, stiletto screw-me pumps to beg tips in. I'm in no mood for a conversation with my adopted mother-in-law. Neecie, I sigh, Just supposing I did call you Mom just once, would you remember what goddamn time it is and quit calling this late?

Oh, well, yeah—hard draw off her cigarette, blow it in my ear—I know, I know, I keep forgetting, you all are an hour later, hah hah, what do you know about that? I gained an hour on my life coming to St. Louis, that's one thing I got from this place. But, the thing is, there's ticks here! she whispers, as if they might hear her. That's what I called to tell you. I got one on me this morning, God knows how since there aren't exactly woods around, just these patches of open space behind the buildings, stringy weeds, some wiseacre put up a sign, says *Prairie Garden*, so the apartment manager thinks he doesn't have to mow. Anyhow, this tick got on my ankle, you know, where the veins are all busted up, varicose, from birthing Baby Girl. I yanked at it so hard, must've got that—what do you call the thing they stick you with?—a proboscis or something, shoved real far in. When I finally pulled the little sucker out blood was spurting everywhere! I think it latched onto an artery. You should've seen the bathroom, Cindra, it looked like a murder scene from one of them TV emergency shows. All over the white linoleum. I'm telling you, they should never use white for a bathroom floor. Beige maybe, or better yet a nice pastel.

Oh for chrissake, get a rug! So what happened? I ask, knowing better, but what the hell. It's not like I've heard any kind of interesting conversation all night in the lounge, just men on the prowl saying the things they say to women and the women pretending they believe them.

Yeah, well, you think any of these neighbors of mine come over, I'm yelling and carrying on and all? I could've been getting a butcher's knife poked in one end of me and out the other, and there they sat, staring at their TVs. Even Ada the psychic didn't come, and she's the one told me on the phone something "unexpected" was going to occur. Who said the Midwest was supposed to be friendly? Isn't that what you told me when you got together with Baby Girl? Anyhow, I called 911.

You called 911 for a tick bite?

This was no ordinary tick bite, Cindra, didn't you hear me about the blood? When they came, the ambulance people, they couldn't believe it neither. They wanted to see the tick. Course, you don't exactly save a tick that's bit you, vicious and all that. I flushed it down the you-know-what, I told them, You think I keep a specimen jar handy in the bathroom? They put a pressure bandage on it, and Arnold even came home early. I had to holler out the whole story to him just so he could hear it, and he ordered up some pizza since I wasn't exactly in any condition to cook for him.

Cindra..., she slides out this next sentence almost in the same breath, so smooth I'm actually listening to her and not hanging up, still thinking about a killer St. Louis tick out for my ex-adopted-mother-in-law's (I'm calling her *ex* but not so she knows) lifeblood... Cindra, what about a makeover? You know, they got those department store ladies, the ones who sell the cosmetics, they can do that for you. A makeover and a fresh haircut, maybe a new dress, short. Baby Girl always had eyes for the legs. Her own are quite good, she gets that from me.

Neecie! There I go again, shouting; my father used to tell me, Modulate, you know a lady by the tone of her voice (this because he was afraid I wasn't...). It's not me, Neecie! I'm not at fault here, damn it, OK? I'm trying to bloody well remember this so you better, too. I got great legs. Any veins in them are pretty well hidden under a decent set of calves. No tick could make my blood spurt out, no miniskirt is going to make your defective daughter come home, and just in case you've been wondering, nothing you can do will make her trade what's under those carpenter overalls for the male brand. She got bored, Neecie. She just goddamn quit sleeping with me. You think I'm going to win that back with the correct shade of eye shadow?

I slam down the receiver and then I run out into my yard, into the Maine September night with a zillion stars and air you can't see, and mosquitoes—maybe not big as bats, but humming crazily around me as I slog barefoot through the clingy, extra long grass she never got around to cutting—just daring them to come and bite me, ticks, mosquitoes, sucking and slurping at my blood, making little red welts and bumps, and itchy, ugly bruises all over my skin. Wouldn't I at least know I've been touched?

When next she calls I don't say her name, won't even grace her with that. It's occurred to me I don't have to listen, if Baby Girl's gone, then she's not exactly my mother-in-law, adopted or otherwise, is she? We don't have any kind of a connection except through her daughter. I don't have to be polite, she was never like a mother, and I don't know what a mother's supposed to be like anyway, since mine's been gone from this world so long I can barely remember her. A whiff of her perfume, Ambush, sometimes, if I'm near a woman that wears it, is all I get. But if Baby Girl's gone, who's going to call me? It's not like I've made many friends in Maine. So I pick up the phone, but I say nothing, and she starts in immediately, as if I really did acknowledge her; or maybe this doesn't even matter.

Cindra, she says, The thing about her, she isn't perfect.

Well, duh! I want to tell her, but I don't. I'm giving her the silent treatment. And anyway, there's not much I can say that hasn't been said. She's gone, I'm not. End of story.

What I mean, Neecie says, She was never perfect. From the start. One of those crying babies, couldn't make her settle in to save my life. God knows I tried. I nursed her until my you-know-whats were sore and wrung out as rags. I rocked her and held her, sung to her into the night. Her father just slept, of course, said *he* didn't have the kind of ninnies that could nourish, so what good could he be? Ain't that the truth, but that's another story.

I sigh, so she knows I'm listening, but still not speaking a word. Something in me wants her to continue.

Anyhow, one day I just got fed up with that baby's constant crying. Made me think all the time I was doing something wrong, that I was a no-good kind of mother, couldn't even make my own child stop crying. So I took her out in the yard behind our house, we had a little ranch-style back then with a big wooded yard—you get those in Maine, big yards and greener than green, not like they have in St. Louis....

Bernice! I say sternly, breaking my vow of silence. I can't help myself, the way that woman goes on can drive a person mad! But I use the name she hates, her mother's name. She wishes she'd been closer to her mother, Neecie told me once, but truth was they shared little more than a name.

Bernice, I say it again, finish your story, who gives a damn about the color of the lawn. Greener than green! She has that way of talking, of comparing a thing to its own self, for chrissake.

She humphs, clucks her tongue, I'm almost done, she says, It's what I called to tell you. I took her out in the yard, this bawling little offspring of mine, and I threw her high up in the air. Baby Girl, I said, I'm the only one who's going to catch you. And I did. She was so startled she even stopped crying for a minute or two. Scared the bejesus out of her, I suppose. But she figured out who was holding the net. She got that figured right.

For chrissake, Neecie, you created the danger for her, you threw your own baby up in the air and then you congratulate yourself for catching her? I jab a fingernail angrily into the palm of my hand—though I'm not so deluded, I know it's not really Neecie I'm furious at.

What I'm telling you here, Cindra, is that she'll always need someone to catch her. I figured that out about her, you see, I knew there was something not quite right from the start. So maybe you're just not the net type, you know? Also, guess what? Even if you did have a baby, it's no guarantee that baby will keep loving you. When they're little they love you cause you're all they got. It's like you're their god. Then they start growing up and they're questioning your very existence. You're no longer a god, you're barely tolerated, and that's the loneliest thing in the world, I tell you. You become silly to them. Silly and useless to the life you created. It's fearsome, Cindra, this kind of loneliness. So maybe you're better off without any babies, after all.

I'm quiet again, but not on purpose. I'm thinking here and she's letting me, breathing stifled little puffs of smoke on the other end. Neecie's throwing me some kind of a bone, I get that, but I don't know how to take it. Is she actually admitting I'm too good for her daughter, this mousy midwesterner, that I'm better off without her? That it's OK I was with her in the first place? God knows her own daughter never calls her Mom; never calls her at all.

How's your tick bite? I ask finally, since I don't know what else to say.

Turns out that tick was probably an ancestor, she says, if you can believe that. I met the people who live directly upstairs, finally they come down. I guess they heard about the ambulance. They're Chinese, real Chinese, from China. Now that's something you don't find much of living in Maine, people from anyplace else.

I'm not from Maine, I remind her.

Oh, well, Neecie sighs, Ohio. She's a pretty one, this Chinese woman, Neecie says. She's got that crispy kind of a voice. Of course, she doesn't speak English too good, though a darn sight better than I could speak Chinese, I'll give her that. She told me in their Buddhist religion, I think it was that, when something like this tick bite happens, it's a good thing, she said. An ancestor maybe, who wanted to be remembered, so he holds on. But I'm thinking while she's saying this, that it's probably not a direct relation. It's probably Baby Girl's father who died doing the you-know-what to another woman. He had a heart attack and they had to pry him off her. He was a big man,

Baby's Girl's father. I used to think those kinds of things only happened in the movies. We were already divorced, so I didn't begrudge him. He was always trying to cling to something.

That's when I laugh. I don't know why, but I can't help myself, short, sharp little barks, ripping into the silence of my house. It's a fakey kind of laugh, out of the throat instead of where it's supposed to come from, deep down inside, but it feels damn good for a change. Maybe the thought of my ex-partner's father coming back as a tick, trying to have a last go at Neecie, who hates bugs more than anybody I know. I know this about Neecie. I know quite a few things about my adopted mother-in-law, I realize, even though most of these add up to a giant pain in the posterior. Did Neecie's ex-husband ever regret leaving her?

Neecie says, Well you can laugh about it, Cindra, but those nice Chinese people invited us to have dinner with them. And it's OK that Arnold can't hear a blasted thing, since he wouldn't be able to understand them anyhow. I'm going to try though, to understand them.

Maybe you could take a Chinese language course, Neecie, I offer, trying to swallow down my giggles. You can find those types of classes in a city like St. Louis, you know.

Wonder how they say *Mom* in Chinese, Neecie says, but she's laughing now, too. She sucks in a big breath of smoke, I can hear that poison as it swims down her lungs, over a thousand miles of telephone signals.

Neecie, I start, then hesitate a moment. I take a big breath too, that fine, invisible Maine air. Neecie, if you don't stop smoking those damn coffin nails you're going to end up deader than dead. Then who in this world have I got to call and pester me? My own mother died of cancer, did you know that? I don't tell her my mother died of skin cancer, melanoma, nothing to do with smoking. Because that's not the point.

She's actually speechless for a moment. I can hear the fuzzy sounds the distance between us makes, those thousand or so miles, St. Louis to Hope. Well! Neecie says finally, It's a lot to ask, don't you think? I could try to quit, I suppose. Maybe next month, or in January after the new year. Maybe the new millennium's a good time to not be smoking, who knows what'll happen to us all then. What you don't understand, Cindra, it's the one dependable thing I've got. Children, husbands, they come and go. Cigarettes are always in my pocketbook, even though I got to buy them to be there.

Then she says, Cindra? Describe what you see out your window where you're sitting, OK? Describe Maine to me, I swear sometimes I can barely remember it.

For chrissake, Neecie, exactly what time do you think it is? Do you ever call at a decent hour? It's dark! I shriek, I can't see a blessed thing.

Oh, well, Neecie sighs, Same here in St. Louis. What do you know about that? Cindra, she says again, what's the prettiest time of the day for you? She doesn't wait for me to answer, but I shrug anyway. These days all my hours look about the same, whatever the view out the Breakwater Lounge, grey and flat, shine and flat, or a flat, hard dark, it's all just hustling tips to pay this rent.

Early evening for me, Neecie says, That's when I miss Maine the most. How the light takes on that pearliness, almost iridescent, and then it just quietly fades. It used to make me feel quiet, too. Do you suppose that's how it will be when we die? The light going soft around you, and then maybe things don't matter so much anymore?

I hear the flick of her lighter followed by, incredibly enough, Neecie's own breath blowing the flame out. She moans, I don't know about this quitting business, Cindra, my little nicotine pals have accompanied me through just about every event in my life.

I lean forward in the overstuffed chair I had collapsed into—a yard-sale find, even my chair used to belong to somebody else—toward the picture window framing the darkness outside. The night is black, a tough, leathery darkness. What I see is my own self reflected in the glass from the lamp behind me, my face, wide-eyed and worn out at twenty-eight, a wan scowling in the window. I slide on an exaggerated, unreal smile, twisting my mouth into the mirrored black.

You know, Neecie sighs, wouldn't you think I could at least dream of Maine when I go to sleep? That I could escape St. Louis in my dreams?

I groan, still plastering on that false grin—I look like some sort of maniac, a psychotic clown trapped in the glass. OK, Neecie, you win! I'm going to give you Hope so you can go to bed and dream of it, and let me go to bed, too. I'm telling you, I work for a living, Neecie! Imagine a mountain of spruce, I say, Pines, tall and waving, a wind blowing up from the coast, shaking these trees that are *greener than green*. Smells like salt, I tell her, This wind smells like salt and, of course, you can't see it.

Invisible air! Neecie chuckles. Are there any bugs? she asks. I seem to remember bugs back there until the killing frost, mosquitoes and maybe even blackflies too. That's one thing I don't miss, those horrendous blackflies, when they sink their mouth parts into you it's worse than a tick.

No little suckers in this dream, I tell her, shaking my hair into my reflection, a shimmer of light, almost the shade of blond Baby Girl had wanted me to create for her, dye my hair, wear what she wanted me to wear, and what I am realizing is something I should have known from the start—I was bloody fine the way I was. What will she want from her carpenter? Leather overalls to hump those nails in?

In this dream we don't have bugs, I repeat, because we're expanding from Hope to the ocean, where there aren't any. Listen, OK? You're on the Breakwater strolling out into the harbor, the sea is silvery and sleek as skin. The moon's rising, fat yellow lantern on one side, the sun's going down over the land, and the sky is pink as....

Pinker than pink, Neecie finishes, she doesn't miss a beat. Am I with anybody? Is Arnold there?

He is or he isn't, that's up to you. You're walking into the sunset, the moonrise, perfect sky, those tall evergreens ringing the land on the one side, and there's that pink horizon, endless space just waiting.

Waiting? she whines, What's there to wait for?

Well for chrissake, Neecie, whose dream is this anyway? Must I always be the one who does all the work? I cluck my tongue at her, a gentle enough reprimand. Then I'm grinning for real, into the receiver at my mother-in-law, a lightbulb coming on in my mouth, dazzling as that giant moon, ear to ear like my father used to say—Smile, he'd tell me, Then who gives a damn if the world smiles with you?—glowing like something new. I don't have to see my reflection through some dark window to remember this is possible.

DREAM LIVES OF BUTTERFLIES

In the work named after him the great Taoist Chuang-tze tells how he dreamed that he was a butterfly. On waking and pondering upon his dream, he came to doubt his own identity. "Who am I? Chuang-tze, who sleeps and dreams that he is a butterfly, or a butterfly that is awake and imagines it is Chuang-tze?"

—Sbordoni and Forestiero, *Butterflies of the World*

I

There was the time when collecting them meant killing them. You got out your aerial-insect net, the lepidopterist's net or butterfly net some called it, slogged off in your knee-high rubber wading boots, your camouflage-type jacket with its oversized pockets, each with a share of glassine envelopes, specimen jars with chloroform-soaked cotton, potassium cyanide, or some such snuffing chemical. Small species, like the Lycaenidae butterflies, were pinned in the field immediately when captured, as they were hard to set after they were dried. Zygaenidnae have a highly elastic exoskeleton; one way to kill them was with pins dipped in a solution of nicotine, made by soaking a cigar in water. Of course, you would have the cigar handy.

It seemed a blameless death, hands-off for the lepidopterist—except for the ones whose chosen method was to exert pressure on the thorax using their own index fingers and thumbs. Then the butterfly was put into a freezer or placed overnight in a receptacle to humidify, perhaps softening it first by injecting hot water or ammonia into its thorax. It was set, wings spread open on two parallel blocks of a soft wood such as balsa, a groove in the middle where the body was placed. The base was a strip of cork or polystyrene, and into this the insect pins were fixed. The butterfly was held in position by a pin inserted through its mesothorax, a label underneath indicating where it was caught, the card with its name, species and behavioral information already there, a grave marker before the body was tucked away.

When the butterfly was dry it was taken off the setting board, pinned again with its label underneath and placed in an insect storage box. Now the lepidopterist owned the butterfly, possessing something this glorious, this rare, in some cases.

My father was this kind of a collector. It was his hobby, the way others might ferret away uncommon coins or stamps, and when he died my mother inherited his numerous books about collecting butterflies, identifying butterfly behaviors and habitat, classifying species of butterflies; over four hundred insect boxes with their pinned-in specimens carefully mounted on polystyrene; his labels underneath identifying when and where these were caught; and under these the index cards with the more specific information, all anchored into little Plexiglas drawers inside the glassed-in shelves of his collection cabinet, preserving them—these small deaths—indefinitely.

There is a certain kind of light that falls into my apartment in the afternoon sometimes, mid-afternoon when the day has been warm, but a fine, clean warm, the kind of warmth more from my memories of Hawai'i than this steamy St. Louis September. Beaming goldly through the windows, lighting up the white walls of my apartment, its clarity, even the pure, uninterrupted smell of it somehow, brings back my father, his room he kept his butterfly collection in, the room that was his heart. White walls, the white cabinet with its glass shelves and glass doors—nothing but a clean and colorless background for his butterflies, and for him as well—an antique white swivel chair with the plastic dustcover still on it, his enormous mahogany desk with its rectangular white blotter and the stacks of white papers at either end, arranged, even categorized with little notes on top held in place by clear glass paperweights, detailing the contents of each stack.

My father was a short man. Perhaps he felt that this oversized desk, built for a bigger person, made him big. He was a compulsively neat man, and one day his life in tropical Hawai'i, with all of its brightness, its colors and chaos, the jumble and small terrors of family living, became just too unordered for him. So he shut it out. Even my mother, her June Cleaver dresses, starched eyelet-hemmed aprons, her floor-length mu'umu'us to "dress for dinner," her choked and desperate ways of trying to fit in with whomever she believed my father was, whatever she figured he wanted her to be, was no longer allowed inside his antiseptic little world. He retired his professorship in biology at the University of Hawai'i, where I was also a new graduate student, and he remained in our house for several more years, inside his room, out of contact with everyone and everything but his books and his butterflies. A couple years later my father had a heart attack and slipped permanently away. But he had been gone from us a long time before that.

And now it is my mother who is slipping, though not consciously, and not to a finer, more deliberate world. Her slipping is messy, unordered, and unpredictable. I hadn't even been in St. Louis long enough to feel the degree of familiarity it generally takes me to call a new place home, however temporary, when my sister called and said I needed to take care of our mother.

Bottom line, Maggie said, I can't do this any longer. It's your turn.

You're delusional, Maggie, bring Mother here, to St. Louis? Uproot her from Honolulu, the only home she's known?

It's not about home, my sister said, It's about survival. Mine, she said. Her house is sold, she can't live alone anymore, so where can she go? We can't put her in some nursing home, she's not so bad as that. My God, she's not even seventy yet, what would people think? They'd think we're putting her away, is what. If I keep her in my house any longer I'm going to lose my own family. Maggie sighed, long and pronounced over the telephone. You don't have one, Julia, she said. You understand what I'm saying? No family, except for Mother and me.

Maggie was the pretty one who took after Mother, and I was the smart one like Dad. That's how they saw us and what they called us. And it's who we became. It's as if there was only enough love for one of us, and the two halves they imagined us as, brains and beauty, formed some kind of a whole. My little sister Maggie at forty is on her third husband, married to Brett, the divorce lawyer of her second husband.

He took me to the cleaners, Maggie said, but he was so goddamn commanding about it. I didn't have a thing to lose anyway, except for Bob, and Bob's lawyer did a damn good job of that. Brett is born to succeed. It's different for you, Julia, she said, You're able to live with less.

We've always talked to each other this way in our family, second-guessing each other's motives, figuring everything we do has a motive. Which is why I had to wonder what Maggie was up to when, despite nights of frantic, pleading phone calls from me—Think about it Maggie, what in God's name are you doing? She'll be lost here, St. Louis is the middle of nowhere she's ever known!—Mother arrived one garishly bright afternoon at Lambert Field International Airport. She was confused and lightly sedated, in the company of a paid traveling "companion," who looked and smelled like she might've helped herself to some sort of sedation as well, the bourbon kind.

Twenty-four hours later the butterfly collection is delivered by UPS to my apartment, packed in a heavy crate. There are instructions taped inside, Maggie's childlike scrawl, explaining how to reassemble the glass shelves, the numerous Plexiglas drawers, glass doors, the polished brass lock, reversing whatever she did, or more likely what she made her lawyer-husband do, to take these apart. Our father's books are at the bottom of the crate, underneath identifying cards and boxes and over 400 dead butterflies.

Christ! I mutter, gazing at these, my father's life, Why on earth would Maggie send us this?

My mother doesn't answer, not that I expected her to. She's sitting in the front room of my apartment where the collection lands by default, the only place there's remotely space for it, and she's staring out the window into that clear afternoon light. A shadow from the honey locust outside plays across her cheeks, making them appear more sunken, powdery and worn. Her face is vague and unreadable, but then it always was, even before she started to decline, as Maggie calls it.

Honestly, Julia, Maggie said, one of those interminable phone calls, can you imagine? The neighbor found her taking a bath in their tub. You know how humiliating that was for me? You'll have to keep her locked inside at all times, because when you turn your back for just a minute, poof, she disappears.

I'm tempted to not set the collection up at all, just shove everything back inside the crate, throw a paisley sheet over the outside and call it a table. Moving around the way I do I've never acquired real furniture, and a large box, a crate, some fold-up metal job or primary-colored plastics from Wal-Mart assembled into a whatever-it-is-you-need, are as Martha Stewart as it gets. There are people who buy furniture and people who move on. But the intensity of my mother's stare after I pried open the crate made me wonder if, perhaps, any recollection of home is better than none at all.

Why, Maggie? Will you tell me why in God's name you sent that damn collection? I ask my sister on the phone when she calls later, to see if I was able to assemble "it" all right.

Well, you study butterflies, she says. You're a bug scientist of some sort, aren't you? You're the one like Dad.

I'm a naturalist, I remind her, These days this means I prefer my subjects alive.

Of the ways my family and I have never known each other, what we do to survive is right up there. I know my sister gets married, but surely there are things she does in the off seasons? I am a naturalist, a lepidopterist. I write articles for professional journals detailing things like disappearing butterfly habitat, that other naturalists read. And I write books about butterfly behaviors with full and half-page colored illustrations for lepidopterist-wannabes and a public-parks population nostalgic for nature. In the photos the butterflies are always alive. I don't make much money from these, rarely does reading about lepidoptera rank for most as top-of-the-list escape, but universities and nature centers hire me as a visiting scholar, to lecture, teach classes, be affiliated with them without having to be part of their permanent payroll (as in benefits), so I get by. And this suits me. Most of the time. The idea of a permanent anything curls my eyelash-thin hair, my father's genetics. Butterflies are in vogue these days. I get more temporary job offers than even I can move to.

To my father a naturalist meant an "unearned" Ph.D. Flimsy, not a "real science," a waste of his DNA. I was the smart one, wasn't I? My father tried to pin me down too, classify me like one of his butterflies. I was to become a biologist, like him, even study at his alma mater, the University of Chicago—as removed from the University of Hawai'i as it gets. Any variation on this theme was not acceptable to him, only barely interesting as a "mutation."

To my mother and sister, what I am means I move around a lot, so whatever it is I do I am probably not good enough at it to do it in one place.

And anyway, Maggie whines into the receiver, before hanging up, dead butterflies don't exactly fit into my living-room decor. I've got a Victorian contemporary thing going here, a lot of mauve. Ever notice how many of those butterflies have orange in them? Of all the colors, orange has got to be the most troublesome with mauve.

The mating cycle of the monarch... I write, our fourth day together almost over, Mother asleep on the chair, silvery halo of evening light about her making her look almost new again, pancake skin, the stoic June Cleaver from my memory, her youth used up trying to please my father. *One day after mating, the adult female begins laying eggs on milkweed plants, one per leaf, up to 500 eggs. The egg hatches a caterpillar, and as it grows it becomes a feeding machine, increasing its weight 3,000 times, shedding its skin four times before transforming into a chrysalis, then shedding its skin one final time....*

Was there something so wrong with me, I didn't want a child? My mother asked me this once, on a visit home. Julia's still not married! she observed to my sister, their mutual appreciation for the obvious.

There was the one I almost loved, I almost told her. What I couldn't tell her was, when we were making love, for some reason I wouldn't do it face to face. More like certain insects or dogs, him behind, busying himself over me. Even then I'd get these insane urges to swivel my neck around, whisper biological oddities to him… Did you know butterflies have no ears?

I didn't do this, of course, but thinking about it was distracting enough, so that I almost always lost interest in our lovemaking before he was finished. I'd imagine him pulling out of me, No ears? Is that a fact? grave interest, puzzled brow, tug of his lower lip between his teeth, his look of curiosity and intellectual concentration, and I'd dissolve into a barely smothered laughter. Which, it turns out, is not a plus for the male erection.

Don't bother saying you'll try to change, this man told me before striding out of my life, Your nature is as reversible as an orgasm, something you wouldn't know a hell of a lot about.

Later, after feeding my mother dinner, pasta with jar sauce and an Italian salad from the Schnucks Market down the street, I turn my back to do the dishes and she disappears. I had locked the apartment door, I always lock the door—one thing about living in strange city apartments, you always lock the door. I read the statistics, how many days of sun an area gets, the crime reports, before I move to a new place, then when I get there I mostly stay inside, doing my work behind the locked door.

Do you think Mother's so far out in *pupule* land she can't figure out how to work a deadbolt from the inside! I shriek to Maggie later on the phone. *Pupule* is Hawai'ian for crazy.

Luckily she didn't go far. I rush outside preparing to journey hollow-eyed and heart-hammering through the St. Louis streets, her name on the tip of my tongue, but not wanting to shout it, not wanting others on the streets to know a pupule woman is loose somewhere. But she didn't even make it out of the complex. I find her in the manager's Prairie Garden, his justification for not mowing the generic long grasses still attempting in inconspicuous places to reclaim St. Louis. She's crouched in the middle, and the way the waving slender stalks curl up delicately, almost protectively around her, it's as if she's always been there, a monument to the what-was-once.

Come back inside, Mother, I plead, You're squatting in the dirt!

Sometimes I miss him, she says flatly, Do you know that, Julia? I just plain miss him.

I take her hand, ease her up off the ground (my impulse is to yank, yank, yank!), tell her that I know this, I know she misses him. But I don't. How can she still miss my father, twenty years after his death? It seems any missing should've been done a long time before that—when he was alive, a stranger in our own home!

Later, I shout at my sister over the phone, 4,000-and-then-some miles of utter frustration: I don't know how to be with her, Maggie! Slap a hand over my mouth, remembering Mother is in the next room, my bed, hopefully finally asleep.

You mean you don't know who to be. Be a person, Julia, her daughter for chrissake. Honestly, you can be just so…frozen.

Oh! I start to shriek again, then force my voice down into its lower, tighter tone. This coming from a person who makes a career out of trading up husbands?

Well at least there's love, she says, At least there's always been that. You're just like Dad, Julia. So bloated in the brains department that the rest of you, where your heart is, didn't have room to grow. You're like a bonsai tree, stunted at the base. The top part is everything.

I sense my sister's satisfaction at having stumbled upon this analogy; she hesitates, as if waiting for me to compliment her. Maggie, I say, go fish. It's what we used to say to each other as kids, Go fish! From the game Mother played with us, until Dad snatched me away, taught me chess. If you must play games, play something that has strategy involved, he snarled, that's not just luck.

Arctic butterflies can live in severe cold in a resting state called diapause. They don't need to respond to outer stimuli, because inside they're quietly surviving.

In the morning I turn up my *Coltrane Live* CD to maximum volume. It's not that I'm such a jazz buff. I call this Retaliation Music. When the people upstairs play their fifties and sixties nostalgia, their TV Best Buys too loud, I put on Coltrane or Miles or Bird, as pumped up as my own system can go. I don't know who the people upstairs are, but their taste in music doesn't invite an introduction. I know other things about them that confirm I don't want to know them. They cook with garlic three times a day, and they go out every night at 8:00 and are back at 11:30. The predictability of this is chilling. It reminds me of my father.

I explain this to my mother, yelling it over Coltrane, handing her a mug of coffee and the *Post-Dispatch*, wondering if she even still reads.

And the person who lives next door, I tell her, on the left side, gets picked up every morning by someone who sits in the driveway below, blasting his horn. I wouldn't want to know someone who knows people like that, I say, horn-blasting people. It's what's interesting about living in apartments, I tell her. You know all these things about people's behavior and you don't have to know them at all.

My mother stares at me, puzzled. She looks older this morning, older than when I picked her up at the airport just five days ago. There's no hint of the mother in Cleaver clothes. She seems smaller than even my memory of her.

You didn't used to be interested in music, she says, nodding her head, as if her own statement requires her confirmation. Maggie was the musical one.

True enough, I say, if you consider being musical developing an ear for disco. Donna Summers blasting through the house was my exit cue, I tell her. Though really this had been dwarfed by the much bigger reason I had for leaving home as a graduate student, despite the ease of living within two blocks of the Mānoa campus, a free room and a mother who made real spaghetti sauce (I doubt she's pried open a Presto jar in her entire life). My father was the reason I left, a status he would have approved of if he still had the capacity to care. How long can one's mind stand the subtle and not-so-subtle reminders of how deeply it had shattered someone else's expectations for it? Maggie was the heart. Sometimes I'm not so sure I was even given one of those.

It occurs to me we're having an actual conversation. I reach up to the top shelf, the front room's grand display of three built-in shelves, where my mini-portable stereo sits (what you sacrifice in sound quality you gain in movability), and I switch Coltrane off. I'll put up with Ricky Nelson's "Traveling Man" thumping through the ceiling, for a conversation with my mother. In the end his travels didn't take him so far, anyway.

So what exactly is wrong with her? I ask my sister during what seems to have become our nightly phone ritual. Did you take her to a doctor, or is decline your own diagnosis? She seems pretty normal most of the time, then other times she's...

Not, Maggie finishes. Yeah, exactly. That's what's wrong with her and it's unpredictable. Yes, I took her to the doctor, and she said it isn't Alzheimer's, but it's probably some sort of aging-related dementia brought on by...

Now Maggie hesitates, and I'm silently filling in the blank with whatever human ailments I can remember from the various classes I took in physiology—though really studying humans, their quirks, their frailties, has never been my interest.

Depression, Maggie finishes. Mother's clinically depressed, Julia, and she won't take anything for it, refuses to. I don't think she understands she has it, depression, and half the time she doesn't remember anyway, so what-the-hell difference does it make?

Well what's this all supposed to mean? I ask dumbly, not knowing what else to say.

Do you think…, Maggie hesitates again, her voice quieter, that it might be genetic?

Butterflies see more colors than humans do. They appear to prefer red, orange, yellow, purple, and dark pink. Butterfly wings are actually clear; the colors we see result from pigment on the undersides of millions of tiny scales that cover the wing, the way light refracts from the surface of the wing. The combinations of refraction and pigment create this diversity of patterns and colors. The scales protect the wing and are slowly lost over the life of an adult butterfly. Scales are what make butterfly wings velvety to the touch. If you handle a butterfly, the powdery residue on your hands is its scales. To touch a butterfly is to lessen its life span.

Since the age of twelve I've had a recurring dream about my father, a nightmare though I try not to name it as such. As a child I used to watch him pin his butterflies into the insect boxes. If it were the first butterfly of a particular species, he would display it so it appeared whole, setting it first so that the wings were spread as if in flight. But if it were the second or third he would take an Exacto knife and cut the wings off, two sharp slices, either side of the thorax. Using clear tape and Elmer's glue he would place the butterfly's right set of wings with the upperside (dorsal) showing on the right side of the box, and the butterfly's left set of wings with the underside (ventral) showing on the left side of the box. This, he said, made for an easier comparison between individuals of the same species and different species. His object was always to obtain more than one butterfly of each species, to show variability in size and patterns. Some individual butterflies are runts, he told me, often due to problems with the host plant (drought, cutting, etc.) in the caterpillar stage.

In the dream my father is slicing the wings off an American Lady, explaining how this one's a runt, that it never fully developed as a caterpillar before forming its chrysalis, so the butterfly that emerged is smaller than normal, inferior. Suddenly he reaches across his desk and grabs my grandmother's old cut-glass butter dish, which in real life would never have been on his desk—things from the kitchen, or any other room for that matter, did not belong in his room. But in the dream it's there and suddenly very large, child size, and he pops the glass lid on top of me where I stand beside him. Now I am trapped, pinned down under the glass and his scrutiny of my imperfections, whatever will reveal me as an inferior of my species, a runt offspring of my father's.

What makes this dream particularly troubling now, I realize, dreaming it so many years later, so many states and cities from my home in Honolulu, is the butter dish. My mother tried to give me that butter dish several years after my father died, after the first time I left Hawai'i, for an adjunct professorship at the University of Oregon. When I returned to Honolulu for a visit that summer, bloated with the expansive possibilities of the mainland, the potent green wetness of the Northwest, a life free from family, my memories of them, she was giving her things away.

Here, she said one morning, handing me the butter dish, take this when you leave. You must have a refrigerator in your apartment in Eugene?

Sunlight exploded into the kitchen, and outside under the avocado tree a shrill of mynah birds, and doves making their cluttered morning sounds. I was still caught up in the not-distant-enough reminders of mornings spent in that kitchen, my mother intent on hushing the world around her so that my father in the next room wouldn't be bothered by it. Things finally felt like they were becoming easier. And so without even thinking, I said, Why on earth would I want that old butter dish, Mother?

She looked hurt, I remember that, then sullenly anxious, her lips pressed into that I'll-be-silent-if-it-pleases-you expression she wore with my father, the days before he retreated to his own room.

It was Grandma's, she said, as if that answered it.

I shrugged, But I don't even use butter. Olive oil is better.

For the rest of that summer she tried to give me things, sweaters of hers (it's colder on the mainland), some of her jewelry (I told her I didn't wear it, that no dangling garnet earrings or glittery necklace could beautify this face), ceramic knickknacks, pans, cooking devices, china, silver, candlesticks. Of course, she offered all these things and more to Maggie, and Maggie took all of them, except for the sweaters. God, Maggie said, Mother has the world's worst taste in woolens.

I wasn't troubled by her behavior then. I think I chose to see it, if I looked at it at all, as a shedding of sorts, a sloughing off of old skin, a metamorphosis; growing into a new skin, her "autumn years" without my father. I didn't—couldn't!—understand how she missed him.

Some years after that my mother was hospitalized for a fall down her stairs, and her doctor suggested to my sister—I was at the University of Colorado then—that my mother wasn't "viable" living alone, she wasn't eating right and her bones were brittle as an old woman's. Maggie and her new husband sold Mother's house, and she moved in with them, in a wing off their oversized Kahala contemporary, just for guests.

I'm thinking about these things now, having awoke from the butter-dish dream, my mother asleep in my bedroom and I'm on the couch, which I guess has become my bed until either I break the lease here and get a bigger apartment or a different position someplace else. One possibility could present itself easily as the next. Four A.M. and finally quiet, few cars on the street out front, the Metrolink won't rattle by on its early-morning run for another hour, and blessedly my neighbors are asleep: fifties regurgitations retired for the night, the horn blaster not here yet, and the daily tromping up and down the building's back metal stairs hasn't begun. It's not even my couch, loaned to me by the director of the Butterfly Lab, where I'm to give a talk in October, leading a group through their connected Butterfly House—something I'm not looking forward to. The part about being a naturalist I don't like much is educating the public. Writing books is one thing, it's private and you don't have to dress for it. I became a naturalist because I like nature, something I've always believed functions more rationally, more naturally, without people.

Depression, I'm thinking, what were the signs? And how could it get to this point? I have a sudden vision of my mother placed under that butter-dish top, her vague sad face pressed against the beveled glass, and it's me who's observing her behavior, identifying it, charting it, documenting her differences.

For God's sake, I tell my sister during our next phone call, we've got to get some Prozac down her.

She won't take antidepressants, Maggie says. Her doctor prescribed them, assured her they've got the side-effects thing down these days, that taking them is like popping a vitamin. I tried to convince her, too, but she won't do it. Insists there's nothing wrong with her, that she's just becoming "a little forgetful," is how she puts it. You can't imagine what I went through to get those Valium in her before she got on the plane. I had to tell her they were for motion sickness. I had to tell her she gets motion sickness. I was afraid if she didn't take them she'd make a scene, something really bizarre. What was I supposed to do? Brett said we have no legal rights unless she's declared incompetent and one of us is given power of attorney.

Brett, I mutter, lawyer-Brett, third in the succession of Maggie's "B" husbands—Bo, Bob and Brett, all behaving precisely the way one would expect a Bo, Bob, or a Brett to behave—infantile, boring, full of himself. Well, she's not competent, I say, Do you know what she did this afternoon while I was at the University? She walked outside, lifted up her mu'umu'u and peed in our apartment complex's so-called Prairie Garden. One of the manager's repair goons saw her, and when I came home I had this pink "infraction of the rules" slip taped to my door, reminding me that residents and guests must dispose of their "personal waste" inside their leased units.

Thank God she had a mu'umu'u on and not pants! Maggie giggled. Remember how Dad used to say when we were little girls that the only reasonable function he could see for a dress was as an instant "privacy stall," since ladies couldn't just unzip at the side of the road? Everyone else's fathers liked their daughters in feminine clothes, he made Mother put us in pants. Especially you, Julia, you were his son-in-training. Anyway, it's like I told you. You can't leave Mother alone.

Yeah, right! I howl, And you sent her here giving me no information about her condition. She's falling apart, Maggie, and I'm without the instructions to put her back together. You forgot to tape those to the insides of the butterfly crate! She's my mother and I haven't a clue what to do. What do I do when I have to teach a class or give a talk, get a babysitter?

Take her with you, Maggie said, She'll be quiet. She's always been too goddamn quiet, if you know what I mean. Whatever it is you talk about in your talks, she'll probably be so bored she'll just drift off to sleep in her chair. She's easiest when she's asleep. Just like a kid.

The next thing I do is, I take up cigarette smoking again. The next night. I figure if I can't feed my mother some sort of drug then I'm going to need one, and a glass of wine or two isn't enough. I've never been much of a smoker, just something I've done periodically in the past when I've had a need to feel a little adventurous, a little dangerous, a little wrong. This morning after a lecture I gave, a student in her rush to exit the auditorium, dropped one out of her pack (how sluggishly they enter, how aggressively they leave!). She looked clean enough and so did the cigarette.

With my mother safe in bed I sneak out of the building and into the St. Louis darkness, what little of it there is, the unlit corners of my apartment complex. Sitting on the concrete steps

that ease into a crisscross of paths, if I swivel my neck around
90 degrees and tip my head back far enough, and if I stare to
the right of one of the brick buildings, in between the unkempt
honey locusts planted on either side of these paths, I can see
the almost-full moon. The first time I light the cigarette it's
the wrong end, culminating in a terrible smell and taste, but
I trudge on, lighting the right end, determined to smoke the
entire thing. Buried in books and being "smart" I missed the
sex-and-drugs-and-rock-'n'-roll years, the years when the rest of
my generation was having fun. I didn't learn how to have fun.
Whether cigarette smoking can be considered fun, who knows?
It's a drug anyway and it's what I've got.

I feel like I'm living some sort of dream life, somebody else's
dream, where I've been given a shot at my childhood again, only
this time the tables are turned—I am my mother's mother and
my mother is me. I don't know how to be with my mother, how
to talk to her, how to assure her it's going to be all right. I don't
know if it will be all right. I don't know her, and it occurs to me
perhaps I never did.

Head tipped back and dragging off what has now become
a mission, to finish this cigarette, I remember a night with
my mother and father long ago, before my father retreated
from the world, when I still believed my father was my world.
The Hawai'ian moon more perfectly round than the moon I
am peering at now, such a startle of white it could have been
painted on, the air muggy, thick with the fragrance of night-
blooming jasmine, a bufo ragging for a mate from the Mānoa
stream weaving through our yard at the bottom of the hill. We
were going to collect them, my father and I, Bufo toads, for my
ninth-grade science class. I had volunteered to bring in a supply
of them, pathetic when I think about this—not for any innate
curiosity of the science of dissecting animals; not even because
I hoped it might improve my grade in this class. Because I
thought it would make my father happy. A project we could do
together, collecting frogs for the kill.

My mother and father were both on the lānai, he's on a
redwood deck chair, she's on the swinging glider, and all of a

sudden she started to sing. Her voice quivery and unsure at first, I watched my mother glance over at my father to see, perhaps, if he was looking at her, signaling her to stop in the private ways they had. But he just stared at the moon. I messed around a little, a little embarrassed, the pail in front of me for collecting the toads, tapping at it with the wire-rimmed net, small, hollow noises, then I too was still. And she sang. Her voice growing clearer, stronger, luminous as the moon-glowing darkness. I don't remember what song she sang, only that I didn't realize she could sing. For that night anyway, my mother singing, her voice becoming something almost unbearably beautiful.

II

Warning! The distinct colors and patterns on butterfly wings warn predators to stay away. For instance, the bright orange on a monarch signals "I will make you sick!" The eye-spot pattern on the owl butterfly is a bluff, "I'm an owl. Beware!" Other butterflies blend with their surroundings, their colors and patterns same as a particular plant; camouflaged this way, a predator will not notice them. Some butterflies can hide from predators because they look like another butterfly who really is poisonous....

September wanes into October, the days a little cooler, brighter, the humidity level has become tolerable, almost pleasant. My mother and I have developed a routine of sorts. It occurred to me to do this, make a habit of our days, that it might make Mother feel more comfortable living with me so far from her home. To know what to expect is to feel part of one's surroundings. Take away or try to change a particular butterfly's host plant, and it will die.

So this is what we do. I wake up first as a rule—I've been having that troubling butter-dish dream more often than I care to examine—and I put on a kettle for tea along with my coffee. I discovered Mother drinks tea now; she'd been politely sipping a half cup of coffee every morning, before I thought to ask her.

I was surprised at this change, something so common yet so preferential. (If you are a tea drinker you are fundamentally different than a coffee drinker in motivation, drive, general serenity and settlement of mind. My father and mother used to drink coffee, lots of it and throughout the entire day.) I make us both instant oatmeal, something Mother prepared for us, though hers was not instant, of course—Oatmeal sticks to your ribs, she would say. My mother is thin now, gaunt, ribs poking out like spikes on a comb, this plush beacon of our childhood, the one whose arms you sought if you needed a touch to sink into. Quiet as she was, you'd think she was part of the living-room scheme. As Maggie would put it, a something that blends comfortably in. But soft, willing as dough.

I didn't seem to crave that touch as often as Maggie. Or maybe I was afraid to appear I needed this, my father constantly cautioning me to "pick myself up," "buckle down under," "move on." Failure was not to be cuddled away, it was an indication to do the thing differently, part of the scientific process— elimination of one hypothesis, a persistent striving toward the goal, using a different method this time. It didn't matter if the goal was balancing a two-wheel bike, or trying to get others to like me, to accept me, hell, to acknowledge me, in high school. Crying in my room was not a productive striving toward that goal; sleeping with whomever paid the slightest attention to me was, I thought. It worked for Maggie, anyway. And it was a solution my father wouldn't have come up with.

Loneliness gripped me, burned in me its shameful flame when I realized I could be this close with another person and not want to know him, know he didn't want to know me. I may have longed for my mother's arms then, but instead I shut my bedroom door. We were door shutters in my family, my sister's slammed at the climax of her tantrums, mine more gently but insistently closed, my father's symbolically then permanently locked. Only my mother didn't have doors.

Sometimes, these quiet mornings now, of oatmeal, tea and coffee, quiet because my mother just is and I don't seem to have much to say to her, I regret not seeking her out when she was there for us to seek. She's distant now, closed off into some intense vagueness, if one can pair such words. How do I reach her? If I ask her what she wants to do she tells me whatever I want is fine; if I ask her what she wants for lunch, for dinner, whatever I eat is fine. Who is my mother? What does she like, besides tea? Did I ever bother to wonder these things, when there might have been some hope of finding them out?

Tonight we will go out to dinner. A celebration, I tell my mother. My agent has placed my new work in a Young Adult Nature Series, published by a textbook company, adapted in numerous schools, libraries, and maybe I'll actually make some income. Not that I know a thing about young adults, YA they're called in the industry, I babble to my mother, who's said nothing at all. But if you make the language simple enough, lots of people like to read about nature, I tell her; Maybe they'd rather read about it than be out in it. It's not so messy, I say, combing her hair, still part auburn, part gray, and shoulder length like it's always been. Not so messy as slogging about in boots and insect repellent, mosquitoes and horseflies dive-bombing your head. Of course, I tell her, twisting her hair into what I hope is the makings of a French braid and bun (Maggie taught me these hair tricks, though I didn't take to them, my own hair web-thin and pliant as dental floss), I rather like going about in the muck and bugs. Various butterflies are attracted to mud, did you know? They call it puddling. They gather together, quite social really, sipping nutrients. That sort of cocktail party is more to my liking than the human kind, and you don't have to dress for it.

I realize I'm chatting incessantly at my mother, something I never do, chat, but it's as if she won't move unless I move her, remove her from this chair she's turned to face the window, staring at the parking lot below. She's like a doll, and mechanically I position her arms inside her yellow silk blouse—Such a pretty blouse, Mother!—I say, expressing an enthusiasm I rarely feel for clothing, help her step into a pair of black polyester slacks, her hands on my shoulders for balance. She's not fighting me on any of this, just accepting it because I am doing it for her. My mission tonight is to feed her some really good food, rich food, saturated with fats and taste. Zipping up her pants I notice they're at least a size too big, her clothes hang on her like some drugstore Halloween costume. When did you get so skinny? I ask my mother, and for a moment there's a flicker of interest.

You're the too-thin one, my mother announces, Maggie has the perfect shape.

Yes! I nod ferociously, encouragingly, though I used to bristle when she said things like this: You are..., Maggie is..., and the labels would rarely be flattering, at least not to me. My mother valued beauty. My father, I had once thought, valued me.

The restaurant I select is reputed to have very good, very normal food—"down-home cuisine" they advertise, meaning nothing ethnic, nothing spicy or overly interesting, nothing my mother wouldn't recognize on the menu, a variety of pasta dishes, chicken, steak, salads, no challenges here. I order a bottle of Chardonnay, and though my mother shakes her head I pour her some anyway.

It's a celebration, Mother, a really good book contract. Amazing what well-positioned-full-color photos will do.

Does this mean you finally get to live in one place? she asks, easing her hand across the checkered tablecloth, fingers lifting, flitting over a vase of mums and baby's breath like an insect might, scouting the potential for a landing. She folds her hands back into her lap.

I shrug, doubting this, but then it occurs to me maybe she's worried she'll be stuck moving with me. I tell her, You never know.

Well, my mother shakes her head, maybe it's best, you not having a real home. You lose your home a part of you gets lost too.

I peer at her sharply. She's frowning, staring intently into the pale globe of her wineglass. Ah ha! I think, now we're getting somewhere! I have visions of peeling away the layers and uncovering this, the source of my mother's depression, getting the appropriate treatment for her, then shipping her back, a contented woman, to my sister. Maggie and her lawyer-husband could buy her her own little house, maybe in their own neighborhood so they could help her when needed, and all will be well. When one method doesn't work you just tunnel back in and try another. I glub down the last of my wine, pour myself a second glass.

So, I say to my mother, sipping my wine confidently, you must really miss our old house, it was home for so many years. A pan is dropped in the nearby kitchen, clattering hard, echoing.

A strange look passes over her face, a sort of darkness, though not vague, not vague at all. She stares toward the kitchen where the sound has stopped, chatter of voices, silence, then back at me. The Mānoa house, Julia? Your father's? Oh sweetheart, but how can you think that? No, she says, shaking her head so hard I'm afraid my clumsily bobby-pinned bun of her hair will tumble down onto her bony shoulders. No, she repeats, I have certain fond memories, of course. But most of me was gone long before that was. By the time that house was sold, sometimes I couldn't even remember who I was.

Do you know..., my mother hesitates, then leans over the table closer to me. My instinct is to pull back. But I don't, I stay there, force myself to move toward her, too, the smell of her faintly sour—perhaps it's the wine—and perhaps it's the wine that has loosened her tongue so that she's actually talking to me.

My mother's face in front of mine, a good face, classic lines, fully symmetrical, cheekbone hollows where the hollows should be. A study I read defined the perception of beauty as that which is normal in every respect. My mother's face is the kind of drawn and fine-boned woman's face that in our society anyway, loses its "beauty" after fifty, becomes "attractive" instead, a good subject for one of those matronly portraits. I think of the way butterflies age, developing little chinks and chunks, little chips off their wings, growing more and more ragged as their days are numbered. They too appear less beautiful, to some. But I think of them as butterfly warriors. They've fought the good fight, just staying alive. I peer into my mother's face and my heartbeat, for some reason, accelerates.

Do I know what, Mother?

Don't tell anyone, my mother whispers, but sometimes I have a hard time even remembering my own name. Carol, I remind myself, like the songs, Carol. Caroline, pronounced mine, not in. Nobody uses it. You think of me as someone who has a name? You and Maggie call me Mother, of course. Your father didn't call me much, did he? He didn't have to. I was there. My name is Carol. It bears reminding. Someday someone will ask me my name, and I won't know what to tell them.

Restless after our long dinner, the wine, perhaps even talking so much, a monk who has broken her silence, it takes Mother a while to fall asleep, but when she finally does I call my sister. It's late, much later where I am than in Hawai'i, but still Maggie whines: You know, Julia, I always taught my own kids it was the ultimate rudeness to call someone after 10:00.

And how often do they call you now? is on my tongue, but I don't say it. Maggie's two children moved to the mainland as soon as they reached their eighteenth birthdays, a son from Bo and a daughter from Bob, two years apart. She keeps rooms in her house readied for their return, but I doubt they do that often, or for very long. But isn't that what having a family is? You raise them to leave.

I called to tell you something, I say. She's lost her identity, Maggie, that's what's wrong with Mother. She no longer knows who she is.

Maggie lets out a sharp little yip of a laugh. My dear brilliant sister, that's a pretty new-agey diagnosis, or retro-1960s, or something, isn't it? For a scientist? I'm not so sure she ever had an identity to lose.

Well you've sure got one! is what I'd like to shout. Instead I say the gist of this—As opposed to you, Mrs. Social Butterfly?

That's what Mother used to call Maggie, Social Butterfly. She meant it as a compliment. To our mother success in school had more to do with the activities you were in, clubs you joined, offices you held, parties you were invited to, than any mere report card. I failed miserably as a Social Butterfly.

Do I detect a note of jealousy, Julia? I don't know…, maybe because I have a real life?

Your real life gives life a bad reputation, I mutter, loud enough for her to hear though.

OK, let's suppose you are correct, big sister saves the day, solves the problem, gets results, as Dad would've said. It's not going to change anything. Mother still won't see a shrink, won't take medication, won't believe there's anything wrong with her, whether she has no identity or she thinks she's Daisy Duck! It's not going to change, Julia. Don't you get that? Nothing is going to change.

There's an Indian legend that says if you capture a butterfly and whisper a wish to it, the butterfly cannot reveal the wish to anyone but the Great Spirit, who hears, sees and knows all. In gratitude for giving the beautiful butterfly its freedom, the Great Spirit grants the wish….

A couple nights later there's another breakthrough of sorts, or I'm trying to see it this way. I make one of my famous one-pan dinners, the kind they print recipes for in places like *Parade Magazine*—a can of soup, chicken breasts, rice, water, and some sort of frozen vegetable, stir and sizzle, a meal in fifteen minutes, my kitchen tolerance. We eat mostly in silence, then suddenly my mother says, Do you remember the summer you came home and I offered you my rice cooker?

I nod, try to smile. You wanted to give me Grandma's butter dish, I say, I've been thinking about that summer, too.

Yes, my mother says, but you should have taken the rice cooker.

I stare at her, puzzled. She stares back at me, then shrugs that exaggerated shrug she used through her long stretches of silence with my father, the one where her shoulders and arms pop up fast and hard, then ease back down slowly, an inaudible sigh. I don't know why she did this, maybe to remind herself she was there?

For heaven's sake, Julia, my mother says, Minute Rice? A daughter of the Islands is cooking Minute Rice? You should be ashamed.

I grin. True enough, I'm thinking. When you move around as much as I do you lose your rights to the heritage of place, to the habits that go along with a heritage. Well at least it's wholegrain Minute Rice, I offer. You know, if you wanted to, Mother, you could do the cooking. It's not a priority with me.

You're like your father, she mumbles. Things you could care less about only become your priority when someone else does them. He was a perfectionist, which meant you did things his way. That's what perfect was, his way. Boil Minute Rice and instant oatmeal to your heart's content, Julia. I'm not much hungry these days anyway.

A part of me remembers I should be angry. The old...*You're just like your father*, whenever it was something my mother didn't like about me. But this is the most coherent my mother's been, the most she's said at one stretch, since the restaurant dinner.

Mother! I lean across the table, take both her hands in mine. Her head droops a little to one side of her neck and she's fluttering her eyes as if fighting sleep. You couldn't be tired, I say, You slept most of the afternoon. She wants out of our conversation and I don't want to let her.

Mother, I say again, stroking her hands, which have an unfamiliar feel to them, her fingers slender and cool as piano keys—but then I remember I stopped reaching for these hands years ago, so how would they feel familiar? I stopped reaching for her, stopped talking to her, stopped talking to pretty much everybody, for that matter, except when hired to do so. I accuse my mother of the habit of silence, yet I have chosen the world of lepidoptera over a world of humans; it's the more predictable.

I suck in a big breath, squeeze her hands, What was it really like, living with Dad? I have visions of talking this way to my mother, woman to woman, honesty and clarity, the waterfall of truths pouring out, cleansing, renewing us the way the books and magazine articles, the self-help gurus and prophets proclaim truth does. "The truth will set you free...." Then I say this to her, which was probably a mistake, The truth will set you free.

She pops her eyes wide open, but she's not looking at me. Her gaze rests somewhere above my head, where bland, white walls meets bland, white ceiling tiles, this home that isn't, this St. Louis apartment. Then she yanks her hands away from mine, flinging them out into that exaggerated shrug, focusing on me for only a moment.

I wanted for us to be happy, Julia, that's what I wanted, you, Maggie, Dad, me. A family together who wants to be together, not just that they hadn't learned how to be apart. Was it so bloody much to ask? My mother squeezes shut her eyes.

III

Aristotle studied the life cycle of the cabbage butterfly. Winston Churchill converted a greenhouse into a butterfly house where he raised butterflies from eggs. Vladimir Nabokov, the Russian-born novelist, was also a renowned lepidopterist, discovering and naming several new North American butterflies. Edward Lorenz's butterfly effect is a fundamental part of chaos theory, defined as "sensitive dependence on initial conditions." This means that very small differences in early conditions can create large differences in later stages. According to the meteorologist Lorenz, the flapping of a butterfly's wings in China could alter the weather in the United States by creating a chain reaction of turbulence....

A few nights later I wake with a start, that feeling of not being alone where you're supposed to be alone, heart tapping some crazy rhythm, snare drum ripping in my chest. My mother is sitting at the end of the couch, the space where my feet don't quite reach, the part closest to my father's butterflies collection. She's unlocked the cabinet and a beam of yolk-colored light shining through the window from outside illuminates the flung-open glass doors, a glowing, pollen-like tinge. Her face, too, is yellow, flat and glassy. There's a sound in the room, low and trembling, strangely melodic, and I realize it is her, humming. I snap on the lamp above my head that rests on the cardboard-box end table. It teeters crazily for a moment, its uncertain perch, its light white and jarring, cutting back and forth in the darkened room. Mother, what the hell?

She's tugged one of the Plexiglas drawers wide open, pulling out several of the insect boxes onto her lap, and her hand flutters over the pinned butterflies, lightly stroking the air above their wings. Her humming is the sound of mourning, tremulous, tragic.

They're dead! I say inanely, because I haven't a clue what else I should say. She turns toward me, humming silenced, and I can see she's been crying. Your father loved them, she says.

No! I shake my head emphatically, He didn't love them, he loved owning them. There's a difference. He owned us all, I say, That's what it was about. Anger washes through me. I'm shaking so hard I have to grab onto the couch to steady myself, its ratty arm, hold on like we are a train about to throttle out into some impossibly long night; I have no choice but to be part of this ride. I squeeze shut my eyes, unable to bear looking at my mother sitting there with those long ago murdered, those magnificent, dead creatures.

There was a time I used to imagine a life for myself, my father's dream for my future having long since died. I would have the job I am doing now, but I wouldn't do it alone. There'd be another naturalist, maybe even another lepidopterist, handsome, of course, it was a dream…communicative when needed, but mostly we would share a comfortable quiet. He would love me unquestioningly. Whoever I am, what I am, would be enough. Sometimes I dreamed a child into this vision, this pretend life, but I never really felt that urge, the need for children. Perhaps I was afraid they wouldn't be who I wanted them to be, they would not be my dream of them, and then I, too, like my father, would be disappointed. I, too, would shut them out of my world.

The next day I sneak out while my mother is napping—her naps are growing longer each day, it seems, then when she's awake she's drained and mournful as if she'd rather be asleep—and I bring her home a cat. The cat, a little black-and-white, neutered male with ears like floppy banana leaves, too big for his triangular-shaped face, is from the animal shelter. He howls all the way back in the car, biting my hand the minute I release him from the pet carrier into the apartment. The woman at the shelter told me this cat was from my own neighborhood, that someone in my apartment complex took pity on him being homeless and dropped him off. He'll feel right at home, the woman said, after charging me fifty bucks for his neutering, his shots and the carrier. I had read that pets were therapeutic for older people, for depressed people, and indeed my mother, who is awake when we come in, finds the cat's biting me quite amusing.

Haven't you heard, you don't bite the hand that feeds you? I mutter, sulking a bit. My idea of rescuing an animal from sure annihilation is that it should show a little more gratitude than this.

For the rest of the week the cat does take center stage, as I had hoped, but not for its cuteness, its cuddliness, its ability to heal through innate innocence or some such nonsense. This cat is a psycho-attack-cat, and I seem to be the source of his profound unease. He lies in wait for me in whatever of the two rooms I am not in, crouching behind the door, and as soon as I enter he springs out, leaping gracefully up on his hind legs like a circus bear, aiming for my kneecap like some Mafia hit-cat. But this is a little cat, so instead he gets his front paws around my calf, sinking his teeth into my flesh.

Maybe he's upset you won't let him go outside, or about having his you-know-whats cut off, my mother offers, Male humans would be.

I have a memory of my father when I was ten, showing me a male butterfly's genitals. With a big specimen such as this Mangrove Skipper, he said, If it's still fresh you can squeeze the abdomen and study them as they protrude. Otherwise you have to remove them. He showed me how he had done this on a Tawny Emperor, storing the tiny genital organs in a miniature glass test tube containing alcohol and a drop of glycerin. Of course, they were properly labeled. I glare significantly at the cat.

I don't let him out for his own protection, damn it! I say. You think anyone's going to take care of a cat like this who's got identity issues, thinks he's a pit bull? How do you guess he ended up in the shelter! I push the creature's face away from my legs and he howls in indignation, lunging forward again and sinking his teeth into my flesh, then rearing back he leaps at me yet again. I grab a pillow off the sofa, fending the cat off like some feline matador. This animal has got to go! I shriek.

Julia, my mother says calmly, is it because he isn't behaving the way you expected him to, like you believe a cat is supposed to behave? You don't get to make those rules, you know.

Which, even though I'm angry, I realize was a pretty savvy thing for my mother to say. Later on in the week, just when I'm beginning to think things are going to be OK with my mother, that yes, maybe she sleeps too much, and yes, she stares vacantly out the window into the asphalt parking lot, and of course she was humming a lullaby to dead butterflies—nonetheless she's beginning to seem back in control. So she isn't particularly happy, who is?

Just when I'm thinking these things I get back from a quick jaunt down to the Schnucks Market for our dinner, leaving my mother quietly curled up with psycho-cat in her chair (the cat has decided my mother, anyway, is not his personal vendetta); twenty-five minutes tops it takes and there's the pink slip on my door. Mother has urinated in the Prairie Garden again—second warning, the third time we are out.

I needed to go, she shrugs, They want me to hold it until I burst?

That night I call my sister and I tell her I don't give a damn if it's ten minutes past her witching hour for phone calls, that now not only Mother has to be asleep when I call, the cat does, too, so I don't have to be on twenty-four-hour kneecap guard! You have to take her back, Maggie, I demand, or I'm going to lose my apartment. I can't do this anymore. Nothing in my life has equipped me for this. I'm a middle-aged scientist with a piece of paper that says I have a Ph.D., and another one confirms I have nothing in the bank. I will not be out on the streets with a clinically depressed mother and a psychotic cat!

Yes, well, Maggie says quietly, Bottom line, I can't.

What do you mean you can't? You did it before, you had her before. Surely you and Brett have room in that gargantuan house of yours, if not in your hearts?

There's a long silence. I can hear the white noise of those miles between us, her exhaled breath on the other end of the telephone. OK, Maggie says finally, here's the reason. Brett and I are getting a divorce. It's why I sent Mother to you in the first place. I just didn't want to tell you.

The hell! I whisper.

What I am is pretty, Julia, you know this is true, it's what I've got and it isn't enough. I'm forty now and soon the prettiness will probably leave me, too. I didn't go to college, I had kids instead and now they're gone. Nothing stays in my life, Julia. What do you think I've got, in the long run, to offer someone like Brett? Good breasts does not a future make, and they're moving south too these days, getting closer to my stomach. I don't know, maybe I should get a boob job?

I'd like to say the right thing to her, the thing that might somehow make a difference, but our family has never known how to do this. To say the right thing sometimes you have to be in the habit of talking to each other. Well! I clear my throat, I doubt silicone is any kind of a solution. I'll keep Mother a while longer, Maggie, but I'm taking her to a shrink. If she kicks and screams the whole way there, we are going to see someone. I've known depressed people, and they don't just walk outside on a whim, drop down in the dirt and pee.

Maybe I should try it, Maggie says, Who knows, maybe Mother's on to something.

Several weeks pass before I'm able to get an appointment, and when we're finally there I remember why I share my father's disdain for psychology. Purely speculative, he would say, A social science, not hard science.

She should be on medication, the psychologist states authoritatively, speaking to me like my mother isn't even in the room. I facilitate a group, he says. Your mother is feeling isolated. She could take part in a group with others who are feeling the way she is.

We're not group people in my family, I tell him, And Mother refuses to take antidepressants. But thanks anyway, I say, helping my mother back into her jacket, practically pushing her back out his door. I brought in the wrong patient, is what I should have told him; I have a feline who could use some socialization therapy!

When we get back to the apartment psycho-cat ambushes me the minute I walk inside. I spray him with a water bottle, advice I read in some veterinarian's column, makes a whole lot more sense than anything that psychologist said. The cat retreats to the corner, glaring at me, his huge yellow eyes.

He wants to be free, my mother shrugs.

Well, don't we all! I say.

I can get out, my mother hums, *I've done it before, I'll do it again, you can't catch me I'm the Gingerbread Man.*

What? I drop the spray bottle on the hardwood floor and psycho-cat makes a beeline for my mother's chair. What did you just say, Mother?

You remember? I used to read that to you girls, it was Maggie's favorite story. Dad pulled you away eventually, insisted you learn to read yourself. He gave you Mr. Science books.

I nod, I remember those. I liked the nature ones.

Right, my mother says. And then when I offered to read to you again you said no, you'd rather read yourself.

I have a sudden image of her in my room, I'm a little girl, and she's sitting at the foot of my bed, much like the way she sat at the end of the couch, humming to the dead butterflies. Did you ever sing to me, Mother? Sometimes I think I remember you singing to me. I remember coming upon you once in your own bedroom, you were making the bed, and you were singing. You stopped when I came into the room.

Hmmm, she nods, a vacant look, but not her usual empty sort of look; more like she too is trying to remember, sitting in this chair, staring out this gritty window that faces a half-empty, St. Louis apartment-complex parking lot, a drooping cottonwood tree on one side of the paved entrance. Not the lush Mānoa valley where we lived, not the verdant green, the tropical fullness, not the same.

I used to want to be a singer, she says, when I was a girl. I thought maybe I'd grow up into one, it's the one thing I did that was any good.

What happened? I frown. Dad make you stop?

Oh, heavens no. Your father liked my singing, when I sang that is. It's how we met. I sang at a mutual friend's wedding and your father came up afterwards, introduced himself and told me he liked my singing. Didn't we ever tell you how we met?

No! I practically shout it. You certainly did not, and you never told me you sang at a wedding, either. My God, Mother, you sang at weddings? These days, do you know what some do? They release hundreds of monarch butterflies into the air that they've raised only for this occasion. God I hate that! Creating life for a wedding spectacle. So why didn't you keep at it, your singing? I imagine my mother and father young and in love— The Scientist and his Singing Wife—almost a vaudeville thing, snappy tunes, a few jokes, and Maggie and I born into a house full of laughter.

She shrugs, her exaggerated shrug. Well, I was good Julia, but I wasn't that good.

IV

An adult butterfly's primary purpose is to reproduce, to locate a suitable mate and go through the mating process....

It almost doesn't matter which city I'm in, I'm thinking, sitting outside in the dark, the concrete steps, smoking again or trying to, staring up at my present apartment. City apartment buildings, they're mostly brick, squared and bulky, a fortress of sorts, but whether to keep a population out or hold them in, who can tell? Enough light or not, they could be anywhere. They are anywhere. And they always belong to someone who would never live in them.

I don't know why, but suddenly I'm crying. Alone in the night with another student-bummed cigarette, and crying! It's just that when I grow old I don't want to be listening to other people's music piping down through other people's floorboards, other people's footsteps over my head. I sit outside in a shroud of darkness and still they surround me, other people's lives; they walk near me, up the path and the stairs where I sit, and I turn my head to avoid eye contact, force myself to smoke so I look like I have a purpose for being out here. I'm forty-four years old with no savings to speak of, no means, as my father would put it. I know the differences between a butterfly and a moth: An adult butterfly emerges from a chrysalis, a moth from a cocoon; a butterfly has a slender thorax, a moth's is thick; butterfly antennae are clubbed, moth's are feathery; butterflies are active in the day, moths mostly at night; butterfly wings fold upright, moths fold theirs along their sides, a triangular shape; butterfly wings have separate front and hind sections, moths can "hook" these sections together; there are approximately 150,000 species of moths, but only about 20,000 species of butterflies.

I know these differences, but I don't really know the difference between a stock or a mutual fund. I don't have the money for either, anyway, and I don't know if I sat down and actually took stock of my own life, if I would even like it, just a little.

I walk back inside, dragging up the building's back metal stairs, the slow ringing sounds of my steps, hollow and unsure. I'm thinking about how I haven't called Maggie for a while, how I should call her and see how she's doing, her divorce and all. It occurs to me I never call her to see how she is doing any more than she calls me for this reason. I call to tell her how I am doing, or not doing, taking care of our mother. And this is pathetic, two middle-aged sisters, one who marries and one who does not, consumed in the smallness of their own lives.

The next day at the University I'm in the middle of a lecture on climax community: A climax community, I tell these undergrads who appear not in the least bit interested— they scratch their heads, necks, their hands, staring up at me with their glazed eyes—is when a biological area reaches its maximum in diversity, a sort of terminal diversity, all the niches are filled. A climax community is a community that has stopped succession, I tell them. A cough, someone drops a notebook, the slap and flutter of pages diverting everyone's attention for a relieved moment.

It has achieved its dominant plant life, I continue. For example, grasses on the prairie, and it remains that way until an outside force changes it, such as fire, or humans uprooting the dominant plant to create farmland, or strip malls! My voice is suddenly louder, commanding them to pay attention, take heed. Big Mac or big bluestem! I shrill, You see how this is a choice?

The reason a community changes over time and doesn't just start up again as a climax community, is because the characteristics of an organism colonizing a place are different than the characteristics of the organisms that can survive in the place after there are already other organisms there. So here it is! I hiss, Your answer to a question that should have been asked. Survival not of the fittest, but of what can fit in! It's been proven, I emphasize, trying hard to modulate my voice, though maybe they'll mistake volume for passion?—in the biological kingdom two or more similar species cannot permanently coexist in the same environment, using the same space the same way, with the same food source. And guess what this is called? I ask the students, their bland, restless faces, as if they would know or care. This is the principle of competitive exclusion, I say. In other words, one of them has got to go!

I hang over the podium a bit, staring at these separate faces, but united in their disinterest, dependent on me only for something as insignificant as their grade: so they can exit this university with a degree in econ; so they can enter graduate school, get their MBAs, rise up in some tech-based company whose sole reason for existence is money; drive showy cars, marry showy wives or husbands, money in their bank accounts, mutual funds, stocks, and someday when they have little else to think about, reinvent their lives as having been somehow lived. Again I have an image from my dream, the butter-dish nightmare, only this time I am an adult, aging like a butterfly, becoming ragged and worn, my whole life spent pressed down underneath the glass barrier, and I don't even realize it. I just keep doing whatever it is I am programmed to do.

Twenty minutes later I'm headed home, skipping my office hours—nobody will miss me, I'm not a permanent part of their community, after all, a drifter, transient weed, lighting down for a semester or two, uprooted and onto the next. I park and race up the back metal stairs to my apartment, steps clanging and echoing in my wake.

Mother! I shove open the door and she's in her usual chair by the window, staring at the TV that isn't even turned on. Psycho-cat lunges off the couch toward my knees and I fend him off with my worn-out leather attaché case, the color of old skin, tossed like a decoy in his path.

He cut out on us, Mother, how can you forgive him? He collected us, studied us, then left us when we were no longer of interest! How in God's name could you ever forgive that?

She whips her head around, shoots me a hard, hurt look, crinkles up her forehead like she's going to...what? Cry? Laugh? Oh, for heaven's sake, Julia, *cutting out* is staying out at night, having an affair, even moving out. Your father was there at least, wasn't he, in our house? You're the one who left us, the house, Hawai'i, didn't return but for the occasional obligatory visit. It's natural enough I suppose, but you have to understand, your father was the bigger part of my life.

I can't imagine how you can say that! He deserted you in your own home, and then he died.

My mother nods. Yes, she says. Don't you get it, Julia? Honestly, don't you? You're like him! You study so hard to know things and you don't have a clue. For years I felt the presence of his absence. I still do. It's how I know there was love.

I'm shaking and tears are sprouting at the corners of my eyes. I swipe at them furiously. I am not a crier, have never been, my father saw to that! And here I am, less than twenty-four hours after I cried last night, bawling again.

My mother rises, tottering back a little as if the thin sticks of her legs cannot quite bear the weight of the rest of her. For a moment I think she's going to walk over and put her arms around me, and for a moment I want this. But she stands, a little distracted, as if she forgot why it was she bothered to get up at all. Then she shrugs. He wasn't so bad, Julia. He was the best he knew. So this wasn't always enough, what is?

I turn my back on her, march over to my desk, to the article I'm working on for a journal. Psycho-cat follows me, a safe distance, then sits on the floor beside my feet staring up at me suspiciously, but also expectantly, as if waiting for me to do something of significance for him. This cat thrives on the sounds of anger, I think, perhaps it's what he's known. We embrace the familiar, what we think we want, however absent of whatever it is we need.

The collecting of lepidoptera is an educational activity that should be pursued in a manner not detrimental to the resource involved. Collecting should be limited to sampling, not depleting, the population. Where the extent and/or the fragility of the population is unknown, restraint should be exercised....

I swivel around in my chair, my mother still standing, gazing absently about the room. Tomorrow I'm giving a lecture at the

Butterfly House, I tell her. It's one of those places where they raise butterflies in a nursery, they call it, raise them to live in a big glass dome with their proper host plants so they never have to go out into the real world. It's an artificial world, created to please the public. I've never been to this place, I don't go to these places, they're becoming too popular these days, butterflies are in vogue, but I have to go tomorrow and I want you to come.

She frowns. I'm not inclined to go out, Julia, you know this.

Well, you seem to manage to go outside and pee in the manager's garden, so I guess you can do this.

To my astonishment my mother actually grins. Yes, she says, I don't plan it, you know. I just somehow find myself out there and that's what I do. She smiles a satisfied smile. Then, in almost the same breath, But why should I come with you tomorrow, Julia? You've always preferred doing things on your own.

I feel suddenly like a little girl, knobby kneed, unsure. I don't want to go there alone, is what I'm thinking, I don't want to be alone. Though I don't say it to her, this is the truth.

We arrive early, which I had intended, before the public I am supposed to lecture to gets there, before the Butterfly House officially opens. I have felt increasingly unsettled about this venue. I've lectured to a general public, outside the realm of academia enough times—like writing one of my "other" manuscripts, the ones that sell—the differences-between-butterflies-and-moths type of thing. Piece of cake, as Maggie would say. It's the glass house I'm nervous about, hundreds of butterflies raised to drift about in this little world, where there are the host plants they need, trees, flowers, particular weeds planted only for them, where they can find each other, mate, lay eggs, then die. Like being born into and living out one's life inside an incubator, someone else's controlled world.

It's not natural, I tell my mother, walking beside me on the petunia-lined path that leads to the Butterfly House museum complex. She's humming softly, one line from the same tune over and over, a way, I suspect, of reigning in her own unsureness at the unexpected, the unforeseen, hmmm.

I tell the flat-faced woman at the front desk who I am. She smiles thinly, tells me what I know, that I'm early, then shows me the auditorium where I will lecture. Asks if I need a slide projector, the overhead, whatever I need, she says, she will get me. I ask her, since we're early, if my mother and I can go into the Butterfly House. I'd like to check it out before leading a group through, I explain.

Oh yes! she replies eagerly, relieved, I imagine, that she won't have to make conversation with us. We follow her and my heart knocks about inside my chest like it wants to jump out of my throat. She ushers us into the waiting room before opening the door to the dome.

I know I don't have to tell you this, she says, looking at me, but I'm supposed to say it to everybody. When you leave, see these mirrors? Check to make sure none of the butterflies are hitchhiking on your clothes anywhere. We got blowers right by the doors, so it's probably not going to happen, but just in case. Some are exotic. If they get out they won't survive St. Louis.

I nod politely, well duh! I'm thinking, then she pulls open the door to the Butterfly House and we step inside. My mother gasps and I can feel her shaking, her arm pressed up against my own, our hands entwined. I am a lepidopterist, yet nothing I've researched or studied in the field has prepared me for this moment. They are everywhere, flights of color and light filling the air above us, drifting through the branches of trees, lighting upon flowers, nectaring the flowers, lifting off, hovering like dainty colorful umbrellas, then dipping down for more. It's as if our own small world we inhabit, my mother's and mine, has suddenly been illuminated with every species of butterfly, shimmering in their iridescence and colors, their various shapes, their incredible loveliness, around us, above us, beside us; as if we could breathe them in and they would fill us, but lightly, helium with wings; breathe them back out and they would be here, dazzling.

A Mourning Cloak lights on my mother's arm. Don't touch him, I caution. If you touch him you lessen his life span, let him touch you. I start to tell her he's a Mourning Cloak, identify him, classify him as one of the longest-lived butterflies in North America, so named because their colors resemble cloaks once worn by people in mourning, then I stare at her face. She's smiling ecstatically, and tears are in her eyes.

They're what he was searching for! she says, Such beauty. Who could settle for less, if they knew?

Beauty wants to be alive, I'd like to tell her, you can't own beauty! But I don't. Because my mother has started to sing, her voice lifting up out of her throat, at first a bit tremulous, then suddenly clear and buoyant, as radiant in its sound as the vision of butterflies weaving fantastic arcs and circles around us.

Sing with me, Julia! she cries. This makes me want to sing!

I can't sing, Mother, you're the one who sings.

Anyone can, you just open your mouth.

Instead I open my arms, wrapping them around her. I'm crying again, too, and it's OK. We sit down on a stone bench by a tiny waterfall, its steady whooshing rhythmic as a heartbeat, the miniature stream created for the butterflies. She is singing, high and ebullient, a song I almost recognize. Like the child I suddenly long to be, the child I never was, I want to crawl on top of my mother's lap, have her sing to me. Grasping onto her shoulders tightly, her voice flows like liquid over us both, rich and vibrant. I metamorphose into my mother's voice, spiraling up and out of her throat, with hundreds of butterflies beating the air, lifting and rising to the top of the glass. Then, as if in the end the glass is really nothing, particles of sand, of dust, of old skin cells; as if all along the nightmare has been only nothingness, out we go, up into the sky where the Great Spirit whispers that secret we're beginning to remember, in our blood, our scales, this fine new skin, these damp and uncertain wings, too long forgotten in those long-ago dreams.

FLY ME TO THE MOON

This middle-aged man sitting beside me on the plane from
Boston to St. Louis starts coming on. Least I think it's a
come-on, who knows anymore? He says, Could I interest you
in sharing my bottle of wine?

I'm a woman whose husband of fifteen years has left her
for another man. And the other man is better looking than
me, nicer legs, a more ready smile, anyone could see that. I've
got seashells in my handbag wrapped in newspaper and when
this middle-aged man, who's not so good looking but not bad
looking either, leans closer to me, his leg pressing against my
bag between us on the floor, I think of them breaking, pale
fragments of shell drifting coarsely about in the black leather,
the lining torn and already sporting eye-pencil shavings, bits
of ancient tissue, the litany of everyday refuse purses seem to
acquire, like old stars in some neglected sky. And this makes
me start to cry.

Naturally it is just what he needed to start a conversation,
offering me his handkerchief, which I eye suspiciously but I

can see it's clean, folded, someone loves him enough to fold his handkerchiefs, or perhaps he loves himself this much.

It's the shells, I explain, and I take them out of the handbag, and we both stare at them in my palm held out like an offering, a large, bleached half of a clamshell with the little yellow and orange translucent shells, the eggshell ones and the zebra striped, all small enough to fit inside. Luminescent, these little shells, like miniature pieces of a rainbow, a reminder of what nature can do when it's of a mind to do it.

They're nice, he says politely.

So then I'm telling him about leaving Massachusetts, about the job I took in St. Louis just to get away but now it about breaks my heart, I tell him, like I'm deserting my own life, the eastern landscape, gritty to be sure but beauty is where you look for it, isn't it? These shells, I say, are what I have.

He nods sympathetically. Well, he says, You won't find many seashells in St. Louis.

A half hour later we're working on our second round of baby airplane-sized bottles of wine, like pouring from a perfume decanter, I'm thinking. I'm thinking I'll take the bottles as souvenirs too, more things that started out in Massachusetts and are no longer there, a document of sorts, of leavings. Then I'm telling him about Rob, as if there's a sudden need to confess it, how he left me for Mick. Such masculine names, I say, moving my hand against his for just a second, his arm using up all of the armrest between us, just long enough to see that flicker of something, a sort of recognition go off in his eyes. He has nice eyes, grayish and plump, small and almost circular, like two lima beans.

I don't have a problem with Rob deciding he's gay, I say, I don't have a problem with gay. It's those years of feeling I just couldn't make myself good enough for him. I mean, wouldn't he have known it before we met? By the time you're out of high school don't you know if you prefer tuna or peanut butter, if you're good at math or can draw a straight line? Wouldn't you know if you like boys better?

The man sighs, stretches a little, nods thoughtfully, as if he's pondering the likelihood of this; which part, I wonder, the tuna or the boys? He's rather small, this man, his knees don't even come up to the seat in front of us, and then he slides over his leg in its perma-creased tan pants until it's touching my own. I'm big enough, a size fourteen, and Rob used to make it his sacred mission to whittle me down to a twelve or a ten, like nagging at a hunk of wood: If you would just do fifty sit-ups every morning, slow on the pulling up, and avoid desserts. Why do we have cookies in the house? Cookies are for kids.

I stare out the window at the land underneath, reddened with the colors of fall, the east disappearing behind us. I never used to think the middle of the country accounted for much, I tell this man, that it was just the part held in by either coast.

I live in St. Louis, he says. It's not such a bad place but I fly to Boston a lot. My daughter has a rare childhood cancer. She's in a special treatment program at the Children's Hospital there. Her mother's with her. My daughter lost all her pretty hair, from the chemo, you know. Sometimes when I look at her naked scalp…, he hesitates, sighs, those lima-bean eyes rolling up, down, then focusing on my own face, hovering there; I remember how it was the day she was born. That was a good day for me, the best.

Oh, God, I'm sorry! I say, my hand fluttering above his knee, lighting down for a second, the need to touch him of course, let him feel my sympathy, but of course. A chill of something creeps up my spine. He's one-upped me here, that's for sure, our confessed despairs spilled out like the cellophane packages of airplane food on the puny tray tables in front of us: rubberized chicken? genetically engineered lasagna? canned fruit in a urine specimen cup? His is the entree. I glub down the last of the second glass of wine and he's ordering a third; Just one, he says when I start to protest, to go with our desserts. We'll share it. But I am sorry, I think, truly, truly.

I had wanted a daughter but I don't tell him this, not when his own has cancer. I wanted a daughter, and a son would have been OK, too. But there's the thing you've got to be doing more

than once every other month or so, if you get lucky, if he gets
drunk, to get these.

If I had a daughter I wouldn't leave Boston, I say, She'd be
a reason to stay.

My daughter was at the National Cancer Institute before, he
tells me, In Bethesda. So then I was flying into DC all the time.
They had her in some research program where a control group
gets the real medication and the other group gets a placebo, only
they didn't know if the real stuff worked either. She was in pain
all the time, so we took her out. At least in Boston they tell you
what they're giving her, even if nobody really believes what good
any of it will do.

I'm staring into his face as he's telling me these things,
and his grayish eyes are meaty, moist, he closes them for just a
second like he's blinking back tears, so naturally I lay my hand
on his, of course I do. And he lifts my hand up under his, as if
to return my hand to its proper place, only when we arrive his
hand plunks down heavily on top of my thigh, my own hand
there, too. And I think how if I move my hand, then his will
still be on my leg, which is kind of like an invitation for it to stay
there, but if I don't move my hand then we're holding hands,
flesh to flesh.

My palm is beginning to itch, to tingle, a burning sort of
strangeness as if I put it in a terribly wrong place, on a stove
burner for instance, but it's numb and would take a great effort
to lift it. His hand under my hand begins to move, slowly,
almost imperceptibly, the fingers like little pudgy animals, each
one lifting up after the next and beginning their slow crawl to
home, the waistband of my pants, side zipper sliding easy as a
tongue. He eases back his seat, sighs like he's falling asleep, and
this hand, well, this hand this wayward hand beneath my own
has apparently chosen to lead its own life, doesn't need a nap,
the man, or maybe even me, the me I believed I was when we
flew out of Boston just a short couple hours ago.

My heart hammers against the inside of my chest like it
wants out, like it could jump the cage of my ribs, race down the
slope of my belly and join those errant fingers, slithering fast

and snakelike now, zeroing in on their prey. I force my head to turn away, my head that is foggy and floating in its residue of baby wine cocktails—but I can't pretend that's the reason this is happening. And it is happening, of course, isn't it? I stare out the window, flying west toward an eternally setting sun. The sky is flushed with swollen, pink clouds that roll and lick and bump and unfurl into each other. My face too is flushed and I think about taking my other hand, the one that is not powerlessly hitchhiking its way down my own crotch, take my other hand and yank both hands away, just yank them; my other hand that is on top of the tray table beside the empty baby wine bottles, and everything else going on below.

Out of sight, out of mind, I whisper inside my head where the sound of the jet's engine races between my ears, the roaring of wind and then a waterfall of it, tumbling down with the greatest ease.

There is a moment or so, flying into a sunset, when you feel a sense of dislocation. The sky opens up out of the clouds below you and it's colored like the sea, aqua, turquoise, with the red of the sunset above that, and more clouds, lavender, salmon; and you have a sense of a world turned upside down, that maybe there could be an ocean above you and the massive expanse of the middle of the country, flat and spread open, raw and brown as a wound, this new land is the top of the world and you are below somewhere, drifting in an opaque sky. It's that turned around.

I look back, staring hard at the lights twinkling behind us, the part of the world now covered in darkness, the east I have left. And I think of the people inside these lights, people who have children and women who have husbands who love other people; people recovering from broken lives and those who will never recover; people who are dying, who are losing their families, and the ones who have lost themselves.

The man, his head tipped back, those lima-bean eyes still shut, lifts up his hand, sliding it out from under my own, which immediately settles back down on the warm place that is growing colder, the place his hand left. I press my forehead against the glass window. And there are the ones who dream, I'm thinking, war dreams perhaps, nightmares that might really have happened and happen over and over, again and again every night. No sleep so sacred that real life can't intrude.

My husband fought in Vietnam and he was never the same afterwards, I tell this man, without turning to look at him, without seeing whether or not he's opened his eyes, if he's looking at me, if he's interested and understands the portend here, understands how irrevocable, no turning back, this is. It won't top childhood cancer but there's truth in this.

Still gazing out the window I can hear the man opening up his briefcase now, imagine him staring at the contents, tidying the crease in those tan pants, snapping up his tray table, his seat back, checking his seat belt like they told us to do on our approach into St. Louis.

There are the things you don't recover from and the things you can't forget, Rob once told me, And these are the things that end up controlling everything else. Life in the hands of whatever it is that damaged you most.

I'll probably get a cat in St. Louis, I say, a perkiness to my voice, a devil-may-care-who-gives-a-damn nonchalance, I'm hoping. You see, the apartment I'm moving into allows pets, though I'll have to pay a nonrefundable deposit, I tell him. Even a cat who prefers other cats still has to depend on me for its food, I'm thinking, but I don't say this out loud.

I'm babbling, I realize, and still not looking at him, but there's that awkwardness of the formerly intimate between us, or the maybe formerly intimate, or the potential to have been intimate, however the hell you define intimate! and until this plane is at its gate and everyone begins their grabbing and gathering of their things, the hustle out into their own lives, there is this emptiness that begs an attempt at filling.

All things considered, it could be a busy time for me in St. Louis, I tell him, louder now, he will hear this, as the jet bumps the pavement lightly, lists and rocks into its landing, the bellow of its brakes, then taxies slowly off the runway turning in a wide, smooth arc at our gate. What with a new job, a cat, who knows? I chirp.

As soon as the plane comes to a complete stop, this man, this exceedingly polite man, steps back from our little row of two seats so that I may get out. He lifts my carry-on down from the luggage rack above our heads, even though as I suspected I am taller than him, as if he believes my arms, my own two hands, are incapable of this. I feel a deadness, a uselessness, and there are new tears dulling my eyes. I am determined they will remain uncried.

I walk out of the plane in front of him, heading into the Lambert International terminal, and when I spot the middle-aged woman in a business suit waving in our direction with the girl of about twelve or thirteen, somehow I know they are his, he is theirs. The girl has lustrous hair, and the woman wears the confidence of someone who is sure who she is. I don't turn around to see what look he is wearing. I stare at the girl who is smiling, but shyly, the uncertainty of one fast approaching the age when she will feel disdain for her parents, but right now she's glad her father is home. I'm glad she isn't in Boston. I'm glad she has beautiful hair. In a year or two she will maybe razor-cut that hair, or dye it some strange rebellious color, and I'm glad she will be around to do this.

It occurs to me whatever look he is wearing doesn't matter. It doesn't matter if he feels guilty, or even if he's sorry. It doesn't matter if he believes he's one-upped me, our tales of woe offered to strangers during the hours when our worlds are temporarily skewed, transported to someplace else. Because these are the moments when our separate lives are joined, and we can become who we had hoped to be, who we are not, or nothing at all, just floating up there like a birdsong, a cloud, bit of space debris from another dimension, suspended for however long it takes to get to wherever it is we think we are going.

PART TWO:
"AND THE RICH GET RICHER,
AND THE POOR HAVE CHILDREN"

"...these are the ashes we rise from."
—Charles Wright, *Appalachia*

2000

AND THE RICH GET RICHER

ADA

There is this that makes you think: November, December, days too warm like summer still and still too dry, as if the moisture's been sucked out, decaying pink this thin light. Did you know this light? Something terribly unfinished in these lingering days.

Feel the thinness in my skin too, prickly, worn tender, spots and bumps like the scraggly coating of a lychee. There are no lychee in St. Louis. I suppose you knew that. But isn't this amazing? Almost sixty and only recently has my skin begun its release, that certain slide, marks shaped like broken leaves on the backs of my hands. Even the leaves didn't turn this fall. St. Louis nights weren't cold enough to awaken this inside the trunks of trees; instead, leaves browned in the sun, shriveled and dropped like old, useless things. Or else when the wind picked up, a dry rattle like a box of matches shaken into the branches sent dead leaves twirling, gracelessly as bent kites. Some speculated it's the millennium, apocalyptic signs, earth parched, a decade of avarice; the rich get richer, as my mother used to say—welfare reform for the rest. Saw it all from my apartment windows. 1999 ends. 2000 begins. Dull leaves scatter, dry out in the sun.

Watch now as I blow smoke out the kitchen window, ancient red scent of lentil soup, window wide open to the night finally cool. Circles back again, lazy haze of cigarette. Not even this deserts me. Sharp press of the cold air, cold flesh; all my life there were those that hung on, but not what I needed, not you.

Watch me, OK?, light the bayberry-scented candle atop the fake-wood kitchen table, where in someone else's kitchen there would be food, bowl of fruit, flowers, a newspaper, scattered mail, signs of the life lived. I have my telephone. And this candle. Firing the sandalwood incense up next, thin stick of it bent like a praying mantis over the pressed-wood cupboard, flip on the fan over the stove, rush of stirred-up air—all to cover the gnarly persistence of Marlboro mingling into the lentil-soup smell I don't even recall making. Did I cook? I didn't used to smoke. You didn't either, ironically enough. You went right for the throat, the jugular, skipped the cigarettes, the beer; far as I know you didn't even go for sweaty teen gropings in my old Falcon wagon. Those rites of passage held your interest about as much as the board games I used to try to play with you, Monopoly, Checkers, Yahtzee. Engage you, your teacher told me; He's living in his own little world, she said, Bright enough, just not with the program. Bored games, you called them. You were never much interested in anyone else's program.

Something about how I need it, this cigarette, how this need burns the back of my throat, hunkers down inside my chest like some stubborn furry pet refusing to go outside, refusing to take a walk, to go away. After I smoke it, for a while I don't need it and this comforts me, sure as my own heart's beating. Is that how you felt about cocaine? A need you could satisfy, if only for the moment, your own tremulous control?

It's like this every night. Every night I turn out the small living-room lamp, the kitchen overhead, pull up a folding metal chair to the darkened window. Every night I think, maybe this is it, the moment when I'll say, OK! the hell with it! and just walk out, closing the door firmly behind me. Like any normal person, JUST WALK OUT, down the three flights of stairs, only three, out onto the concrete walk, the narrow strip of stony white below my window illuminated by the lights from nearby apartment buildings, mine and the ones on the other side of the path. I live inside this secondhand light. Imagine the concrete beneath my feet, unyielding, certain, maybe I would feel its cold under my shoes. I can return whenever I want. My key opens this door. Just walk out.

I want you to watch as I blow my smoke through the open window. Somewhere in this January night, easing into the millennium with hardly a whimper, a sigh—nothing changed, didn't I tell you? ADA SEES ALL, or most things anyway—thin trails of white become a single cloud then disappear, up into the atmosphere where perhaps there really is a heaven and you are there. This is where the world's smoke, its exhaust, fumes of the living drift; its grit, its poisons, its losses, the used-up yet stubbornly lingering odors, an interminable needling of where you were, who you were, what you left. This is heaven. This is hell.

TROY

Her name a chant, a prayer, part voice, part breath, part not anything lucid at all, in, out, looping, swirling, a jig maybe, the Irish in me, dances in my dreams as if I really do have some secret right to be happy. Her chest, her throat, her mouth, the smoke she's gusting into the darkness, believe that I am part of it, riding its wave back to her. The spirit of Jim Morrison, she told me; fierceness of my mania when I couldn't control this, the despair. Nobody but me is allowed inside Ada Kamuela's apartment. Rider of this storm.

Met her nearly eighteen years ago, back on O'ahu where I

had known her son, had been a friend of sorts to her son, though after a while nobody could be a friend to Kai. I'm Troy, I said, when Kai didn't offer an introduction.

Nope, shaking her head, tinkling of those long, glassy earrings against her long, pink neck, I think you're Jim! Grinned and her teeth were small and very white, like slivers of shells.

That's your mother? I whispered to Kai when Ada shimmered out of the room, satiny tight pants, flip of her hair the color of wet brick settling about her shoulders like a cape. She doesn't look like someone's mother!

She doesn't act like someone's mother, Kai said, that violent tremble, began in his shoulders then shivered down through him, a full skeletal rage. How many mothers you know rag at you for things you haven't done, says she can see them in your future? How many mothers give you a cup of tea then read your fucking fortune in the dirt at the bottom? How many mothers have a PSY-CHIC phone number, for chrissake! *ASA*, her business name, she's printed it on cards, *ADA SEES ALL*. Christ, give me a fucking break! Please, I've got to speak with ASA! they whimper on the phone like it's life or death, like she's some kind of doctor, somebody you really need. My father was half Hawai'ian, his great uncle a kahuna, Hawai'ian priest. If Dad hadn't died already he'd die now, this haole hoo-doo. I'm sick to death of it. I'm going out, Kai said, Somebody I got to see.

Somebody I got to see. Sudden rat-a-tat-tat chatter of a gecko on the window screen, Hawai'ian evening too warm, too moist, cloying scent of night-blooming jasmine. Ah man, I said, didn't I? Didn't I at least say this? Do you have to go? Then I shrugged. Kai's powdery quest, who was I to object? Makes me feel normal, Kai said, What others feel, nothing goddamn better than that. I could barely get by in my own life without some help at that point, even worse, I hadn't discovered what that help should be. Who was I to say coke wasn't some kind of a solution, some kind of god? And selling it? Of course you had to, the outrageous expense of using it. Small time, Kai said, I'm peanuts man, not worth a hill of beans. Try some! he grinned, mouth widening, no smile in those eyes.

What I tried: psych ward, Hawai'i State Hospital those black manic months, scraped off Kamehameha Highway playing chicken with the traffic, steel against flesh, machine versus God; if there is a god, shouldn't he have won? The woman I played house with in Punulu'u to figure out what love was, who I was if I couldn't love. Tried that too. It was lithium, finally, took the crazies away but it made me not want the woman. Unexpectedly, a child on its way. Shrugged when Kai said he was going out. Nothing seemed quite real enough.

Until I met Ada. Ada, my hand in hers, palm up. Felt the shock of her touch go through me, sizzle of her fingers like small electric eels wrapping around mine. Skin glowing as if a fire had been lit just under its surface. Wanted to crawl inside her warmth, take my hand hot and heavy as a rock inside hers, slide both my hands up her arm, her hand, my hand, twirl our fingers through that crimson hair, wrapping them inside.

You're the age of my son? Ada asked.

Four months later Kai disappeared. St. Louis was the last place he was seen after leaving Honolulu only weeks before. I shrugged. Ada trembling like something needing to erupt, something volatile and sour that began beneath the surface of her, plunging deeper, powerless to work its way back out. I held her and she let me, and later I lay with her and she let me do that too, let me stroke her, rock against her. The scent of her, apples, crisp and red and good. How could I have known the ways I would come to need her?

I dreamed of him in the Mississippi River, Ada whimpered, choking out each word, each syllable a glitch, a sliver off a sentence, a shard. But I would know! she cried. I see these things! Why don't I know?

They don't know, I had reasoned, wheedled, Kai could be anywhere. They'll find him, I said, clear voice, confident smile, nothing I was really feeling, this want, this crazed maniacal desire. Hungrily, guiltily, wretchedly, slide back down between those sorrowful thighs.

When Ada moved to St. Louis I did, too, leaving the woman I couldn't love and the baby girl I might have loved. I couldn't

stop myself. Tried telling myself I could love this woman, mother
of my baby daughter. But more and more living with them I felt
the weight of my own life pinning me under, the weight of this
wrong that could not be helped, a wrong love—but how could
love be wrong? What force is it makes us pick one woman at
one time and try to make her the right woman at the right time,
then along comes the right woman at the wrong time! If she's
right, you love her, what makes this wrong? This weight like a
sack of cement, crushing bones, settling inside, irreparable.

Left her apartment less and less, then comes the day she
couldn't leave at all. Felt the river rise up in her throat whenever
she tried to step outside the door, the cold push of it. She'd close
her eyes and the pattern of dead leaves floating on its surface
grew over her and she was dragged down under it, struggling
only to breathe.

I don't understand river water, Ada told me one day, sky
outside the color of hamburger, rippled and meaty and darkening
all afternoon like a storm was moving in. We're sprawled on
her sofa and I slip further down into its grainy surface, pulling
her closer. Rain-scented air blew through the partly opened
window, but there was no rain, nothing cleansing out of that
harsh sky.

Let me hold you, I said.

I don't get it, its depths, what fish swim there, Ada
continued, my hand pulled by some invisible cord on her breast
now and she's gazing at it like it's some kind of annoyance, a
bug? not threatening, just out of its element, something that
doesn't belong.

I don't get what animals crawl in its silt, just once I slid my
foot into it to feel if it's cold or warm. Do people around here
grow up knowing these things, the river like the ocean is to us
in Hawai'i, in their veins, their blood? Could that long stretch
of brown be their lifeline, for God's sake? I don't get it. Which

was it? Cold? Temperature of rain? I used to take Kai to the beach when he was a child, Ada said, brushing my hand off her breast then grabbing it, squeezing it hard until my fingers burned, red as her hair. Kailua Beach. I want to think of him there, aqua water the way his eyes were.

Kai was part Hawai'ian so it's doubtful he had aqua eyes. I nodded, pressing myself against her. If there was a way to become her I would have done this. If there was a way to take her loss inside me I would have done even that, if only to have her inside me too. Slowly, no sudden moves, I eased Ada Kamuela down flat on the couch and myself beside her, turning her, stiff yet ultimately yielding, a kind of compliance that happens when you just plain give up, until she's facing me, her body's perfect fit against mine. Rocking my way inside her, imagining what she breathed was me. Like drowning but easy, without that struggle, the need for air that makes us all slaves, wanting to be free of it yet knowing it's impossible, impossible to be God.

ADA

I did go to the Mississippi, once with the detective when I was finally able to persuade the police and one time alone. I did go to the river. Searched for you there.

It was February that second time, and there were the browns and grays of the land on either side, icy wind through bare trees, brown and yellow marsh grasses dead in the mud at the sides of the bank, the mud-colored, icy water. Cold, I remember that part all right, that day the air frigid as death. There were at least fifty ducks circling as I approached the bank, and I noticed what looked at first to be a pile of dead ducks but turned out to be plastic decoys—lure live ducks into becoming dead ducks. I saw the raw-wood duck blind like some slapped-together Hilton for beavers, covered in dead marsh grasses, anchored at the edge of an inlet off the river, a slough of sorts. Had a webbed lounging chair inside; even in the kill, the comforts of Kmart. Sheet of ice floating beside it, flat and shiny as cellophane.

As children growing up in Hawai'i we used to play a singsong game that spelled *Mississippi*, the island ripe and green around us, M-i-s-s-i-s-s-i-p-p-i, skipping to a jump rope, miss a letter you're out. What was it to us but a way to win? No feeling at all for the wide, bold, brown river of these letters, carving up the middle of a country I could never imagine myself part of. Hawai'i wasn't even a state until 1959, the year I graduated from high school. No feeling for the turn of my future, sudden and hopeless, this river would bear. No feeling, even, for you.

Water the color of nothing, mud underneath gave it its brown, at the sides a dull brown gurgling over the dark brown loam of the bank, pushing against it, sucking back, making small, almost ocean-like sounds, in, out—if I closed my eyes I might have imagined this, my Pacific, lulled and sleeping beside me like a lover, something I could wake up to, open my eyes and what is there is who you dreamed would be there. But that river-water smell! of wet earth, jumble of dead stumps, twigs poking out of the shallow like antlers. At its middle I could see boats, and long freight ships, dragging their cargo from state to state. The mighty M-i-s-s-i-s-s-i-p-p-i that had you, my Kai, trapped somewhere in its thick mud. I'm sure of it!

There was a steady drip, drip, dripping, dirty icicles off the exposed roots of the dead tree I sat beside, half in the river, half out, the in-the-river part green with a luminous algae. I pushed my red sneaker against the exposed bark, swiping at the mud that clung like sludge to my shoe, brown on scarlet like dried blood, something that wouldn't let go. Kai, even your name means water; but the ocean was what we named you after, the achingly blue Pacific, not some river, not this brown water.

Hundreds of mallards dotting the middle, a wave of them lifting up, taking off. I could hear the rush, a whistlelike singed air, frantic beating of their wings as they rose over me. A bit of rubbish, an old translucent bag floating by like a jellyfish, puffed out and bloated. It caught on a branch, then the trunk of the dead tree, then onto a dead vine, drifting like hair.

I saw you under it all. Imagined the moment when the river first filled you, weighing you down. Was it a relief? Bleeding perhaps? The detective, glasses thick as spotlights— they let them be police, the ones who can't see?—speculated you might have been shot. Drugs, he shrugged, what could I expect? That greed, hunger, some chronic dissatisfaction, this need for more and more, becoming more and more a part of you. Hefting your own personal thunder about like it was some sort of dignity. There had been times, years before, when you seemed to reach out to me. Whatever I did for you, however I responded, it was always somehow wrong. And never enough. I was not enough.

Did you think of me, my baby boy, my blue-eyed Kai, sinking down into the water, cold sheet of mud tucking you in the way my own hands used to? Ceiling of roots above you, a hollowed-out tree (alive it must have been magnificent!), now pinning you down, holding you under, forcing you to give up the one thing I had given you that mattered. And this but a breath away.

AND THE POOR HAVE CHILDREN

TROY

The apartment doorbell chimes and Troy opens the door expecting who knows what. She's a tall, broom-thin girl about the age his daughter would be maybe, one of those indeterminable teenage years where faces appear bland and ecstatic in almost the same breath. This girl, though, has a mask at the top of her head, which she suddenly yanks down covering most of her face.

He asks anxiously, It's not Halloween or something, is it?

She lifts a spidery finger, points at the mask. It's thin ceramic, or a very smooth plastic made to look like ceramic, painted white to resemble a geisha perhaps, that stark sense of skin, blood-colored lips pooching out like a goldfish, black-lined eyeholes and the girl's own eyes blinking rapidly underneath.

Are you meaning about this mask? she says. Her voice is lower, much less irritating than he would've thought possible from such a gaunt and stretched-out frame, almost husky, almost pleasing, a voice like Debra Winger's, somebody like that. Debra Winger! an actress, for chrissake; how many times did he sit through *Terms of Endearment* with Ada, her moist eyes fixed on her television watching Debra Winger, Emma, die. The part Ada waited for, loss of the child and the mother goes on.

It's my alter ego, the girl says, That means another me. When it's on I'm Marta, spelled like Martha, but you got to drop the H when you say it. Otherwise it's just too Martha Washington, know what I mean?

Troy shakes his head; I doubt it, he says. He shifts his weight from one leg to the other. Who are you? What do you want? Are you selling something? I've got everything I need.

You sure about that? She lifts the mask up again, placing it like a second face across bangs the color of a thick, coarse paper. They need trimming, Troy notices, needling about her eyes, making her appear cross-eyed at times. She blows up at the bangs and they scatter like tossed weeds across her forehead, drifting back down below her almost nonexistent pale brows. You think I need a haircut? she grins, like she's reading his mind. Her own skin is thin and bleached looking, and she pooches out her two-toned, lipsticked lips—a brazen mauve with a hint of brown, or are they brown with waves of purple streaked in?— slings back a bony shoulder, says, What do you think?

About what? he frowns. He decides she's not the age his daughter would be after all, more like twenty-one or twenty-two. Too much wear on her. And anyway, he doesn't like to imagine his daughter's face with lipstick on, with any makeup at all. He tries to picture his daughter's baby face, only face he knew, those little circles of cheek he remembers her having, the rumply forehead that's become every baby's face he sees these days; how it might shape into the lines of a young woman's face, but still its freshness, still with a sense of hope. Well, he says, inching the door closed a little, stepping back.

I'm studying to be a Victoria's Secret model, the girl tells him, popping her hand up on the door frame so he can't shut the door. Underwear, you know, the sexy type—they call one of their lines "second skin," if you get what that means, but they have real clothes, too. You've got to be skinny as spaghetti to be a V.S. model, and sort of disappointed looking, like you've been spoiled all your life but even so you never really got what you wanted. They like you to have fat lips and big yoohoos. So, what do you think?

Big what?

Yoohoos, you know, breasts. I wasn't sure you'd want me to use the b-word, seeing as we're just getting to know each other. So?

He inhales a smarmy breath, that baked-brick smell from the hallway past his open door that leads to another door, then the stairs outside. The sun sinks heavily into the roof and sides of the building by noon, even in January this year. You'd think he lived in an adobe, New Mexico or some such place, hardly St. Louis. The world is going down hot, he thinks. Troy's eyes slide briefly off the girl's face, down her neck to her chest, which he can't help but note for all her scrawniness is indeed substantial, then back to her eyes. You go to school for this kind of thing? he asks, cheeks flushing. He can't remember ever having had an actual invitation to look at some stranger's breasts.

Oh, yeah, like there's the Community College of Underwear out there! I'm talking about studying catalogs, geez. I can give you the names of the models in the V.S. catalog, Victoria's Secret Angels—Naughty Angel is my personal favorite—what they like to eat, when they eat, which is hardly ever, that sort of thing. I copy the way they stand or lean up against a wall, their stilettos balanced just so to get the right torque on the calf muscle, like they could stay that way forever. I do what they do with their mouths, their eyes. Most of them get their lips blown up with collagen, that's why they're so poofy, but like I can afford that! I got enough troubles just finding food to put between mine. Mick Mouths I call these, after Jagger. The real secret of modeling is in the eyes, did you know? It's a certain look, some got it down better than others, and you better believe it, they're the cover babes. It's in the way they pop off the page, like they're staring right at you; eyes that say, take me away with you! Only not really, cause why would they want to be taken away? Those babes got it all. Like, what do you think?

Her face grows suddenly serious, something sad in its peaked concentration. Troy can see the outlines of her cheekbones, two little drawer knobs under the bluish, almost translucent skin beneath her eyes. He wonders again about his daughter. He hopes she's not studying to be an underwear model, for chrissake! That would be very disappointing if this was Lucy's goal. He likes to picture her maybe going to dental school someday, solid and predictable, a profession everybody needs at some point, so she'd always be needed.

Troy frowns, What is it exactly you want from me? Why did you ring my bell? He stares past her through the open hallway door leading to the outside metal stairs. Beads of sunlight burn through, lighting up a side of the girl's hair, making it appear a fleeting brilliant yellow, wisps of it like golden feathers, a canary caught in the light. He can smell the fall that didn't come to St. Louis, a drained and squeezed-out harshness in the new winter air. And besides, he mutters, that hall door's supposed to be locked, so strangers don't come through.

Well hell's bells! she squeals, stamping her foot impatiently, You think I'm some kind of stranger? I'm no stranger, I'm going to be your neighbor. I signed a lease on 201, right across the goddamn hall. Paid the damage deposit and all but, here's the rub—I love that expression, don't you? Sounds like it comes from some sucky 1950s detective novel—I don't have enough left to pay my first month's rent. For a lot of reasons, none of them worth getting into. I wouldn't want to bore you with my personal problems. So, what I'm wondering is, can I stay here with you, just for the month I mean? I could sublet my apartment, I met a couple gay guys willing to pay for it. They're movie makers from someplace else, doing this kind of documentary on St. Louis. They're calling it *To The Middle of Everywhere.* It's about the gilded age, they told me, when everyone was supposed to be rich and happy, only most of them weren't. Only the rich were rich, and who knows if any of them were happy. It's not like happiness is automatic when you're rich, I guess, though I'll tell you what. If I had money I'd for damn sure take a stab at happiness, wouldn't you? If nothing else you'd have some time to go out looking for it, instead of where your next meal is coming from or how to come up with the damn rent. They'll be neat, neater than me; gays are, you know, and nice, too. I've always believed the best kind of boyfriend would be a gay man. You wouldn't sleep together, but you could trust he wouldn't be out sleeping with some other babe either, whose legs, yoohoos, hair, who knows? are better than yours. See, if I could stay here with you I'd be close. I can check on things and when the month is over, I just walk across the hall and I'm home.

Troy scratches at his two-day chin growth; should've shaved, he thinks. What the hell is he supposed to say here? He shakes his head. Look…, he starts, and she gives him that and-what's-more look; he can tell she's about to open her mouth again, erupt into more babble. He holds up his hand, Stop! I don't even know you! You're asking if you can stay with me? Why me? Why did you come to my door? You regularly ask strangers if you can move in with them?

Well geez! she says, You're right next door practically to where I'm supposed to be living. Besides, you'd be surprised, she adds, her eyes squinting, darkening for a moment; Not everyone gets to have their own keys in this life. Slides the mask back down. And anyway, she mumbles underneath its (ceramic?) surface, I rang the bell, you answered. Your choice, so you got some responsibility in this, too. OK, so here I am, Marta, spelled Martha. She lifts the mask back up, And now who am I? You don't know, right? Because I haven't told you my other name. Who do we really know, anyway? A stranger could be your own wife. You don't have one of those, do you? You don't look like the married type. I'll cook for you, do your cleaning, whatever you want. Consider it rent. You got a two bedroom, right? She slides the mask back down. You have the unique opportunity to do someone who needs it a favor, she adds, her voice suddenly quieter, flatter, To be a nice guy. Call it karma building, for your afterlife. I happen to know something about being dead. Dead people don't just disappear into the sunset. Turns out living good might be some kind of answer, after all.

Troy tugs at his chin, turns and stares doubtfully about the room behind him. I don't know, this is pretty sudden, I mean, what the hell is this all about? Not even people I know ask me if they can stay here, and here you are, asking me if you can stay here, mumbling on about dead people! Can't you see how odd that is? I need to think about this. The other bedroom is my studio. I paint sometimes. When I can. When I'm in the mood. But I like it there in case I get in the mood. I'm not exactly set up for a guest here, even a guest I've actually invited!

Great! so I'm no guest, do I look like someone's guest? I'm an artist's model. Could you guess that? Nude is not a problem, not for me. So, is it settled then? Did you think about it? Can't think too long about things in this life or they'll just pass you up. Now watch this, my name is Lucy, Juicy Lucy. She grins, lifting the mask up high off her face so he can see she's grinning and winking at him, too. That is, when I'm not Marta, she says. Now you know the both of me. So, please? pale eyes clouding again for just a second. I don't know what I'll do if you say no. I'm so tired of having to figure these things out.

I can't call you that, Troy says quietly. I can't call you Juicy Lucy. I happen to like that name, Lucy. *I Love Lucy.* She was my favorite comedian. That's before your time.

Well geez! Don't you think I know who Lucy Ricardo is? It's not like I didn't spend half my childhood watching the reruns. She pops out her mauve—Troy guesses that's the shade it would be called—lower lip, flutters her eyelashes at him, Ahhhh, Ricky…, P…lease? So call me Lucy Luck if you rather, that's honest-I-swear-to-God my other name. I bring good luck to people that need it, and I really can talk to dead people, too. That's what I meant about the karma thing. I hear them in my head, kind of freaked me out at first, but I got used to it. Is there anyone from your life long ago you want me to ring up? Just tell me. Especially if they were a writer. I'm a channel for writers, can't tell you why. But I can contact anybody most likely.

Right, Troy shakes his head, Dead people. What about people you don't know whether they're dead or alive? Troy thinks, though he'd never say it. He thinks about his daughter, his Lucy, what she looked like back then; he remembers her hair, sparse and white as a daisy, just a baby, beginning to get about on her knees, crawling to him the day he walked out. Troy didn't look back at her, couldn't look back because if he did he would have stayed there, would've been buried there. He heard but didn't see it, the way his daughter's mother grabbed her up off the floor, said, Shush now, though Lucy hadn't made a peep; We don't need him! Troy wants to imagine her a strapping young teenager now, not down on her knees, not on her knees to anybody, least of all him.

Troy stares at this noodle-thin girl in front of him, mask down again, a hollow eagerness in her eyes burning through the black-rimmed eyeholes, peering back at him. Just give me a chance, she pleads, Won't be for that long, only a month, I promise. Don't make me beg, OK? It's not like I've got a lot of options here. I was so happy. Only a week ago, I really thought I was going to finally be in my own place. I just didn't have enough, turns out.

Troy gazes past her, that drift of hard light like a spotlight off the sun, illuminating the space through the open hallway door, fingers of it reaching out to where she stands, slumped now, shoulders boning up under her gauzy green shirt, which he notices is torn in several places, covered in part with the black canvas pack she's slung over her back. The light of the afternoon closing in. He says, There's nobody else? Family, friends, nobody? Troy doesn't wait for her to do anything more than shrug. He's embarrassed for her, for his own question. When you get right down to it, where would he go if he had no place to go? There's only Ada, and when push comes to shove, Troy doubts she'd take him in.

Outside a wind has suddenly picked up. Troy can hear the skittering of dry leaves on the concrete path below, feel a sudden chill darkening the air, the absence of sun. He imagines telling Ada about it later, this strange girl, the evening light through Ada's kitchen window a gritty, wintry gray. Troy to the rescue! Ada would smirk. And maybe he could. Maybe for once, he could give it a shot. OK, he sighs, We can try it I guess, if it's just the month. Give me a moment to think about how best to arrange it.

But before Troy can figure this out, the best way, if there is a best way to bring a stranger into his apartment, his life for chrissake! Lucy Luck wriggles around him through his half-opened door, makes a beeline for his living room, striding across the ancient green carpet like it's grass, the earth, hers! Flops down on his favorite chair.

Thanks, she says, that huge white grin. Geez, you can't even guess how good this feels.

ADA

It's like this in the waking dream: she's in her recliner, a Goodwill purchase, perfectly good, too, just the color is one nobody wanted, mottled and pink as a tongue. Ada likes to conjure up the image of a wild beach plum, though she doubts this color really occurs much in nature. Not so many years ago, it seems, she dyed her hair a shade of red just a little deeper than this and the men went wild. Back when Kai was still in a place where she could open his bedroom door and he'd be inside, or traces of him would be there, balled-up socks, crumple of sheets, the scent of him, a part of her yet apart from her—Ada's son, what was left of the man she had loved, not just made love to but loved—her husband. Their home, Nu'uanu, Hawai'i, chattering of crickets and bullfrogs deep inside a milky darkness, sweetness of night-blooming jasmine. The men had come, mostly after Kai was asleep and later when often he was not even there, slipping in and out of her bedroom like shadows. A widow, beautiful, and lonely. So lonely. Rolling over in the koa-frame bed, middle of the night, that half-awake place feels like a half-remembered dream, like nothing's changed, like she could reach out and her husband would be there, his body still whole, not the shell it became, husk of the man she loved. Wake up and it's a changed world. Could Kai have blamed her that much? She let the men stay and then she could sleep, a little less alone, for that night anyway.

But this dream is not the going-to-sleep type. It's when Ada tips her head back against the rosy pink recliner, shuts her eyes, follows it down to where the kinds of dreams that let her know about everyone else are, that unique concentration, a hum thrumming inside her chest, fingers tingle, eyes pop open and she can tell them the truths they need to hear. This dream is different. Defies truth, becomes too close to habit. Over and over she has seen it and yet when she finally convinced Detective Mallory to search at the spot in this vision, his divers sliding slowly over the silt-bottom dregs of the Mississippi, nothing. Kai still considered a "missing person," her son, Kai Tristan Kamuela. Ada half expected to open her mail one day and discover in the coupon packet from local businesses she would never frequent, Kai's face next to some ad for a free car wash perhaps, oil change and a lube job: Have You Seen This Missing Person?

I'm afraid your son was just swallowed up, Detective Mallory told Ada, Drug culture, they play by their own set of rules.

Swallowed up, so poetic a way of putting it. Like the mouth of a wave, mouth of a river, swallowed up. Consumed, digested, yesterday's flesh and blood, history. Disappeared, the way a moment of life is a part of us, then it's not. Becomes a memory, a dear and distant dream.

THE GIRL WHO'S LIVING WITH TROY

Another St. Louis day the color of paste, no sun, no cold, no warmth, no air, nothing; he feels like nothing, a man, come home from work, used up. The sky behind him a huge white field, like the world's been tipped upside down and what he's standing on passes for cloud, for breath, nothing solid at all. The prairie garden, the manager's answer to nature, boxed in, just enough space where it can't become anything else, glows golden and dead in the late winter light, thorny bushes, sticks, skeletons of things formerly alive. Drags up the concrete stairs. Unlocks his apartment door, the key jiggling this way, that way trying to find the connection and when it finally opens Troy's staring at the watermark, hunched and squiggly as a giant spider on the wall beside. Somebody else's leak. Somebody else's weather. Steps into the room and she says: I brought these cats here, you mind awfully?

Troy stands there blinking. Then, J. H. Christ! he wails, What the hell, Lucy, you've got three cats in here! A black-and-white one with big ears and yellow eyes hunches and glowers

in one corner of the room under the long narrow window, a
fat puffed-up one the color of marmalade or some fleshy, half-
ripened orange is on top of the opposite window ledge, and
the little gray tiger, an old soft sausage on her lap. Lucy Luck
sprawled out, her legs stretched taut as pulled rubber, in Troy's
favorite chair.

What the hell? he says again. I don't even like cats and
there's three of them in here!

At the sound of his voice, raw and elevated, the fat orange
one plunks down off the window ledge, waddles over to where
Lucy sits, gazing up at her for a moment, then jumps on her lap,
too, causing the gray tiger to scatter. In the lap world, evidently,
fat rules. The little tiger shoots a hard look at Troy still standing
there with his mouth dropped open, steals a glance at the yellow-
eyed beast glaring in the corner, then leaps up on the back of
Troy's couch, digging its claws into the fabric. A sort of comfort
test? The way a human might pat the sofa pillows, fluff them up
for the perfect place to plop wearily against?

That's my goddamn couch! he sputters. Not that I care so
much about some old couch, far be it for me to give a damn about
my own furniture, but that cat's going to ruin it even more than
it's already ruined. What can you mean by this, Lucy? Cats are
about as destructive as they come and you've got three of them
here! Did you even ask the manager about this, what their pet
policy is in the complex? Did you think to do that, let alone ask
me? You get us kicked out and you and those cats won't be the
only homeless around here. I won't make a polite beggar either,
I'll jangle my little cup of change in your ear nonstop till you
think it's the devil himself got in your brain!

Lucy Luck screws up her forehead, scrunches her eyes
half shut like there's tears behind them, or she wants him to
think there are tears behind them, pops the pale smooch-lipped
Marta mask down over her face from its perch at the top of her
head. When she first appeared at his door he thought it was
Halloween or some such craziness, but No! she tells him, it's her
alter ego, Marta spelled Martha but you pronounce it without
the *H*. Fine! she says, from under the plastic (he's determined

this much anyway, what the damn thing's made of), a muddling of her voice; I get it, you can count, three cats. Geez, OK, I'll just throw them out in the cold. It's bound to snow any day now wouldn't you think, almost February, will that be enough suffering for you? The marmalade cat twists its fat neck around, staring accusingly over at Troy scowling near the door, a you-still-here? kind of a look. The one in the corner seems like he'd as soon take a chunk out of somebody's ankle.

Three cats! he sputters, I don't believe you've brought three cats into my apartment. People who beg the favor of a place to stay do not commonly behave this way. Three fucking cats!

OK, OK, what do you know, three of them, I can count too, I'm not exactly ignorant, you don't have to swear at me.

That one in the corner looks a mean son of a bitch, Troy adds. Lucy...

Marta, I'm Marta when the mask is down! Geez, how many times do I have to tell you that, anyway?

Lucy, Marta, whoever the hell you are, you've been in my apartment less than a week and you're moving three full-grown cats in? I mean, don't you think that's a little bit, I don't know, over the goddamn top on your part? How did you expect me to react? Oh Lucy, oh Marta, how nice, what a surprise—three fucking felines!

Hey! She slides the mask up again, shrugs violently, and the marmalade cat drops soundlessly off her lap to the floor, a furry jam bomb. It's not like I'm bringing people in here, huh? she says, Other guys, nothing like that. They're just cats, aren't they? There were the two from where I stayed before, Sylvia and Virginia, but then a lady, one of the neighbors in the building on the other side of the path, saw me carrying them in and she asked if I would take Ernest. She said he's been neutered and all, and he's had his shots. She said she and her mother couldn't take care of him anymore, so what am I going to do, let the poor thing be homeless? I know how that feels, Troy, and I'll tell you what, you can make your little beggar jokes, but it's no good, that's what. It feels like no damn good at all.

Ernest? Troy peers at the glowering cat in the corner, those disagreeable yellow eyes, two radioactive yolks. That cat's named Ernest? He looks more like a Spike, or a Chomper! Ernest is a name for some dorky guy who ends up president of a bank or a software company.

Ernest Hemingway, geez! Hardly a dork, he was a hunter. I named him that because the lady said she never gave him an actual name, just a nickname she said. The other two are Sylvia Plath and Virginia Woolf. They were writers. Not the cats, I mean their names are the names of famous writers.

I know that! Who's thinking who is ignorant now? Look, Troy starts, stops. He moves closer to her and the orange one makes a chuckling sound, rolls over in front of Troy's feet, exposing its fat underside. He frowns at it and then at Lucy. Virginia Woolf likes you, Lucy says. Right! Troy says, Now get this. I got one piece of furniture I actually do appreciate in this place, and that happens to be the chair you're sitting in, you're always sitting in. So when I come home, since I'm the person who has a job to go to around here, I'd like to be the person who gets to sit in it.

Well geez, OK! Lucy pops out of the chair, shimmery unfolding of that noodly frame, like wire pieces angled and tied up into some semblance of a human, standing in front of him. He's aware they are the same height; if he put his arms around her and pulled her close to him all their body parts would match up. He's also aware of that look in her eyes, he keeps seeing it there, a used-up sort of expression, eyes that have known something too soon to be knowing it. And this, for some reason, makes him think of his daughter. Though whatever is in his daughter's eyes now, Troy wouldn't have a clue.

OK, he starts again, sitting gingerly down on his chair—he made an issue of it so he'd better. He's too aware of the three cats in this crowded room, like maybe one might sneak up behind him and steal his chair out from under him. He knew a cat that did that sort of thing, one of his brother's cats, long ago when Troy still felt a part of his family, part of something besides this diminished little life of his now. Sit down, OK? He points at the couch, You're making me nervous standing there.

Lucy shrugs, tossing her sand-colored hair back off her shoulders. Meanders over to the couch, perching delicately on the right side where the spring isn't poking up under the cotton slipcover (she's that familiar with his furniture already), crossing her long legs at the ankles she slides her denim skirt further up over her knees, slips one dangle of an arm back behind the couch, says, Am I a Secret model or what?

Troy rolls his eyes, scratches his neck. Look! he says, Lucy, Marta, whoever you are…

Lucy, Lucy Luck! she shrieks. Hell's bells, I mean it's so easy. Why do you have such an issue about this? I don't have the mask down, do I? I'm only Marta under the mask.

OK! Right, whatever! I let you live with me for the month, sleeping in my studio room because you said you had no place else to go and you'd be living across the hall from me anyway, so it was the neighborly thing to do, I figured. But it's odd. Can't you see that? I don't know you from Adam, and now you've brought these strange cats in here, too.

Eve, Lucy says, I'm a girl, aren't I? You don't have issues with my sex, do you? Would you have preferred an Adam? You don't know me from Eve. Or is it that you want me to prove to you I'm a girl? I could do that, you know, means nothing to me. I can do it as a favor, a chance to be nice. You like girls, huh? She leans toward him, sliding her arm back off the couch in one fluid movement, lizard-green of her eyes, the gauzy blouse slipping off one of her bony shoulders then lower still to expose rich cleavage, two rounded hills in the valley of those snaky arms. Something about the contrast of actual cleavage on such a wasted-looking frame gets to him; sad, really sad. Like maybe she could have been someone else, if only she weren't her.

Christ! Troy mutters, forcing himself to look back into her eyes. Will you just listen to me for a moment here, goddamnit? I'm not asking you to do anything but that, just listen. First you tell me you're going to cook for me and all, and you made one meal burnt so badly I almost didn't recognize what meat it was.

Well, I'm a vegetarian! she growls, a guttural sound, that husky voice. Flesh is flesh, DNA, formerly alive. And anyway, I didn't tell you I could cook, I said I would cook. I'd be willing, is what I meant.

Right, so then you bring into my already-small-enough apartment, three cats! I mean, what gives here? Where do you get off doing stuff like this? Troy's heart starts racing and he rubs his chest, snagging a deep breath. It occurs to him he's almost lecturing her here, the punishing tone of his voice, sounding like he's her father or something. He feels that roaring inside him thinking about this and for a terrible minute Troy wonders if despite his popping the lithium his mania's coming back, and this whole scene, the cats, Lucy Luck offering herself to him, that skinny chest's pumped-up cleavage may not be real at all. But he'd have to prove it, prove to himself it's not just, after all, another delusion. Force himself to think it: that once he was a father, but the dearest memory of this is the top of her head, hair finespun and white as a daisy, on her knees as he walked out.

Lucy lowers her eyes and stares at her crossed feet. Troy follows her down. She's wearing a beat-up pair of combat boots, looking like they'd already done some kind of war and had been retired to her feet, untied, no socks. Her ankles are too delicate, he thinks, little bird legs, how can they possibly support the rest of her?

Where I was staying before, she says quietly, they weren't such nice people. So when I heard they were going to get rid of the cats, I came and got them. I didn't want them to be just tossed out of the house, out on the street, you know? What if someone did that to you? Do you know what that's like? My mother used to do that to me and my sister. We'd get off the school bus and my little sister always had something to show her, a picture she colored for her in school, a good grade on her spelling test. My sister never got it, but I knew. I knew we'd come home, most every day we'd come home and the door would be locked. We'd knock and our mother would be in there, but she wouldn't answer the door. Maybe she's not home, my sister always said. But, like, where would she go? She didn't work. She didn't have friends. Maybe some boyfriend before she'd chase him away. She'd let us in eventually, whenever it was she decided she couldn't get away with keeping us outside any longer. You know how that feels? Sylvia Plath and Virginia Woolf scratching at the door and nobody opens it for them?

Troy pulls his gaze away from Lucy and stares out the window. The late January afternoon is fish colored now, a hard, silvery gray. The few trees in the complex that still have their leaves look bare nonetheless; he can see the deadening light through their branches, through leaves that are brown and shriveled. Should've dropped off long ago, he thinks, part of the soil, the earth, or carted away in piles pushed out on the curb for the garbage trucks, on their way to some landfill. The orange cat rubs up against Troy's leg and he reaches down, running his hand tentatively over its back. The fur feels coarse and thick as a fine-grained wood, not what he'd expect a cat to feel like. The cat purrs, a rumbly, steady sound of someone snoring.

Which one is this? Troy asks.

Virginia Woolf, she's the most social. Sylvia's a little shy, but she'll sleep pressed up in a warm ball against your stomach. I love the feel of her there. It's like you're not sleeping alone, and you don't have to do anything but just be with her. I don't know about Ernest Hemingway. The lady said he can be a bit unpredictable. She said he's got an attitude problem. She admitted he liked her mother better than her, but that he didn't like either of them all that much. He needs a cat person, she said, and she prefers butterflies. And anyway, she said, they're moving to Chicago in the spring. She wouldn't want to bring a cat to Chicago. When I brought Ernest in here he wasn't so sure about Sylvia and Virginia and they're not too sure about him, either. So for now they're all kind of keeping their distance. Reminds me of a seventh-grade dance, they eyeball each other but no real contact.

Troy lifts his hand back onto his lap, sits straight up, and the orange cat jumps up on his lap. He decides to let her stay there, for the time being.

Well, he says, It doesn't take a genius to believe that one in the corner has an attitude problem. Why did you name them after writers? Are you a reader or something? I don't think I've seen you open a book since you've been here. I knew somebody once who read all the time, every living, breathing moment she read, no room for anything else in that woman's life, she preferred a life madeup.

Lucy grins, pulls the mask down over her face. Guess which one of me likes to read? she asks, then slides the mask back up. The thing is, they told me these are their names.

Troy rolls his eyes again, shakes his head. Oh, I see, you talk to cats?

No, dead people. I told you that before. Virginia Woolf, Sylvia Plath, and Ernest Hemingway all killed themselves, did you know? They weren't so happy, I guess. I guess even being talented and famous isn't enough sometimes, do you think? Now I can give them another shot at it, or their names at least.

Troy sighs, I bet they were only famous with people who read. I bet if you asked our manager if he knew Sylvia Plath, he'd search through his ledger to see if she's rented from him.

The light outside is growing darker, color of a street, that concrete gray. Troy thinks about Ada in the building near his, maybe sitting there, too, staring out her window. He wishes he could touch her, that's all, just hold her again, one of these long nights. It isn't about sex, he thinks, though God knows he wouldn't say no. Just the need for another's skin up close against your own. He can't figure out why, after all these years, he still loves Ada, why he even started loving her in the first place. A woman old enough to be his mother, what is it she has that makes it impossible for him to stop thinking about her? A woman who's never loved him back, just let him love her. He couldn't figure it out then and not now either, after all these years. Here sits Troy, a middle-aged man in this crummy St. Louis apartment, its watermarked walls, scraps of old carpeting curled up in the corners like toenails, with some incredibly weird girl and three unwanted cats.

Troy slides Virginia off his lap. The cat bitches a little, a whiny, clucking sound. He stands, stretches, then shuffles into the kitchen, reaching into the cupboard for his lithium; tugs open the refrigerator, pops the cap off a Bud and downs the pill.

What are those for, anyway? Lucy calls out, I've seen you do those.

Troy stares over the kitchen counter at her head, turned sideways, the same angle as her again slung-over-the-sofa arm. She's peering back at him expectantly, almost innocently. There's a sweetness to that hair of hers, he thinks, fine and straight and light, wispy in the places where it sticks up around that silly geisha mask, anchored on top of her bangs.

They keep me balanced, he says. Otherwise, you see, the world doesn't always seem such a good place to me either, and I'm not famous at all. Nobody's going to name their cat after me. How old are you, anyway? he asks. We should probably get that much straight.

Twenty, she says, But don't worry, I won't go into your refrigerator and chug down any of your beers. I don't even like beer. I'm legal enough, you can't get arrested letting me stay here.

So, when are you going to get a job? You said you were going to get the money to move into your apartment next month, and it's getting closer to next month.

Lucy Luck studies him, a vaguely eager expression on her face. Guess what, she grins, I got one. At the Sonic, taking food orders. I start in a couple days.

Good thing they won't have you cooking the food! I don't guess mystery meat is an option on their menu. Troy winks, trying to put her at ease. He's been a bit of an asshole, he figures, and he sees she's still got that anxious face. He's relieved to hear about her job, almost proud. She said she'd get a job and now she has. Maybe there really will be an end to this craziness.

Well? Lucy pleads, So, what do you think?

OK, OK, Troy sighs, Christ, what choice do I have? They can stay, for as long as you stay, and as long as you're the one taking care of their cat box or whatever the hell it is they better use. But if that nasty-looking one, Ernest Hemingway, starts schlepping a rifle around I'm going to get a little nervous here. Don't think I won't do something about it, too.

Lucy shrugs, I'll pray for his soul. My mother used to do that, though I never saw what good it did her. She'd clasp her hands together so tight her fingers would go red at their tips, and she'd mumble things, face burning up at the ceiling like it's the Lord himself lived in those cracked tiles. She'd wail God God God! as if repeating it's the charm, three times and you win. I'll pray for the real Ernest Hemingway. Maybe when they're dead it's easier to get an answer. You know what I mean? Because nothing's at stake anymore.

THE MANAGER'S SON

The manager's son hovers behind the leafless oak, huddling there as if it could cover him, shade him, though it's January and there's no shade or any need for it. He scratches at the baby fat on his cheek, tugs it a bit, both cheeks, in the upward direction; up and away, like being lifted by his face one moment, and when he's set back down he's magically older, more fully formed, the sculpted perfection of the man he wishes he could see himself becoming.

He's watching the pregnant girl from 211-D, who's staring at an empty wooden crib stuck there between his father's prairie garden and the garbage dumpsters. The crib is white, a knot of little yellow ducks painted at the head. She's just standing, leaning up against nothing at all, though her posture is thrust back a little as if she really is leaning, short pale hands anchored on her narrow hips, maybe to support the weight of the baby, he thinks, poking out in front. Otherwise, she's the slick straight shape of a pencil. You'd never guess a baby's there. In fact, the first time he saw her from the back, that sort of jaunty walk of hers, no hips, sleek hair streaming off her neck, dark yellow arrow of it pointing down at nothing in particular, he had thoughts about her and immediately needed to see her face. It's in the face you can tell about a person. But her face, when he saw it, was blank.

A cat leaps from out of nowhere into the crib and it startles them both, she jumping back a little, he letting out a sound he should've (oh man, why didn't he?) kept to himself. Because then, of course, she whips around and sees him there, watching her. And it's not the first time.

She sucks in her lower lip, You again? I've seen you before. Whose cat is this anyway? I've seen this cat before.

He walks over to her stiffly, a scratchy, uncomfortable sort of walk propelled by something stronger than his shyness, his reluctance, but not too close. He feels his own heart pounding like it's been unleashed in his chest; don't look at her! he warns himself. They both gaze inside the crib at the black and white cat, the long ears and golden eyes, lounging about on the plastic mattress with its yellow ducks, its blue daisies, its puffy, cheery red steam engines; the cat lolling on his back like all of this is his, his personal world, white belly exposed. The manager's son has a sudden longing to be there himself, contained and safe, eyes shut.

That cat keeps turning up here, he says, his voice cracking a little at its own unfamiliar sound. (A quiet boy, his mother always said; know when to keep your mouth shut! his father's words.) My dad took it to the shelter when some people complained, but it found its way back again with a lady who lives here, only then she didn't want it either. The manager's son gasps a little, realizing he's rattling on about this and maybe the pregnant girl couldn't care less? Anyway, he adds, I don't know who has it now, but someone's feeding it. That stomach's fat as…

The girl rolls her eyes. Oh, great! she says, Just great, I'm happy to make your acquaintance too. So go ahead then, finish your sentence. Weren't you going to say fat as mine?

The manager's son's face burns.   He fixes on the girl's painted fingernails, a sort of purpley-maroon or dark aubergine, something like that, like the blaze of his cheeks.   No, he mumbles, shaking his head, this way, that way, anyway but her way; I'd never say that.   I just couldn't think of what to say is all, the best way to complete the sentence.

Her eyes crinkle up, light eyes, not a lot of color, that drained green shallow of the ocean the manager's son misses like it's his own blood.   Bloodless, he thinks of it this way sometimes, living in a place he never dreamed he would be, no ocean to speak of, how this feels—bloodless.   He guesses she's probably laughing at him, the white flash of her smile, then she turns away, back toward the cat.   Who are you? she asks.

He's staring at the curved slope of her back, and he jumps a little at the nasally sound of this, her voice; though why should he jump?   They've been talking, haven't they?

You some kind of English class flunk-out?   Can't complete a sentence?   One of those genius math kids, only functions if there's numbers and a grade?   What's to finish?   You just speak.

The manger's son shakes his head, strands of his dirt-brown hair leaking into his eyes.   I'm not very good at algebra, he says, But I don't mind geometry.   You can see a world in its shapes. The manager's son feels a sudden surge of sickness, blaze of his fat cheeks, the inside of his fat stomach hot and heavy as a slab of meat.   Why is he telling her these stupid kinds of things?   I didn't mean I couldn't finish my sentence, he mumbles, I just needed to figure out the best way to finish it and you jumped in. Can't a person think a minute before he speaks?   And anyway, he says, puffing a little, his round, red cheeks, his freckles, slouching up next to her, but taller than her—he hopes she's aware of this, even if he's not quite fifteen—How the heck did this crib get here?   That's what I wanted to know.   My dad's not going to like it, a crib stuck out in the middle of everything.   He doesn't like things out of order.

The girl leans toward him, an exaggerated sigh, flipping those shiny noodles of hair off her neck.   Heck? she says, You say heck instead of hell?   Where you from, Iowa?   Maybe they don't have hell in Iowa. I'm from the prairie. Even people in the prairie say hell. You say shoot instead of shit? Jesus! she shakes her head violently, Well, so happens I've got a daddy just like yours. Things not in order, a major tragedy, you know? She glances around, sweeping out an arm—her too-big nylon jacket is torn at the elbow, he notices. Did you say in the middle of everything? she asks. Looks like the middle of nothing to me. Your daddy's plot of dead grass he thinks will bring the wild back to the metropolis of St. Louis, and the garbage dumpsters. So what kind of idiot can't guess this crib's for my baby?

He stares at her face then focuses down on her feet, embarrassed, then back up to her forehead. He likes her face, short, ragged bangs like the fringed bottom of a particular lamp shade he remembers, his mother's antique lamp, used to sit on the table beside her reclining chair; the pregnant girl's got a forehead that's wide and pale and soft looking as a slice of bread. OK, he says quietly, his heart suddenly thumping, Then what's it doing out here with that cat in it instead of inside your apartment?

They look again at the cat. She reaches down her hand to stroke it and he cautions, I wouldn't if I were you. That cat's got a reputation, he bites.

She jerks her hand back just a little then grins, full fleshy lips pulling up over her teeth. He notices she's got a crooked kind of smile, and this makes him like her all the more. The girl drives her hand back down into the cat's furry, white belly and the cat—still lounging about on his back like he's thinking maybe he's on a raft in some sea, sailing away instead of stuck in this complex, this city, in the middle of nowhere—lets her do this.

Let me tell you, kiddo, I've had worse, she says. I'll tell you something about being a girl. I've never told anyone else what I'm going to tell you. It's like this: You have dreams, you know, of a time when you can just fly away somewhere. Some kind of place that isn't in your life now, but then, you think, maybe. Did you ever play the piano? The better it sounds the more you hope for, like the notes are something real. When you stop playing, turns out it's empty air. She hesitates, sliding closer to him. He can almost feel, almost imagine the touch of her against his arm, his bare wrist where his own jacket has slipped up. Then comes the time, she whispers, When you start to think, so maybe I won't get to have those wings. You see what I'm telling you here? The girl lifts her hand up off the cat, moving her fingers slowly, uncertainly, staring at them like they've become somehow unfamiliar. She pats her big belly. It's like having your feet nailed to the ground, she says.

The pregnant girl's name is Neville. He finds this out from his father later that afternoon, Neville Story. That's not a girl's name, is it? Neville? the manager's son asks. I can't call her Neville.

Call her whatever the Christ you want, his father says. She's got her father's name, that crazy Vietnam vet. I've considered evicting them, but I can't come up with the reason why. Just don't like the man, is all. Has nothing to do with my feelings about that goddamn war, neither. The guy did what he had to do and he got screwed for doing it. So now he's screwing his family in return. That's cowardice, if you ask me. Going to the war or not going to the war, it's all the same to me. It's how you are the rest of your life that counts.

You mean he's the father of that baby? The manager's son's fish-colored eyes grow wide and solemn and slightly crossed. That kind of screwing?

Oh for crying out loud, were you born in a balloon, your mother's sacred womb? Scratching viciously at his two-day beard, the manager mutters, Christ! How is it I remember salt for the goddamn icy paths but no razors for my own face? They don't pay me enough for the job I'm doing. Real life isn't what they show on TV, son, you better believe it. I don't know and I don't care who the father of that baby is, though I'd bet my month's income it's that scabby white kid with the His-Spanic name in Unit C. They were thick as thieves until her stomach pops out. What I'm saying is, the man's an asshole to his family.

Case in point, he's thrown her crib out. Well, I'm not going to stand for it. Do they think I'm running a tenement project here? Most of the people renting from me earn their money the normal way, then there's the subsidized buildings like the one the vet's in. Just because he slogged through the jungle for a year and he gets a nightmare now and then, so now he doesn't have to make an honest wage? There are no dead cars in my driveway, and I'll be damned if a chucked-out baby bed's going to park there instead. You set standards, son, that's what I'm trying to teach you here. You set standards, and if folks live up to them, even a little, you've got yourself a smoothly running deal. Otherwise they walk all over you. You think I grew up wanting a job like this? You think I dreamed of managing someone else's property? It doesn't work that way. You make the best of it, and damn what they say about you in the process.

It's the manager's son who's given the task of delivering the pink slip to the girl's father. His own father said it's only fair, since the boy's come from Maine to live here now. It's about time you took some responsibility, his father said, You think life's handed to people like us on some goddamn silver platter? His father told him he was being coddled by his mother, living the country life in Maine without a thing to do but go to school, sleep, eat and excrete, is the way his father sees it. My turn to make a man out of you, his father said.

The evening is a washed-out lavender, a thin holdout from the afternoon, the light dying so early these winter days, not the woodsy, golden, winter light of Maine, he thinks, short as the days are there now. The manager's son misses Maine. It's a kind of constant longing, in his stomach, his chest, that aching, and his arms—like something you can hold on to, if only he could! just reach out and it would be there, salt smell of the sea, his mother huddled up in her reclining chair by the window looking toward the sea (you couldn't see it from their house, but you could breathe it, know it was close); the chair she grew sick in, grew silent in and, eventually, died in. He didn't know if she suffered, though he thought she must have. Could only guess it, the shots of morphine more and more frequent from the hospice nurse, the setup where his mother could just press a patch of it onto her arm when she needed more. Until she grew too weak for even that. The manager's son knows this: he hates death for what it takes from the one left living, and he hates St. Louis, because this is the place they send you when there's nowhere else to go. He has no feelings in particular about his father. He barely knows him at all.

The manager's son raps lightly on 211-D, hoping the girl's father won't answer, that maybe he's taking a nap or he's already asleep for the night. The manager's son knows he's there because his own father said the man never goes out. When the girl opens the door he's relieved at first, then embarrassed, pink slip fluttering in his hand like a caught bird. A smell of old onions, or maybe garlic wafting from somewhere.

My dad wants your dad to bring the crib back up here, he says inanely, grinning foolishly as if it's a funny request. Maybe he could carry it back up for the girl, he thinks, maybe she'd appreciate him doing that?

She shrugs, eying him up and down. He stands up taller, taller than her he reminds himself, does she notice?

Yeah, she says, Well, but it's complicated. You see, my daddy doesn't want a baby around here, he doesn't want me to have a baby, so he thinks if he gets rid of the baby's things, like its crib my own mother's church gave me for chrissake! then the baby disappears. Or something like that. Poof! Everything the same as it was. We don't take charity, my daddy said.

So you have a mother? the manager's son asks, then immediately regrets this. Why the heck would he ask such a thing? He doesn't like to say that word, even think it too much, *mother*, and now the girl will respond to it, which means they might have to have an entire conversation about mothers. My father just talked about your father, he mumbles, That's all I meant.

No duh! the girl smirks. My mother says my father is difficult and I should just accept that. Come to terms with it, is how she put it. It's the price of war, my mother said. Well let me tell you, kiddo, I've seen just about every war movie ever made, my father makes my mother rent them seven days a week, pops them into our VCR over and over, same damn ones half the time. I know how they're supposed to act, the ones who've been in some war, even the ones who've been totally wasted for chrissake, by some war. There's nothing about not wanting your own daughter's baby just because you were in the war; no matter how screwed up they got, not a damn thing about that! Her voice is suddenly shrill, and the manager's son peers about her face anxiously, looking for what, he isn't sure.

What about the baby's father? the manager's son asks, turning a little so he isn't staring at the girl smack into those pale round eyes, bleary and glassy, like a doll's eyes. What if the father kept the crib for you? He feels embarrassed about this part of it, since obviously there's another guy pretty intimately involved. He's not sure if he should be mentioning this, maybe it'll embarrass her as much as it's embarrassing him. She did it with some guy and now she's got to reap the consequences, his own father's way of summing these things up. The manager's son stares into the living room behind where the girl is standing, a plain, rectangular room, same shape and the same cheap paint the color of milk in all the units, blinds on all the windows. There's not a lot of furniture, but he can see the worn, green couch at the rear of the room, the back of a man's balding head lying on it, and the TV flickering its ghostly light. He wonders about those consequences, whether they'd be all that bad if what you reaped was to have this girl with you every night for the rest of your life.

Well kiddo, guess what? Fact of the matter is, my baby doesn't actually have a father, only Pablo, the one who helped me make it. So, she continues, staring hard at the manager's son, marble eyes narrowing into clear, pale beads like she thinks he's going to protest, You believe God created us right, the Bible says he's our father? So you don't see him hanging around much, do you? Now there's an absentee father if I ever saw one. You're supposed to believe in him even though you can't see him, can't hear him, can't even crawl up on his lap and suck your thumb!

Neville? The bald head from the couch croaks out suddenly, not even turning around, Who the hell you yacking with? That yellow kid? I'm trying to watch something here.

He's white as rice, Dad! she shouts back. Just the color of his heart is sort of yellow, she whispers to the manager's son, I'm meaning about Pablo, the baby's so-called father.

The girl places her hand against the manager's son's chest, pushing him farther out into the hallway and she immediately behind him, shutting her apartment door hard. My father doesn't really hate Pablo, she says, Not in any kind of a personal way. He just hates everything he doesn't have control over. He's not talking about skin color either, you know, He's talking about a kind of courage. It's what the war taught him. He says there's the people who face what they got to face, and then the people who don't.

That's weird, the manager's son starts, then snaps his mouth closed, reddens and looks away. He was about to tell her what his father said about courage then thought better of it. He's still feeling her hand there against his skin, even though it's through a layer of down jacket and his flannel shirt underneath; he can feel the touch of her fingers there, near his heart where only his mother has touched before.

You go out with girls? she asks, as they sidle down the metal steps into the January night, a frigid, snowless cold. You're a bit of a baby yet yourself, I guess.

I'm fifteen! he says defensively, which is almost true.

I was sixteen when Pablo started doing me. I was from the prairie, that's what he used to remind me of. Which is like coming from nowhere, far as Pablo was concerned. Guess he figured people from the prairie didn't know any better, don't know when they're being screwed.

They sit down on the ground under the eaves of his father's building, crackle of dry, frozen leaves, Unit A, near the concrete wall that separates the complex from the boulevard roaring behind, trying to escape the small wind that has risen, its icy breath whistling out a deeper, more burning cold. What will you do? he asks, About the baby, I mean. If your father doesn't want it and Pablo doesn't either?

Pablo's not such a bad guy, the girl starts, staring out into a distance above the manager's son's own head, past the other brick buildings arranged in a long rectangle around the zig and zag of the concrete paths, forming an uninteresting courtyard without even a bench to justify its protected space, to sit on, relax, to just be there; only the paths moving from one point to the next, back to the concrete wall that keeps the boulevard from rushing in. He can hear the whine of a truck passing by too fast.

Pablo's just no kind of a father is all, she says. How would he know what a father's supposed to be? It's not like he really ever had one. The girl shrugs, shivers, Anyway, I guess it won't much matter who wants the baby. It's going to come regardless.

Where will you live? he asks, suddenly aware of her trembling beside him. He wonders if he should move closer to her, or let her have his down jacket—her nylon one is so thin, and torn to boot. When his mom got the chills in her chair he tried wrapping her in more and more blankets at first, but when nothing worked he climbed right into the chair beside her, under all those blankets and held on.

The yellow-eyed cat slides up out of nowhere again, rubbing against the girl's legs. I can't believe that cat likes you, he says. I didn't think it liked a soul, according to my father anyway.

His name is Ernest Hemingway, the girl says, Found that out this afternoon, after you went inside. Probably he likes me because, you know, the baby and all. Maybe he smells my milk brewing or something. Does that embarrass you? Breast milk?

He shakes his head, cheeks burning (breast, she said breast!), but she won't see this in the darkness.

I might've found it embarrassing when I was fifteen. Weird how things change. Well, so anyhow I saw this program on TV, my father had it on, about cats. They said kittens taken from their mothers too soon become permanently antisocial. So what I'm thinking is, maybe Ernest senses I'm about to be a mother, he's relating to that in some strange way, so he likes me but nobody else. By the way, do you know my name? It's Neville, Neville Story. I guess we can get that much straight. Anyway, so Ernest hunkered down in the crib like he was my baby, let me pet him and all, then this tall girl comes out from the next building—maybe you've seen her, she's got this really cool mask, looks like a…what do you call those actors that imitate people without using any words? a mime—and she tells me his name is Ernest. Says that the man she and Ernest and a couple of other cats are living with doesn't like cats. Especially not Ernest Hemingway, she said. Well, I bet you anything Ernest just needs a mother, I told that tall girl. He just needs someone to love him, that's what I think.

The manager's son, cheeks still flaring (can't quite get free of those words, *breast milk*), reaches out tentatively to scratch the yellow-eyed cat behind his ears. Ernest makes a stifled yowling sort of sound in his throat, swivels his head around and sinks his teeth into the manager's son's palm.

Oh, no! the manager's son howls. And then for no reason whatsoever—the horror of this!—he starts to cry. He feels terribly embarrassed, it didn't hurt that much, did it? His fat head between his fat knees, his fat shoulders shaking like that icy wind's blowing through, sheltered as they are, and Neville's petting him, stroking his neck like she's petting that cat. Shhhhush, she's going, Hush now. Did he hurt you real bad? It must've hurt real bad.

The manager's son sniffles, tries to stuff all those gritty, groveling sounds back up through his nose, down his throat, into his gut where they've sat for four months like a belly full of stones; four months since his mother's died and no one's ever bothered to ask: Did it hurt real bad? Are you all right? How do you feel about this? So embarrassed, he never wants to look up again. He'll just sit here on this cold ground in the middle of this cold night, the middle of this cold (Christ! he whispers to himself, just like his father; Christ, this cold, cold place!), the middle of nowhere, his fat head between his fat legs, his mother gone.

Hey! Neville says, You want to feel something cool? Want to feel my baby move? He lifts his head just a little, starts to shake it *No*, but then he sees her jacket is unzipped, her shirt pulled up; he sees her bare, glistening skin in the white of the apartment-complex lights, the round hump of it tight as a doe's belly. He's seen a pregnant doe in Maine, right outside in their own yard, he and his mother peeping from behind the curtains. His mother was permanently in her chair at that point, and he's perching on the arm of it like they were any mother and any son, a moment in eternity spent together, peering out the window. There's life for you, sweetie, his mother had said; Got this way of keeping on.

Here, Neville says, taking his frigid hand into hers, This the one Ernest bit? Her hands feel so warm, profound as those blankets he wrapped around his mother, and for a moment he imagines himself back again, under those blankets, tucked away from everything else. But this can't last, his mother had whispered.

Ernest didn't mean anything by it, you know, manager's son, him biting you that way, nothing personal. He barely even knows you. There, Neville says, stretching out his fingers then moving his hand gently back and forth against the bare, pulsing warmth of her belly. He can feel it, a flutter here and there under her skin, like a flag waving, staking its claim: hello! I'm here.

There! she says it again.

As if that's that.

WHAT LUCY LUCK WAS

What she wasn't those days was lucky. Four years ago, still just plain Lucy Luke, with a mother not fit for their world, a father who might be anyone, anywhere in the world. And a sister everyone loved, including Lucy. How not? Lucy's little sister didn't make waves, was how their mother used to put it; a wrinkle now and then maybe, but nothing that couldn't be ironed out. Juicy Lucy was a name some guy gave her and she thought it kind of cute, rhyming and all, not a bad idea for a V.S. Angel to have a catchy name; Naughty Angel, Juicy Lucy. But it's OK with Lucy that Troy doesn't find this name so cute, that maybe he actually believes there's something more to her, something else going on.

Four years ago, sixteen and leaving home. Not that it was ever a home. Rented houses, the longest for three years, subsidized by the government and Lucy's mother's on-and-off boyfriends, peeling porches, weeds like strands of unruly, green hair wrapped around the railings, stink of rotting onions, potatoes, somebody else's former meals inside. Not theirs, God knows. Their mother didn't cook; That's what the good Lord invented TV dinners for! she'd joke, narrow hands on narrow hips, pointy chest poking out, trying to sound like someone who wasn't her, someone else's mother, or maybe not any kind of a mother at all. And those hallways, small dark rooms pooling off them like blood vessels, stained and faded carpets, the color dirt gets when it's ground in, flattened. Theirs was a fleeting world; in the end, what would stick around? Not the boyfriends. Not Lucy. Her mother's illness was not the flu, she didn't get better in a week. You couldn't just put up with a cough, the sour breath, waiting on her hand and foot because there'd come a day the fever would lift and she'd be normal. *Chronic Misery* was what one of the boyfriends diagnosed; Wakes up every morning when she just as soon not. And there was this: when push came to shove, their mother liked Lucy's little sister better. And it was Lucy's little sister who most needed to be liked. So Lucy left. Not enough love in their family, not enough for them both.

Her real regret was leaving school, that was the worst of it. Lucy liked reading the books they assigned in English, she even kept some. It would've been her senior year that next year, then maybe college, who knows? Who gets to make these choices? Probably not Lucy, she understood that much anyway, not girls like her. Girls named Bethany or Jessica, whose mothers peeked around flutters of crisp, clean curtains watching for them to come home, wanting to see them home safe. Not someone named Juicy Lucy, whose mother locks her out of the house; not the blow-job queen, some high-school-football jock called her. Back then, she didn't even know for sure what that was.

Slogging about with those books in her backpack, underneath the extra pair of jeans, the oversized T-shirt to sleep in, if she was lucky enough to find a place to just sleep, enough socks and underwear to last five days before having to score a washing machine or a not-too-disgustingly-filthy sink. Lucy's underwear had the days of the week embroidered on them, her sister's birthday gift to her: Monday, Tuesday, Wednesday, Friday and Saturday; Thursday and Sunday had disappeared. Thursday's child works hard for a living? Sunday's full of grace? What fates were now lost? Or maybe she never had a Sunday after all; God's day, she could hear her mother exclaim, Is this a subject for underwear? Reading those books is how Lucy discovered Virginia Woolf, Sylvia Plath, and Ernest Hemingway—the poetry anthology with an entire section on Sylvia Plath, *To The Lighthouse* by Virginia Woolf, and *A Farewell to Arms*.

Too many farewells in those days for Lucy, though nobody she ever much missed; what you had to do just to have a bed to sleep in! Think of it like sucking a banana into your mouth then peeling it with your tongue. The blow-job queen. In the morning they'd never want her there, cup of coffee, bowl of Cheerios if she got really lucky. Lucy Luck, she renamed herself, hoping maybe it would be this, some kind of luck that could see her through.

One night the buzz in Forest Park where she hung with the other freed teens, they named themselves, was about a party, some place called the Incredible Organ in South County where they weren't checking IDs. Lucy got very drunk on White Russians that night, the bartender kept feeding them to her; Joey, who became better and better looking after each one, hangdog face of his chiseled and real, even seeming to transform into a nice guy. Like a prince! Lucy thought.

Later he's dragging her, this Prince Joey, up to his room over the bar, tart odor of too much alcohol in her nose, her mouth, trying to suck in little, sticky, half breaths like grains of cement hardening in her lungs. She's gasping and giggling, that empty sort of way—does he think she's having fun? Her head knocking back against the stairwell, and what Lucy longed for was to fall into his bed without doing anything, sleep inside its fluffy give, scent of clean sheets, of home, somebody's home anyway—the smells of normal life, shampoo lingering in washed hair, a cared-for shirt. Please oh geez, only this time let him be someone who liked her.

Lucy got to hurting so hard in her head, her chest, a lump of something sour and grave stuck in her throat, and she heard herself cry out, No! Or maybe she just thought it, no, no actual word, not even a syllable on that spongy thick tongue, and tears sprouting in her eyes as Joey pushed her onto his bed, tugged off her jeans, yanked up her shirt, mauling both of her breasts, fingers, fist, mouth, and without even removing her underwear (maybe it was Thursday's child who's full of woe? or was this the one who had far to go?), just shoving them to one side, took out the rent of his bed. Lucy felt her body suspended there, he's pounding away on it like a jackhammer, like she's something to break apart, slab of tough meat to be tenderized. You like it huh? he asked her, anxiously, almost, it almost seemed. You want it, huh? Well but of course she wanted it, the house, car, a puppy, children, breakfast..., maybe. Lucy, tender somewhere but so far inside herself now sometimes even she couldn't recognize it, understood this—the sum of her life, already the dream of what might have been under those cool sheets.

Later, the bartender snoring, her head reeling from the vodka, stomach churning, kahlúa a sludge in her blood, the familiar throbbing between her legs, Lucy heard the slow spin of those voices inside her. It wasn't the first time. Still, for a terrible moment she thought maybe she was going crazy the way her own mother was most certainly crazy—the paranoia, strange, unpredictable behavior, the crying, icy coldness, those times when her mother's eyes hardened into small, black stones. Her mother would light up a cigarette then, wouldn't smoke it, just let the trail of its smoke surround her, wrapping itself about her as if this, anyway, wanted to be with her. She'd pace into the kitchen, yank open the refrigerator door and hurl whatever semblance of food was inside, milk, sour or not, a frizzle of generic colas, bruised fruit, apples, pears, cheese if they were lucky—cheese could survive the fall—all onto the floor. There! she'd scream triumphantly, as if this was supposed to mean something, kicking at the tossed and scattered foods, these markers, emblems, organic habits of loss. Here's Lucy in some stranger's room, yet again.

She slid away from the bartender, hugging a pillow over her head. Block them, she thought, Go away! But there they are, clearer this time, one with a British accent (that would be Virginia), Ernest's rough and craggy, the shy, slow ponderance of Sylvia. I'm not listening to you! Lucy whispered fiercely.

But of course you are, Lucille! Virginia said, the crisp clip of the English. You can't only read us, you know, then forget us. We have to mean something more than that. Otherwise, what's any of it worth?

Get the hell off the streets! Ernest said. That's what I'm here to tell you. What do you think you're doing? Who do you think you are? Some pathetic Dickens waif? Wrong story, sister! The street's no place for a girl.

Not a thing, Sylvia said, She's doing not a thing, is what she's not doing. She's wasting her life. A small life, too, Sylvia added, Not a lot of it to waste.

Hey! Lucy sat up, eyes swimming across the unfamiliar room, pasty white of the too-close ceiling lit from a streetlamp outside the window, too narrow, too choked, not hers. The bartender groaning in his sleep beside her.

Geez! so what the hell am I supposed to do?

Get a job! said Ernest. I worked plenty in our time.

Go back to school, Virginia advised. An educated person carries a home in her head.

Excuse me, but you can't lie down and die just because your parents weren't the best, Sylvia said.

I'm not lying down to die, I just need a good night's sleep. You guys at least had your own beds.

I'd rather have no bed than share a stranger's, said Sylvia.

Oh yeah? Lucy glowered furiously into the dark, And I suppose Virginia would rather lie down on a riverbed.

Just hold it right there, Ernest said.

We came to encourage you, Virginia said, I had my demons, too, you know, how many books did I write all the same?

I'm making you up, you're not really here, you're voices inside my head. You're not real! Lucy humming a crooked little song about something lost or someone gone, somebody's left behind; that's the gist of it, she didn't remember the words. Her mother used to sing it, long ago when her mother used to sing to herself, when her mother still had a voice that wasn't all anger. Even her mother didn't know all the words.

What is reality, that is not constructed in each of us? Virginia chirped.

The point, said Ernest, Your life's in a pretty sorry state.

Lost, Sylvia added, And there's only so much you can ever get back.

I'm listening to a guy who blew his head off and another one pops hers in the oven! Lucy was mumbling, still trying to sing the song whose words she didn't remember, hummmmm! And geez, wouldn't you know, the third sticks a rock in her pocket and drowns herself in the goddamn river!

Joey the bartender woke up suddenly, slitting his eyes in her direction; What the hell? The way she was sitting, straight up in his bed, rubbing her head, rocking and muttering like a crazy person. You OK? he asked, not a particularly caring tone in his voice, more like a warning, you better be! It's annoying at the least, Lucy supposed, to awaken in your own bed and some girl you jerked up there for an anonymous fuck sits yacking with dead people.

Maybe you should go now, Joey said.

Stones in her pocket, the river a wet, green field, strands of dead grasses waving above…

Do something! Virginia hissed, Before morning, never enough hours.   Not enough, Sylvia whispered, bruised voice already fading.

Lucy yanked the dangling chain on the lamp beside his bed and in its cold, pink light swiveled out of her underwear, her shirt, balling them up, hurling them to the other side of his room. How much am I worth? she asked, angling her chest into his face. She has nice breasts, she's been told this, big enough, perfectly shaped, nipples round and small and dark as olives. In the streets you take stock of what you can carry on your own back.

Joey reaches out, fingers drawn like magnets. Lucy, squeezing shut her eyes, imagining Ernest in his safari jacket, his rifle slung over his shoulder; Virginia, hair swept back into a bun, the fine and haggard cheekbones; Sylvia's eyes, those metaphors nobody got, until it was too late.

RADIO VOICES,
OR THE DEAD DON'T KNOW IT'S RAINING

Hit the road Jack, don't you come back no more, no more....
It's what she wanted to say sometimes, wasn't it? Weren't
those the very words? Used to be she even imagined herself
whispering these words, slipping them into her pretend sleep
beside him, when she still had a place beside him in their bed,
not his, not hers, not separate and alone the way you were never
supposed to have to be again, once you were married. It's the
reason she wanted to get married, before she actually was. One
husband, one wife, one flesh. So she wouldn't have to be so
separate; like having another living within you, always the two
of you. It could have been some sort of a dream voice coming
out, Hit the road, Jack. And maybe he'd think, She's dreaming
of me. Maybe he wouldn't think anything at all. Jack. Carol's
husband Jack. Carol, wife of Jack. Jack and Carol. Jack. JACK.
Caroline...?

There was a time she might've sung it and he would've listened. Singing isn't your real voice, he'd say; Almost as if it's coming from somewhere else. There was a time she had a real voice, before the shrinking. Shrunken almost into a tiny speck, it seemed, like that Dr. Seuss book she'd read to her daughters, Horton the…Who?…a whole little town, a community, an entire world on a speck of dust and no one to hear it but Horton, no one to listen to its cries for help. She read to those girls, holding them when she could, Maggie wriggling so close it was as if she were built into Carol's side, an addition that made Carol feel less small, less diminished. Julia, that probing, triangular little face, not a pretty child, his child, pulling away, taking a little piece of Carol each time so that in the end it evened out—just Carol, becoming smaller.

When Carol bore him Julia, little Julia sharp as new metal, Jack stopped needing Carol. It wasn't a wife he was after, turned out, but an apprentice, an intern, someone smart, to mirror Jack. Carol kept loving him. What else was there, becoming smaller and smaller in the world? Soon she'd be one of his butterflies, encased in his collection, reduced to the size of an index card printed with her nourishment needs, her habitat; Carol could barely give voice to these herself anymore.

Until now, the radio voices. Mostly she hears them when Julia is out doing whatever it is Julia does when she's not inside the apartment, or when Julia is asleep and Carol is not. At first she thought they were coming out of the ceiling, the uneven spackle, the dull, white corners suddenly squirming, alive with sound. At one point she mentioned the radio voices to her daughter and Julia said, It's the people in the unit above, no doubt, they have god-awful taste in music.

Carol shook her head, No, not people, radio voices.

Yes, Julia said, That's what I said. It is a radio. They play that fifties and sixties nostalgia crap, it's what I've been telling you. God, Mother, do you listen to what I'm saying to you? When you don't own a house you're stuck with other people's choices in music, other people's schedules for playing music, other people's idea of nostalgia, for heaven's sake!

You never did have much use for nostalgia, did you, Julia? Carol sighed. Maggie could be sentimental, but Julia was the tough one. She didn't like looking back to see if there was something that, had it been different, would've made all the difference in the world. What's the point? Julia would say.

And then what Julia did say to Carol, was that if Carol's really hearing voices, and they aren't from the neighbor's radio, then this might indicate a more debilitating problem than your basic run-of-the-mill, garden-variety depression, she said. Maybe even schizophrenia! Julia said, though she didn't look so worried, more irritated. That's when Carol decided she would keep the radio voices to herself. She didn't mind them. In fact, she's actually been feeling better since she first began hearing them, less lonely, and most definitely less depressed. If depression was really ever the problem. Is depression what happens when you're not happy? Used to be happiness that Carol longed for, for her family, and if they were happy—if only they were happy!—she could be. But what is happiness? Is it the human condition to think we're entitled to it? Are squirrels born expecting it? Birds flitting about searching for it? They all just go about the business of inhabiting their lives. Carol's been thinking about this a lot these days, the simplicity of it, really. Like reading about someone's life in a book or a magazine article. How quickly it seemed to pass, a lifetime in a couple of paragraphs, tragedies gotten over with in a mere sentence or two.

Lately it's as if the radio voices are telling Carol what to do, what to think. It's as if they are becoming her own voice, her own thoughts inside her head. Radio voices. They do it in song though, which makes this OK. *The cat's in the cradle with a silver spoon...*, and Carol peers around the apartment for their little cat, who spends almost all of his time roaming outside in the complex somewhere, perhaps even crossing the busy street over to the next complex, the row of office buildings, or the strip mall with the haircutters Julia took her to, and beyond that Schnucks Market. Could he be going to all these places, crossing those heartless streets? Is the radio voice directing her to look for him, to bring him home?

It was Carol herself who *instigated*—that's the word Julia used for it—this habit of Little Cat's wandering. Little Cat. Julia calls him Psycho-Cat, which is not a good kind of a name, and it's important to be named right. So Carol calls him Little Cat. She took him out to the prairie garden one morning, Julia at the university lecturing about something or other, and it seemed such a shame to confine him to Julia's small apartment, the restless spirit in that little fellow. He could use the prairie garden for his litter box, she had thought. She's used it herself, God knows! But Little Cat immediately took to wandering, so of course Carol had to follow. After that Julia gave him away to some girl in a mask. But Little Cat comes back. When Julia's not around, he comes back.

Give us a song you're a piano man, Carol sings, her own voice dry as crackers, but isn't this what the radio voice is telling her to do? Give us a song! Little Cat slips back to her like an arcane lover, his special scratch at their door, creeps in when Julia is gone then stalks about the place, his tail pointing straight up like some land shark, cruising. He lets Carol pet him from her chair, rubbing up against her swollen ankles. He is a healer, this Little Cat. Her ankles always feel better after his silky fur has slid against them. She gives him a handful of snacky this or that, whatever Julia has in the refrigerator—Little Cat is partial to tuna, but without the mayo and celery—and then he leaves.

The next time the radio voices speak to Carol is on an afternoon Julia is scheduled to teach. She can hardly hear them, Julia fussing with her things at the door, she's out, she's back in, forgetting something, making an announcement about the weather: Rain, a day the color of dirt out there, she snarls, yanking on rubber galoshes over her flats; Don't go outside, Mother, you know that.

But this is exactly what the voices are telling her, Carol can finally hear them better after Julia has left. *These boots are made for walking, and that's just what they'll do.* Boots are not an integral part of Hawai'ian footwear, and coming to St. Louis from Honolulu Carol has none. So for a moment she plunks down in her chair and thinks about this; does she really want to do it, go out in that rain? Then she remembers Julia's boots, a bit dressy for a weekday February afternoon, more of a spring-evening accessory, tall, black-leather lace-ups, spiked heels, several inches closer to the clouds. Maggie sent them to Julia for her birthday, ordered them out of a catalog, since she'd never be able to buy them, let alone wear them, in Honolulu, Maggie said. But Julia doesn't wear dressy anything, and they sit at the back of her closet, still in the long, tan, boot box. My sister's criterion for a gift for someone else, Julia said, Something she would want.

Carol tugs the boots up over her swollen ankles, over her calves, tucking her aqua knit pants inside, attempting to tie what's left of the laces. Her legs are, let's face it, not as slim as Julia's these days. It's the pills Julia's been giving her, she finally agreed to them (You're wasting away, Mother!), so now Carol's appetite has struck with a vengeance, even relishing Julia's cooking. The laces refuse to form bows and Carol yanks them into knots instead, her double-knit-covered skin pooching out over the tops. It's OK, the radio voice tells her, *These boots are made for walking....*

Carol totters on the high heels once she's outside, that satisfying click, click, clicking over the asphalt parking lot, the sound she always envied when other women used to walk past her, those dressed-up, polished women, like someone took silver cloths to them every day of their lives, making Carol feel even smaller, barely there, eating her lunch on a bench in the Ala Moana Shopping Center. Click, click, click, they had somewhere to go, to do, something important to do, business women. Nowadays Carol realizes they were probably secretaries from the nearby offices, other people's businesses, or clerks from the stores, receptionists at the Waikīkī hotels, all just happy to have an hour off from the drudge. Back then, though, she was sure they were laughing at her, perfectly drawn and profoundly red lipstick smiles for her, sitting alone, nowhere to go.

Whole years of her married life Carol used to eat her lunch at the Ala Moana, Jack never knew. She didn't need to buy so much as to just be surrounded by it, that potential for normalcy. Americanism, Jack called this type of consumerism—but he was a professor and thought this way about things. Ala Moana, peaceful way. The largest mall in the country at one time, maybe even the world, created in 1959 to honor Hawai'i's new statehood, built entirely on coral from the Waikīkī reef. Carol had been impressed by this back then. Imagine, she had said to Jack, It's like walking on the sea. It's walking on money, Jack said, Someone else's profit.

For Carol, Ala Moana came alive in its scents: the slick smells of plastic-encased furniture, precisely folded linens and coppery household goods, the crisp-new-everything smells, floating out the open doors of the department stores, Sears, McInerny's, Liberty House; hot buttered popcorn from Woolworth, clothes, cotton and the fierce, new, shiny polyesters, brassy knickknacks for the home; the spicy aroma of Ala Moana decked out at Christmas, its mainland-imported evergreens, Salvation Army bells tingalingalinging, the fragrance of Hawai'ian greenery and flowers, ginger, gardenia, in the planters behind the benches; and Li Hing Moi, cuttlefish, dried-seed fragrances sifting out of the Oriental shops, they were called in those days. Asian, they would probably call these now; Asian, Julia said, is preferred. All this seemed so desirable, so important, goods, just to be a part of. Otherwise, what would Carol have done? Keep dusting and re-dusting the things in her house, watching more dust dribble down, as it always eventually did, until the girls came home? Working wasn't an option, those days. You're their mother, Jack said. As if that was that. Anyway, what else could she do? Sing?

These boots are made for walking..., past the prairie garden, the long, dead stalks of grasses, short, stubby, brambly things, the empty seedpods, all brown and pokey and blown apart. The day is mud colored and damp, the rain a fine, barely-there drizzle, and out on the boulevard the traffic whizzes past her, slick sounds of tires on wet pavement. Nobody's looking at me,

Carol thinks, shrunken and invisible in these high-heeled boots, click, click, clicking down the sidewalk.

It's a disorienting place, this just-outside-of-downtown St. Louis, no mountains or a seaward direction, *mauka* or *makai* these are called in Hawai'i, to help Carol understand where she is. Somewhere there is the river of course, the Mississippi, and Illinois beyond that. But Carol hasn't quite figured out where. East, she was told, but which way is east? Just the endless march of the brick buildings, dull red, rust red, concrete colored, a deeper red here and there the color of old blood, the apartment complexes, an occasional long, brick building, a post office perhaps?—you can tell these if the flag's out front—and across the busy four-lane boulevard the little strip mall that looks like every other little strip mall, where her hair was cut.

Carol angles an abrupt left down a side road, and immediately she is into a neighborhood, smaller, older houses, these too are mostly brick, but homes—with little yards, fences, walkways going up to colored, wooden doors, decorative lights on either side of these doors. They remind Carol of gingerbread houses, the steep slope of their roofs, painted chimneys, window boxes that in the summer would erupt with some sort of flowers, pansies, petunias, their cloying, urgent scent.

Homes, Carol gazes at them, the afternoon dreary enough so that inside some there's lights on. Through lace curtains Carol can make out bookshelves, lamps, chosen things. There was always that look, homes, defined by the things you put in them. Hers and Jack's where they raised their daughters had the look of order; A place for everything and everything in its place, Jack would say. We'll have a house big enough so everything can be put away properly, he said. And everybody, too, Carol thinks now. She hadn't understood this back then, that they, herself and the girls, would be part of what needed to be put away.

Everything in its place. Different than the Kaneohe Bay Marine Corps Air Station house, the Base, this neighborhood was called, she shared with her own parents and brothers so long ago. Her father a captain, the regimented rows of ranch-style houses, moving from Los Angeles into one of them, 1938, just a few years before Pearl Harbor, as it became known. Their house looked like everyone else's on the outside, but inside was the jumble of the five of their lives comfortably intertwined. The dank salt smell of Kaneohe Bay sucking out its tides, O'ahu lush, popsicle green around her, and Carol still filled with song in those early years. When you have song you carry your home inside.

What Julia can't seem to understand is, when eventually Jack retreated to his own room, Carol felt relief, not abandonment. It was easier to love him from the other side of the closed door. He was in his place. She knew where he was. In fact, before he disappeared into his room Carol used to sometimes (oh so secretly!) wish that Jack would die—long before he did, of course. As terrible as this sounds! But it wasn't out of not loving him enough, it was because she loved him too much. Those years of feeling him just slip away from her; if he died, then not only would she know exactly where he was, but he couldn't slide any further out of their life together. He would die still loving her. So when Jack retreated to his room, there was that relief. It was easier to carry on whole conversations with her husband in her head, when he was behind his door, answering for him as she saw fit, since the reality was Carol had long since forgotten how to talk to Jack and he to her. It was as if they didn't even share the same language for things. But she did love him. There didn't have to be a language for that.

These boots are made for walking..., except by now Carol's ankles, puffed up angrily enough to begin with, have started to really hurt, trapped inside these ferocious lacings, and the way she has to walk, sort of toes forward to keep herself steady on the spiky heels, is beginning to create a sense of almost-on-the-verge panic. Like if she leans over just a little too far forward, she will fall off these high-heeled ledges. Very unforgiving of the reality of the foot, high heels, Carol had forgotten this. No wonder Julia avoids them. Sound thinking, Jack would have said about Julia's refusal to wear anything but flats and clunky "field boots"; That one is our sound thinker.

Carol's eyes burn into the wet and wintry afternoon, and for a moment she doesn't remember where she is, the sounds of a highway in the distance, but this tight little neighborhood could be anywhere, even Honolulu, its parade of houses, the windows like eyes watching her, lives inside so separate from her own. Whatever her own is. Sometimes Carol can't quite put her finger on this. It's as if it's all already happened, and now she's just here to try and remember; as if every moment of her life is just another memory being formed, a memory, almost before the moment has even passed. She's become a rerun of sorts, and she's not even sure it was all that interesting to begin with. *All you need is love!* commands a radio voice, but this voice is blending in with the other ones now so that there's such a frantic jumbling of them, she can't pick out which is the dominant to listen to. Which the one to believe.

And then these boots just stop walking.

The manager's son sees her from the other side of the street, spread-eagled on the curb in those stretchy, old-lady pants, screaming aqua, a color nobody but an old lady would wear, bent over like a collapsed question mark, rubbing and squeezing one ankle then the other, fierce, black Hitler-boots saddled halfway up her legs, muttering to herself. He recognizes her, his father had pointed her out one day. Now there's a Looney Tune for you, his father said, Relieves herself in my prairie garden, if you can believe that. The manager's son had a hard time believing it, that old women like this even peed, let alone outside in his father's garden? I've been trying to find a reason to evict them, his father said, But the daughter's got more education than God. She knows the loopholes. Why would someone with a couple of college degrees live in my apartments? A Ph.D. in something or other, for chrissake, she should be out with the rest of them making her own slaughtering on the stock market.

The manager's son is walking home from school, a different route than his usual, cutting through the neighborhood that stretches behind the complex to avoid busloads of the others traveling home on the boulevard, shouting his name to him through cracks of the forced-open windows, like he doesn't know it and they have to remind him—his father's name that even his father won't use, Lovely! Lovely! Lovely! Just call me The Manager, his father says.

Until now the manager's son had been a speck, a squiggle on the roll books, barely a presence in this new school. But today it was the name that called attention to him, the name that is his father's, not his mother's, he couldn't even keep that of hers. Lovely! He'd bet most everyone else in this school at least has a mother, and a last name like Johnson or Adams or Smith, Ying or Chang, even something totally unpronounceable from the other side of the world—anything but his father's name! Lovely boy, they catcalled him, Lovely boy, jiggle your cheeks for us, lovely fat boy. Are you a fag, Lovely fag boy?

He should never have left Maine after she died, should've just run away, disappeared into the woods. People do. There's folks out there without even a social security number, his father had said scornfully; Rural Maine, his father laughed, like rural was the name of a place to be despised. Maine had been his mother's home, his father was only in it for as long as there was love, his father said. Though if there was love between his parents, it was before the manager's son's memory of things. The manager's son knows he could've done it, lived in the woods, built himself a lean-to out of tree branches, eaten berries, leafy things in the spring and summer, drank from the streams and rivers, trapped animals. Not that he'd want to kill an animal, but there's things you've got to do to survive. He would have stayed alive out there, instead of this slow dying he feels here.

He approaches the woman slowly, uncertain of what to say to her, the way she's mumbling there, sprawled out on the curb. He could just walk past, he thinks, pretend he never noticed her, continue on. What do you say to an adult crazy person, except that maybe if she's lost somehow, he could offer to walk her back? This isn't exactly the woods of Maine. Every sidewalk here leads to another. But if the lady really is loony like his father says, maybe she can't understand that. Maybe she really is lost.

Hi, he says softly, standing awkwardly on the street in front of her.

She peers up at him, wide eyes surprisingly unlined, a bland, doughy sort of face, almost pretty. He can see where she probably once was, anyway. She might've even looked like his girlfriend Neville—he likes to think of Neville as his girlfriend, though they haven't kissed, but she likes him, he knows she likes him because she's told him so—the kind of prettiness that doesn't belong in a city, a mild, almost dazed look, more of the land somehow.

I'm the manager's son, from the apartments? You seemed like maybe…, he hesitates. What if she's not lost? Would she be insulted?

My feet hurt so much! she whines, It's these darn boots, they're not really made for walking, you know. To be admired, maybe, in a shoe store, coveted is how they say in the Bible, glass wall between you and them. Can you help me? If I fall off of them you can get me up. Wearing high heels is like being at the edge of your own personal cliff.

He stares hard at her. The Bible? He hopes she's not some religious fanatic and all this a ruse to make him listen to her, the way they come to his father's door, newly shaven, cheeks white and smooth as an egg, dark suits like you'd wear to a funeral, bearing the word, they say. My word is printed on the sign, can't you read? his father snarls. No soliciting!

Maybe they're too small, the manager's son offers, surveying her thick legs, like shortened tree stumps, laces like vines creeping desperately up them; then he claps his hand over his mouth. His mother used to say you should never comment on a woman's age or her shoe size. They don't much like to admit to either, she said.

The woman offers him her hand and he helps her up, reddening a little at the touch of her skin, moist, yet slippery at the same time, like she rubs Vaseline or something gooey into her palms.

You've got that right, Carol says to the boy, making the emphasis fall on *that*, the way she's heard some of the African-

Americans in the apartment complex say it. You've got that right, a musical way of speaking, like Hawai'ian, even the pidgin English of Hawai'i, so different from the flattened speech she hears here, vowels stretched thick as slugs, words reamed out like an axe splitting wood, tinfoil ripping. No song in the way Midwest haoles talk, no song in the sound of it at all.

Carol says, You're right, young man, these boots are too darn small. It's because they're my daughter's, you know, they're not even mine. Who would've imagined I'd make bigger footprints in this world than Julia? She's our smart one.

He lets her hook her arm around his bent elbow, like he used to walk his mother to the bathroom, to her bed, when she could still get in and out of her reclining chair. That's what he'll think about while he's doing this, his mother, helping his mother navigate her world to its end. His mother would have approved of him helping this old woman. He blushes a fierce pink that lights up the smattering of freckles across his buttery cheeks, remembering the dismissive way his father pointed her out; She relieves herself in my garden.

So what's your name? the woman asks. I'm accustomed to knowing the names of strange men who escort me home, she giggles. My name is Carol. Did you hear me say it? It's Carol, so you can call me that.

The thing is, the manager's son blushes again, I don't particularly like my name.

Oh, Carol says. Well. Half the time I barely remember mine.

Inside the apartment he leads the woman to her chair—he knows without her telling him that this is her chair, a plush rocker by the window. She says, I hate to ask this, manager's son, but could you help me get these boots off? I feel like they're trying to nest inside my skin about now. I'm so tired. I can't believe how tiring just a little walk down the street in high-heeled boots is. The woman, Carol (can he really call her that?), yawns and tilts her graying head back against the chair. She's got one of those old-lady haircuts, the short, crisp ones with a froth of little, whipped waves the color of metal shavings, like she's wearing a bonnet or a textured bathing cap. But really she's not so old, the manager's son thinks, studying her face, smoothed out with her eyes shut now, almost carefree for the moment. His own mother had beautiful long hair, when she still had her hair. She wore a bathing cap over it when she was still able to swim at the Y.

Julia will be furious with me, the woman sighs. I was going to make us dinner. She's no kind of a cook, my daughter. She studies butterflies, just like her father. So what does your mother do, manager's son?

He kneels down, not looking at her, his face level with her knees, carefully undoing the knots in each boot lace, freeing the bubbles of skin hanging over both boots, releasing a violence of aqua, the knit pant legs tucked under them, gently wriggling off the boots. My mother died, he says finally, Cancer. He looks up then and she's staring at him, her head still back against the chair, but her eyes are popped open, moist and bright as a frog's.

She nods, I see. Well, before the cancer, your mother must have done things before the cancer?

He thinks a minute. Before the cancer? So much of recent memory is the cancer, the cancer a part of all that they were, all that was thought, all they said and didn't say, his mother, himself. Well, he hesitates, She used to swim at the Y. Also she had very nice, long hair. When I was little I used to like to wrap my hand in it, play hide and seek with my own fingers. I didn't like it when she washed it. Or when she was walking in the rain, like us, like we just did. I didn't like wrapping my hand in wet hair. When her hair fell out after the chemo she told me to sweep it up; Get it out of my sight! she said. I cleaned it up but I couldn't throw it away. I tied it into a ponytail, the way she used to let me brush her hair, pulling it back into a rubber band. I still have it, my father doesn't know.

Carol says, My daughter persuaded me to cut my hair. She didn't actually persuade me, since I never wanted to. She seemed to think life would be easier lived in short hair. Easier for whom, I wonder? I let her take me to that haircutting place across the way. I did it for her. Julia likes to believe she's in control of things. Even our little cat, she couldn't control him so she gives him away. She's like her father. I let them think they're in control, but they aren't, you know. Life is messier than that, don't you agree?

He shrugs, I wish I had some control. If I did, I wouldn't be living here.

Carol sighs. You got that right, she says. You got that right, manager's son.

Later, after the manager's son has left, her feet propped up on the needlepoint stool he put under them, a pillow on top of it and her head tipped back, Carol listens to the rain, hard now, pelting the window. Julia will be home soon and there's no dinner waiting, but they can whip up some Minute Rice, something like that, and it will fill them, for tonight anyway. Carol feels strangely relaxed. There's that spinning, swimming sensation in her head, receptors she's thinking, like the rabbit-ear antenna Jack used to arrange this way, that way on their old black-and-white TV, foil wrapped, trying to get something, for God's sake! he'd hiss. *Get your kicks on Route 66....*

Carol doesn't have to arrange herself in any particular way to hear the radio voices, and tonight one of them is especially clear. She knows this voice, Jim Morrison's, melodic yet grainy, insistent, the feeling of sand scratching under your swimsuit. A neighbor, Ada's her name, told her maybe Jim Morrison's been reincarnated into someone living right here in the complex. Carol wonders about the manager's son, that dark, curly hair. Carol isn't sure what to think about reincarnation. She's not sure maybe once around isn't enough in this world. Ada is also from Hawai'i, but she doesn't long for what she misses the way Carol does. Little things, fresh papaya for breakfast from their tree off the lānai, a clean-swept path to their door. Those nights when Jack slept with her, the solid shape of him, then the dream of him beside her when he was no longer there.

Carol stares out the window, darkness descending over St. Louis, rain slicing against the glass in little, silvery blades. She would've liked to hold him, that manager's boy, press his head into her chest and rock, the two of them, back and forth, rocking to the rhythm of the rain. *She lives on love street.…* Carol hums, softly at first, then she belts it out—jubilant, she can hear her father bark in his captain's voice, sing with conviction! And the rain keeps raining, and it is her own voice calling them home.

ASHES WE RISE FROM

Cassandra climbing up into the lone oak, up through the gnarl of branches, through a twist of twigs, the scatter of dead leaves hanging; but mostly there are no leaves, just the bare, winter branches, a late-winter sun paling through them like it doesn't mean it, doesn't really mean to be there at all. She climbs easily, sneakered feet sure as if she's on God's good ground, as her grandma would say. Only her grandma says it in such a way as to mean, Isn't God's good ground good enough for you?

It's what Cassandra does, climbing. What she's thinking is that maybe this is where she'll find him, that the higher up she goes the closer she is to him. Grandma told her, You wait and you pray and you fill yourself up with something like hope, and he comes to you, in the middle of the night maybe, at your window he'll be. Cassandra's left her window open to make it easier for him, but the cold night comes spilling in, the sounds of the highway in the distance—Everybody's going everywhere but us! Grandma snarled; and all this noise, this spinning cold makes Cassandra feel like she's got a hole in her somewhere, and the wind, the whole weird rush of the frozen night whistling through.

What she wants to tell him is he should take her grandma instead. It's not so mean, Grandma said she's ready to be taken. Anytime, she said, and that sometimes she can't bear the thought of outliving another daughter anyway. And besides, Grandma said, How do I keep affording this, all the medicines it takes to keep your mother in this world? Medicaid pays only so much, do I keep begging Toby Manza, your grandfather, who won't even live with us? We're just another low-rent tragedy around this place, Grandma said. This place is where they live, Grass Acres Apartments, St. Louis. There's not a heck of a lot of anything but patches of crabgrass, Grandma's pointed out, let alone any real acreage. Cassandra's grandmother comes from the corn-and-the-soy-beans farm country in Illinois.

Cassandra's going to beg Jesus; no, not begging exactly, a trade. Her grandmother for her mother. They already got a sort of relationship, Grandma says, her and Jesus, a history, Grandma says. Cassandra isn't completely sure about Jesus, what he looks like these days, whether he speaks English, that sort of thing. She remembers a story she heard in kindergarten, something about God appearing in a burning bush. So if Jesus is God's son, well, then a tree seems as good a place as any to find him. Plus, the higher she climbs the closer she is to the sky, and that's where they live, Jesus, God, the heavenly angels, Santa. If they're real at all that is, and Cassandra has some doubts about this, but if they are then that's where they live. She can tell it from her grandma's face, turned up and flattened in a skyward direction, red as a ham and mumbling things. A prayer, Grandma says, To keep me going. How much more of this must I take? Grandma asks the sky, flinging out her arms. The sky is generally silent, her arms quivering at it like jelly; then these, too, are still, hanging useless at her sides. Sometimes, Grandma remarks, You just can't tell it when he answers you.

In fact, as Cassandra gazes up now from the highest branch she can sit on—the few above it are too thin, though they might allow her to hang from them, to swing a little if she's so inclined, a cold breeze cutting through and swaying things a bit, rocking her like her mother used to rock her in between her own knees— Cassandra looks into that gray-blue winter sky, the white winter sun that burns your eyes but no warmth on your skin, just a weak light washing over things, and she has to wonder if they really are up there, or if this isn't just some screw-on top to the world, this oval sky, like opening a big jar.

A voice calls out and for a moment she thinks it's him, this voice so close, like it's in the tree with her and invisible, too. When push comes to shove, her grandma admits, it's been a good long while since she's maybe seen Jesus, but he's spoken to her. Except this voice is a woman's. Maybe Jesus is really the daughter of God and all this time people expecting someone with a beard?

Little girl! I said, what are you doing so high in that tree? It's dangerous up there!

Cassandra peers down, but not too far. She sees the woman's head stuck out of the apartment window a little below her, a wide head thick as a cabbage, her red-plaid scarf wrapped around, and red and white hair poking out of it like it's been pasted there, like a clown's, Cassandra thinks.

Cassandra says, So? What you gonna make of it? It's the only one big enough around here. I'm waiting for Jesus.

Is that right? the woman says. She shakes her head, the red tufts bouncing and jiggling out of the scarf, the white at the sides spronging like old springs. Well, she says, Who in heaven's name told you he'd be in a oak tree? Walking on water now maybe, the woman chuckles, But for the life of me I don't remember anything about Jesus in a tree. The woman's face grows serious again, frowning, her round eyes darting about here and there, like there's answers out somewhere in the asphalt parking lot below, or maybe in the winter-dead prairie garden. Look, she says, little girl, bottom line is you got to get down from there. What if you fall? Nobody knows you're up here but me, and I don't want to have to come out and pick you up, thank you very much. I don't do that.

Do what? Cassandra asks, settling herself deeper into the groove of this branch, kicking out one of her bony jean-clad legs so that her heel can bump against the branch below, making the tree shake rhythmically, this way, that way.

Come out, the woman says. I don't come outside.

Ever? Cassandra asks.

Not ever, the woman says.

Not at all? Cassandra says suspiciously. What about food? How you get your food then? Or what if you have to go to the doctor? An ambulance takes my mommy when she has to go to the doctor, whether she wants it or not it comes. She's very, very sick. Grandma says I'm supposed to prepare myself for her maybe not getting better this time, for Jesus wanting her to be with Him, so I'm going to ask Jesus to take Grandma instead.

The woman pops her head out farther at this, staring up into Cassandra's dark little eyes, her squinty pie-round face, tussle of Shirley Temple curls framing this face. (Does that scream old, or what? Ada thinks, Shirley Temple curls!)

The woman nods, frowns, then sighs. OK, she says. I'm Ada, she says. Look, child, it's very cold with this window open. Maybe you can climb down just a bit and work your way inside it. You think you could do that? I'll help you, you see there's this big branch right here beside. We can visit a while, I've got some seed my brother sends me from Hawai'i. Have you ever tried Li Hing Moi, or sweet and sour cherry seed? The kids in Hawai'i love it, it's a real treat there I'll tell you, like buying candy bars or Ho Ho's, something like that. Then you can go back out if you must. It's not like climbing all the way down, just to the third story. I never invite anybody inside my apartment but my friend Troy; he's the one brings me my food, since you asked. So you're pretty special. It will be our secret. What do you think?

Cassandra hesitates, picks her nose, bumps her foot up and down harder on the branch below, causing the branch she's sitting on to sway and bend even more. Then she does this again when she sees the effect this has on the woman, who's grimacing and tugging at her chin, eyes like olives rolling about in their sockets, focusing first on the near-empty parking lot then back again on Cassandra.

So, why would anyone want to eat some old seed? Cassandra asks, And anyways, I'm not allowed to have secrets. (She'll keep this woman's attention on her, she'll make this woman see her!) Grandma said I better not go into a stranger's place. Bad things happen, she said, and you can never forget them or the stranger neither.

Well I'm no stranger! Didn't I just tell you my name is Ada? Ada! Spell it frontwards, backwards, it stays the same. A stranger is someone you don't even know their name.

Do you know my name? the child asks, gap-toothed, smug little grin.

Ada sighs. OK, you got me there, you're a smart little girl all right. Here's the thing. Maybe you've heard of me? My phone number's better known around this place than 911, just about. I'm a psychic, you know what that means? It means I can see into the future sometimes, it means I can know things about people, things other people wouldn't know, things they themselves might not know. So here's the deal. If you come down into my apartment, I'll tell you the things other people pay for. I'll give you a reading on your future. We'll have tea, Li Hing Moi, whatever you want. Like I told you before, nobody but my friend Troy's been inside here. I'm inviting you because I have a feeling about you, and because, to be perfectly honest, I don't want your falling from that tree being the reason I have to go back out into the world. OK? I'm not ready for that. It's a strange-enough fate made me put my face to this window a few minutes ago and see you here, so now I'm involved whether you want me or not. Now I've said too much, so what do you want to know? Ada asks the child. Try me.

Cassandra hesitates. She stares down at the woman, the tufting red hair, the flat, anxious face. But it's a nice face, Cassandra decides, she can imagine putting her hand on the woman's forehead like she does with her own mother, checking for the burning, her mother twitching and tossing, sweating buckets as Grandma says; this woman's skin would feel dry and cool. The woman looks like she could be somebody's grandmother, though she's not yelling at Cassandra to Get the heck down off of that tree, you little monkey! like Grandma would. She's trading with Cassandra. I'll give you this, the woman said, if you climb down into my window.

Cassandra lifts her own face, gazing past the highest branch, through the twiggy thin sprouts of it like a hand stretching up, up, into a long, pale sky. What I want, Cassandra says, looking back down at the woman, Is for Jesus to not take my mother with him. She doesn't like being up high, says it makes her dizzy to even get off the couch sometimes. She wouldn't like it up there in heaven, and Jesus doesn't need my mother. She's just one woman. He's got God and the angels and Santa. He's got enough. Grandma says it's a miracle Mommy's hung on this long, and miracles don't happen much to people like us, she said. My mommy doesn't even believe in Jesus, so it's just not right for him to take her.

The woman frowns, But you believe in Jesus? she asks.

Cassandra shrugs. I'm covering my bases, she says, her little eyes suddenly weary and dark as two stones, too old for the little face; That's how Grandma puts it. If you can make Jesus not take my mother, I'll come down.

The woman yanks at her scarf like she wants to tear it off her head. Oh, child, for chrissake! I'm not some kind of a witch here. Is that what you think? You think I can cast spells, make miracles? *You think I can talk to God?* I can't change things! God, if I could! I'd be back home on O'ahu and my own boy would be little as you, before he became the sort of person trouble just seemed to find. And I'd change that. He'd be with me now. I can't change things. I can only see them sometimes, how they're going to work. I can tell you how you'll be in this world, but it's a question of whether it's with broken bones or not if you don't get the heck down out of that damn tree!

Cassandra's forehead wrinkles up, she rubs her eyes, a scraped, bony elbow poking out of a hole in her sweatshirt. Now this woman is sounding like her grandmother.

For God's sake! the woman says, You're not even dressed for the cold. Your mother let you go out like that, a hole in your shirt and no jacket on? Then she plugs a fleshy fist to her mouth, bites at it gently. Christ! Ada sighs, Me and my big mouth.

I want her! Cassandra shrills. My mommy!

Yeah, well, and I want my son. *Want* adds up to a hill of beans in this world.

So what? Where's your stupid son, anyways? Cassandra sniffles a bit, wipes her nose with her fingers, You're too old to be a mommy.

You're never too old to feel that old pain, child. He made some bad choices, the police are so fond of saying. The way people talk! Bad choices and a person drops off the face of the earth. But you're a kid, you don't need to concern yourself with these things yet. Just know this: right or wrong in the world, my son was everything to me. Can you understand? Isn't that how you feel about your mother? So come down, Ada says, Please, come in here with me.

She stretches her arm out the window into the frigid air, reaching up toward the girl. Ada's flesh starts to tingle, and something punches her in the pit of her stomach, that fierce ache, that familiar loss—or maybe not, nobody knows, no one could tell her for sure what happened and her own keen sense of the world, her way of seeing certain truths, blighted, fogged over, deadened. There's the image of the river, the Mississippi, its colorless water reflecting the deep-brown mud at its sides and depths, the tangle of dead branches, twigs and leaves floating at the edges of its banks; and her vision of Kai in it, held down perhaps by a moss-covered trunk stuck in the murky bottom, not unlike the tree this child is in now, a tree that in its waving glory would have been a monument to all that is alive. Ada breathes inside herself the sinister smell of river water and feels the old sinking. Please! she cries out to the girl again, I can't take much more of this.

Cassandra peers out through watering eyes, swiping at them angrily, rubbing back and forth, clearing them like rain off a window, wipers on a car—and they don't even have a car. We're not the type of people who can afford to own cars, Grandma said, And tears don't do anybody any kind of good, she says. Pray, Grandma tells Cassandra, Try praying for some answer you might understand.

It's late afternoon, that flat pink, clumps of clouds unfurling, wisping like strands of cotton candy. Cassandra can see past the burnt brick corner of one of the apartments, to the prairie garden, the squared plot of it, fenced in like it needs to be contained—As if the prairie's going to come back to the middle of St. Louis! her grandma said. She can see the way the old, yellow stalks light up, the long, dead grasses, all a pale glow the color of butter, almost as if this light can warm them, make them alive again. Like it's summer, two summers ago before her mother got sick. Summer, and the birds so maddening out the window; too early in the morning, her mother would groan. Later, when her mother got home from work, long, lavender twilight, crickety hum of insects, Grandma nattering on and on about something or other her mother didn't make Cassandra do—Put her dishes in the sink, make her own bed, Pick a number, Grandma would say—and her mother just there, with Cassandra. Until she would go out later with her motorcycle men. Cassandra clambering up the sill of the bedroom window to watch her mother leave, the heathery smell of her still sweet in their room, wet-skin scent of her leather jacket, leather pants tight as skin, sputtering roar of the bike and the tail of her mother's hair the color of a shadow, flying out of her helmet, becoming part of the distance then disappearing.

They're the ones made her so sick, Grandma told Cassandra, her head bobbing viciously up and down, back and forth, edgy as a puppet. Lord forgive me this hate, but it's one of those damn motorcycle men got your mother sick.

Cassandra looks down again at the woman, who is herself now leaning so far out the window maybe she'll be the one to fall. Cassandra knows how to call for an ambulance, she's done it enough times. She can see inside the woman's loose sweater, the dangling, full breasts. Her mother's breasts aren't this big. Since she's been sick they've flattened into little mud pies. Once when Cassandra was four years old and one of the motorcycle men her mother liked—A lot! her mother cried, I made myself believe he was the one, goddamn it!—left her, her mother let Cassandra crawl into her bed beside her, let Cassandra suck on her dry little breast like she did when she was small, when her mother could fill her this way, when her mother was everything she needed.

No, Cassandra says to Ada, shaking her own head vigorously, up and down, back and forth, I'm waiting for Jesus. When he comes for her I'll be the one to stop him.

Suddenly she bends way over, toward the woman's wide-eyed, panicky face, grasping the rough branch tightly inside her two balled-up fists. Watch this! she commands. Cassandra kicks off her sneakers, easy enough, they were barely tied anyways—still can't manage a decent bow, her grandma points out—they make a small thudding sound on the hard ground below. She tugs each sock off with the opposite foot then sits bolt upright again on the branch. Cassandra pulls her skinny legs onto the branch, a foot planted on each side of her bottom, reaches up and grabs the thinner branch above her and it bumps and swaggers like the February wind's cutting through. Holding onto the upper branch, she swings her legs off the lower, one at a time, pulling them up and securing first one then the other on the upper branch at her bent knees; then she lets go of the lower, hanging like a bat, wiggle of bare toes, giggling wildly in the swaying oak, three-and-a-half stories high.

Oh my God! Ada cries, Child, you'll be the end of us both! Must I become your parent here, too? For pity's sake will you get the hell down or I'm going to call 911 and tell them there's a wild cat stuck up in the tree and they'll come after you, a swarm of sirens and ladders, they'll drag you out of there and they'll scold you up but good! A smacking! Ada snarls, Maybe that's what you need, a good smacking.

Cassandra laughs even harder at this, one of her dangling hands swiping again at her liquidy eyes. But this isn't even my trick! she squeals, upside down, swiveling her body a bit to get her face back into position to look at the woman. Why you think I kicked my shoes off, huh?

I haven't a clue, Ada says, Please, please don't do this, you must have a lick of sense in that damn stubborn head of yours?

Well, I can do things with my feet, don't you know. I can write my name with them, I can pick up my clothes off the floor when Grandma hollers at me to do that, and I can hang on this branch using only my feet. It's nothing with your knees, even you could do that. You think I'm someone's little girl, she laughs again, fake rattle of a hah-hah-hah-sounding laugh. Guess what? I'm not even part of the family. I'm not my mother's kid or my grandma's neither! Nobody knows who Cassandra is!

Her voice is becoming shriller and Ada peers frantically about the complex driveway for another living being, a car coming in, someone to witness this besides herself, someone else to do something about it, please God! Where the hell is anybody when you need them? She considers running into the next room, grabbing the phone off the table. But in the seconds that takes, what will the child do? Ada becomes aware of a sucking sound like a person breathing, the early evening wind pushing against the screen of the window beside this one, then pulling away, the window Ada couldn't fully close so she taped plastic over it this winter. The wind works its way inside the screen, then breathes heavily against the plastic like it wants to come in the rest of the way. Recently she asked Troy if he could fix this window and he said, in the most exasperated tone he's ever used with her, I can't fix things for you anymore, Ada! I've got a twenty-year-old underwear model and three cats she thinks are the souls of dead writers living with me, and now her teenaged pal from the next building drops her baby into the mix. They've taken up permanent residence in my place, looks like, do they think I'm some sort of shelter? The baby wails, the cats yowl, those girls giggle and I'm the one supposed to be in charge. I don't know whether I'm coming or going anymore!

So who the hell is in charge, anyway! Ada cries, to the girl, the tree, the frozen, tin-colored sky.

What am I, squeals the child, Can you guess? I'm a monkey! I live far away in a big, old forest, not in this stinking, low-rent Hilton, Grandma calls it, not Grass Acres at all. Watch!

she commands, and slowly one of her bony knees releases the branch, the short jean-covered calf slipping down it, the little bare ankle then the top of the foot hooking itself precariously against the creaking, jiggling wood. And then she does the same with her other leg.

At this moment it seems to Ada she has never seen anything as vulnerable, as breakable, as heartbreaking as those small ankles, the crooked little feet, the rigid toes stuck out helplessly in their wake. Oh God, she says, I don't believe it. I don't believe some funny-looking little seven-year-old—you're about seven, aren't you kid?—is the one to make me do this. Keep her talking, thinks Ada, keep her distracted, just keep her going. OK, she says, If you won't come down this minute I'm climbing out there into that tree, do you get what I'm saying? After you.

I never asked you, Cassandra whines breathlessly. One of her legs, the one whose knee was first freed from the branch, is beginning to shake.

Yeah? Well, just who you think is going to come along out here with a written invitation? Not Jesus! Ada says, her own voice becoming louder and more hysterical now too, watching that little leg, the intermittent trembling. I'll tell you that much, she cries, Not Jesus! There's only me, goddamn it, there's nobody else! The person least likely to manage in this world gets to crawl out there and save your little butt.

Ada yanks up the window high as it can go and the child whimpers, OK, OK! You don't have to have a cow about it, I'm coming down. Ada hears these words and in the hollow of a minute she knows. Sees the shivering leg loosen, the foot pale as paste. She hoists her own leg over the windowsill, the cold air squeezing round it like something solid, something she could hold onto, pops her torso out next, other side of the glass. Staring at the child's sweatshirt crumpled up around her shoulders, the bird on it, a St. Louis Cardinal—and she imagines this child a bird, those scrawny arms bone-light and tenuous as feathers, soaring. Ada is conscious of the world again, rumble of a distant jet, a yellow-eyed cat with big ears slinking underneath the tree, peering up. Her husband, sick in Queens Hospital that final time (they had known it was coming, kidney failure then everything else shutting down), told her when a soul flies free for a moment everything stops—a glitch in the movement of things—clocks lose a fraction of a second, machines, things that run on electricity blink, an electrical surge, most would believe, then it is normal again. Probably no time to even wonder if Jesus would be there, if he could arrange a trade after all. Ada would gladly have done it, just reach out her arms like some fleshy red-haired angel, and let go.

PART III: METAMORPHOSE

"this is living beyond
the reach of
death."

—Charles Bukowski

TAKING HOLD

I

Spring settling like a hand, fingers of warmth scratching lightly into earth made new, flutter of a monarch on and off my transplanted milkweed already fast in the ground. He whispered, Something to take hold! Watch for me, Jesus said, words growing faint, In some miracle? So barely there, how can I know for sure?

A miracle Sandra is alive, no doubt about that, Toby Manza snapped. Thinks it's because of the medicines he helps to supply. Sold his fancy house with the golf-course lawn and one of the show-off-mobiles just to keep those medicines pumped into her. Sandra has no health insurance and Medicaid pays generic, not the good ones, Toby said, and not enough. Why should only rich AIDS patients get to stay alive?

Toby rented an apartment in St. Louis and I told him, Welcome back to how the rest of us live! Which was mean, especially since in the process his pint-sized girlfriend traded him up for someone more property prevalent. Toby has someone else now, a pretty, slightly plump, middle-aged woman, not so different from me when you come right down to it. Lately he's been talking about divorce, something I just can't hear. I told him, You keep those cocktails pumping into our daughter. Our daughter, I repeated.

Jesus told me plant a garden, put the seeds in, something to take hold. Then I'm going home. I'll take Sandra, bring her for as long as I've got her to where the other is, too. The one with the wrong name. Rock back on my knees in the garden's dirt, warm tingle of sun on my shoulders, my arms. I'm remembering the Shady Tree town graveyard, back almost to the edge of the property where the scrubby trees are, papaw, honey locust, redbud, nothing holds its leaves in the winter. Late winter that time, thin, glaring sun, pink rays knifing through the bare trees. A flock of Canada geese waddled about where the babies are buried, by the wrought-iron gates—baby graves, each one somebody's tragedy. Some lived a few weeks, a couple months, one for over a year, most an hour or less if they breathed at all. Brass heart markers on these, a name and one date, birth, death. On the grave where she is buried, the rose and the name I would not have chosen carved into it, sat a Canada goose. I stared and it stared back at me, intense, glassy, little eyes.

Names are important, I mutter to the manager's son and the young mother, as if we had been conversing about names. Though maybe we have? I lose track of things these days, the world in my head, world outside, hard to know the difference sometimes. They are helping me plant. Neville's put the sleeping baby inside the portable bassinet her mother's church gave her, she said, zipping shut the shade cover so the baby's marshmallow skin won't blister in the hard, new, sunshine. The girl's not much more than a child herself, I think, peering sharply at Neville. Ferret out packets of seed from my big, plastic bucket. Earlier I had jam-packed the bucket, various garden-center-suggested seed packages, fertilizer, a bag of mulch for the transplants.

This is switchgrass, this is big bluestem, I inform them, handing each a packet, And here we have spiderwort. I'll tell you something about spiderwort. Flowers unfold in the morning and by noon they've shriveled up into fluid jelly, like a tear. When I was a girl I thought they were crying. Those poor spiderwort flowers, I thought, start out pretty enough but in a few hours they're ugly as warts. Hairy filaments look like a spider, sticky threads from the stem. My father said in some the hairs mutate from blue to pink if they're exposed to nuclear radiation, so they planted them around a reactor in Japan to monitor low-level radiation. My father knew things like that. He could name everything that grew in Shady Tree, give you a little history for each. He's dead now and so's my mother. Farm's gone, too. When I go back home I'll be in someone else's place.

Close my eyes for a moment. These days Jesus is inside my dreams. Sometimes I'm on a tower and there's nothing but cold, white air around me. Higher than the earth, than the clouds, and afraid. He makes the water rise up to me, deep and black, an ocean? I cry, I can't swim! Marybeth, he says, Take hold.

Later, sticky, humming afternoon, I'm sowing more seeds, talking to these seeds, willing them to split apart their tender husks and grow. Plant the garden, he said. Grow, I mutter. How could you have believed you wouldn't be made to suffer guilt again?

Lithospermum croceum, the Latin name, hairy puccoon, dry prairie, flowers golden yellow. Last night I soaked the seeds in hot water the way *How to Plant a Prairie Garden* told me. It lists companion plants, plants that grow well with hairy puccoon, big bluestem, sideoats, bush clover. Father told me Native Americans were said to have used hairy puccoon as an oral contraceptive. Which is a sin, but they didn't know any better, he said.

Work the seeds into the ground with my fingers, into cool, grainy earth, seed too tiny, too delicate for the trowel. Plant on the surface, they need plenty of light to germinate. Top layer of soil grainy and light as sand. Alumroot, dry prairie, flowers a greenish white. Native Americans made these into a poultice, an antiseptic. Father said the juice was used in 17th-century England for secret writing. Can't be proven of course, he said, Being it was a secret. Ha ha. Father told a joke. So little laughter in our family, after all.

I know secrets. Secrets are what you never breathe a word of so your husband will keep his love for you alive. So that your husband's love can live, you let the secret die inside you. Poisonous gasses from its dying fill you like a balloon, seep stealthily out of your pores. No one can see, no one will know, but it infects the air around you. How not? Poisonous secret gasses seeping out. The ones who breathe this air become part of the secret without understanding there is a secret, filled with the poison without ever knowing. And for each the poison takes (Cassandra!), the secret—its death inside you—resurrected.

So when your husband's love dies anyway (Marybeth, I think it's time we talked about divorce…), you grow bitter, even vengeful. You have the secret's born-again arms to crawl into, to stumble into bed with at night; you let the secret hold you like a lover, sharing with you what no one else can know. It's not too late? you whisper. And the secret, sated, its job nearly complete, nods sleepily inside you, belonging to you the way a dream belongs, personal, private, yours, whether you hoped for it, longed for it, prayed for it, even dreamed of it or not.

II

I believe in God, the Father almighty,
Creator of heaven and earth.
I believe in Jesus Christ, his only Son, our Lord.
He was conceived by the Holy Spirit
and born of the Virgin Mary.
He suffered under Pontius Pilate,
was crucified, died, and was buried.
He descended into hell.
On the third day he rose again.

There was the year my father decided we should go to Mass, and every Sunday he drove us forty miles into the next town since there was no Catholic church in Shady Tree. We'll give her a try, my father said. I'm not so keen on having to get up at the crack of dawn, I do that every other damn day of the week. But we'll give her a try.

And then one hot summer Sunday, a fiery afternoon, last time we went to the church, stopping afterwards at Foxtail Pond, a small, man-made pond named for the foxtail grasses all around it. You can eat those grasses, Father said, but they're miserable. There's a tribe in Africa, puts foxtail over the opening of their grain storage. The mice and rats get their fur so damnably tangled with the husks they keep the hell out of the grain.

I nodded, as I always did when my father went on about plants. It would be impolite not to. It was what he knew best. Better with plants than people, though I'm not sure he recognized much of a difference. Beans, corn, his fields, things that grew, required water, oxygen, roots dug into a good solid base; what's so different with his family?

No one else at the pond that day. In fact, thinking about it now, I have to wonder if the pond was really intended for swimming at all. Probably drainage of sorts, for the nearby farms. I'm eight years old, called Mary by my father, Mary Elizabeth by my mother. Marybeth had not yet emerged. Guilt had not yet taken hold. This was innocence, the belief you still mattered.

We're going for a swim, Mary, Father said, swiping at his brow with his white, cotton handkerchief, his Sunday handkerchief; Too damn hot to breathe.

I stared doubtfully at the pond. An eerie darkness to it, pearly and dull, something thick and unlikely, not clear like the water you drink, nothing the rays of the hot sun could penetrate. Like many of the farm children where I was from, swimming just wasn't a part of what we did. Not enough places to do it, maybe. I watched my father strip down to his T-shirt and shorts, underneath his charcoal colored pants, his long-sleeved white shirt, tossing these down on the foxtail grass. My mother stayed home that day complaining of a headache; she was who I complained to when there was something to complain about. I would've whispered to my mother, I don't want to go swimming! My mother would have glanced at my father, her steely, silent look, pulled me down on her lap and held me there. My mother never said no to my father, didn't say much of anything to him, for the most part. More beans and potatoes? seemed the extent of their conversations.

But I don't want to go swimming, quivering voice, head down. Thou shalt not disobey thy parents.

Nonsense! he said, wading into the pond. It's miserable hot.

But I don't know how to swim!

Then don't you think it's about time you learned? What if you make it out to the ocean someday? Or fall into someone's swimming pool? How would you save yourself? His scrawny arms, white as bleached sand where his shirtsleeves covered and the color of tree bark everywhere else, flayed upwards toward the burning, cloudless sky. Look! he commanded, waving at the sky, then back at me. I'm in the middle, water's not even at my shoulders. You're half my size, so if you come in half as far as me, think where the water will be on you. You don't have to swim. You can walk. Like Jesus did, almost.

I pulled off my dress reluctantly, counting the buttons in the front, four of them gleaming like little white shells, in a straight line under the starched collar. Inhaled the scent of my mother's care, the detergent she used, the iron, the starch, tears fogging my eyes, breathe in, push it out, that ragged feeling of fear in my stomach. Pivoting away from my father—eight years old but I knew our differences—then deciding to keep my full slip on, color of cottage cheese, jagged tear in the lace at its hem. Turned back again, slowly. My mother had tried to repair this slip and when she couldn't she made me wear it anyway. We aren't folks who afford a new thing every time the old one rips a little, my mother proclaimed.

I slid one foot tentatively into the water just under the tiny shore ripple, preparing to yank it back from the cold. Water felt tepid as a bath. Forced the other to follow, small slow steps toward my father. Maybe he'd say, That's good enough! Good enough, Mary, you're a good girl, good enough! Pond weed floating like tangles of green hair, and a fat lily pad with a small frog on it. I took a couple more steps, reaching for the frog just to hold it for a minute. One of my feet slid deeper into the mucky bottom, a soft, squishy, silty bottom; I felt it sucking my leg down, tugging at my leg, begging me to follow. Quicksand! I squealed, Oh, no, quicksand!

Mary, Mary, quite contrary, my father laughed, Don't be a little fool. This is Illinois. You think we're in the Amazon or something?

I stumbled in further and the other leg was in the mud now too, sucking under, slurp slurp. Help me, Daddy! Flinging my arms toward him, little-girl arms that still believed in a father's redemption, that it was he who could save me. Arms that in a few years would stretch long enough to fit around Toby Manza's back as he pumped his seed inside, that would hold for a moment what grows from this seed, its deep and permanent stillness.

My father shook his head, lifting his own arms straight up again toward a blazing sky, fingers pointing toward heaven, away from me. Mary! he spat, This is how we are taught to have faith. That water can't go past your neck and it's God's good ground beneath the silt.

The way my father told it later to my mother, it was out of spite I put my face in the water, he said, Just to prove what couldn't be proven. To this day I don't know why I did it. There was my fear, beating, alive, palpable as the muck underneath, and a memory of the priest earlier that day droning on about purgatory, stiff and sweaty beside my father in the sweltering church. My father smelled of our farm still, of old corn in the sun and that dirt that doesn't go away. I thought of hell, only it wasn't a hell that I would go to if I were bad, if I kept rubbing myself in the secret place, if I didn't confess it; it's hell right here, the murky ground I was falling into. Hell in Illinois.

I envied that little frog on the lily pad, alive without fearing what it might mean to not be, and suddenly I was filled with such sorrow, for what I couldn't even name. Arms still reaching toward my father, who had turned completely away, I let the muddy bottom take me, flesh and bones buckling like chains bending, each link folding in on itself, easy as caving into a bath: chest, neck, and then my face, under the water where it was a dark and ancient green, not the violent red of hell after all, my slip floating out like a jellyfish, a stingray, creatures of the sea I had only seen pictures of, the roar of the damned in my ears, sound of my own smothered breath.

TELL ME THIS ONE THING

She's pulled him into her mother's room, his hand, her hand, a low rectangle of bare, white walls like the other two rooms, ancient framed painting of cows, bewildered and slow, grazing at the edge of the Mississippi where now there are casino boats, where now there is St. Louis. And another, a photograph, the mother, the father, almost as old it seems, spruced up for a hopeful occasion, almost as surprisingly sad. Her father, she says, sleeps on the couch. Sleep is yet another issue around here, she tells him.

The baby is there, in the portable bassinet, and that cat she calls Ernie, sprawled on a rag rug at one end of the room near the bassinet, long ears prickling, yellow eyes fixing on them then closing. The baby isn't really crying, just an on-and-off broken whimper, but Neville lifts it up, her mouth making soothing cluck-cluck noises into its face, its bare, fat thighs hanging from its diaper like two rounded loaves. She settles the baby on top of her, on her mother's bed, forming it against the curve of her arm like a plumped-out noodle. It gazes at her quizzically, a bit out of focus, then a fat, dimpled arm stretches up and pats her on her shoulder. She points at the bed indicating he, too, should sit. Her mother and father aren't home, she tells him, her mother took her father to the veterans hospital for a treatment. Something psychiatric, I'm not supposed to know about it, Neville says.

He sits down tentatively on one end of the queen-sized mattress, and she lifts up her T-shirt that announces *BABY* in bold, blue letters, an arrow aiming down at this baby, sprawled against her stomach, its head wagging and rooting about. Such a fluid motion this seemed to him, her shirt sliding up, bare breast suddenly there, like a wave of a flag, a wink of an eye, she's watching him watch her all the while. His skin feels like tinder, red and prickly as an old leaf. He tries to just look at the flat of her forehead, hair the color of dark corn yanked back into a French braid, she calls it, the plain, steady face fully exposed. The baby's plump hand pinches and tugs the side of her breast possessively, little sucking sounds. He can almost make this out, his furtive glances, pretending he's looking at the baby's head maybe, or its squiggly fingers like little worms—the baby's cherry lips on Neville's nipple, her nipple a darkening ring around the baby's greedy mouth.

Then he wonders if he should turn away as the baby, suddenly asleep, releases that nipple, smacking sound, dappled head drifting back into the crook of her arm; and here it is again, *BREAST*, upright and perky as a greeting, a tip of a hat, naked as the baby's smooth, bare shoulder, that nipple's an eye watching him now. Hot summer air through the open window is a drone of insect sounds, impatient rush of traffic from the highway and somewhere the profound and salty breath of wilting flowers, mixed into the diesel fumes from the passing trucks.

She lays the baby down gently on its back by her side, frog-fat legs, creamy arms, then turns and stares at him, still perched at one end of her mother's bed. As if at any moment he might bolt out of that room, as if it hasn't occurred to him he might never rise up off this bed and be the same again; whoever he was, she's changed all that. He could do it, he thinks, he could be something like a father to that baby, if this is what she'd like.

Come here, she orders him, patting the empty place at the other side of her where the baby isn't. So he does, sliding across her mother's beige quilt, easy as if it's a sheen of ice, eying that breast, a reel, hooking him, dragging him in. He's close enough to breathe the thin, sweetish scent of her milk, and another, duskier smell. It stirs something on the insides of his skin, goose bumps sprouting like seeds, pale arm hairs rippling like tiny, golden waves.

She clucks her tongue, Haven't you seen a real boob before? You haven't, have you? kisses the top of his forehead where the shock of his hair begins, where a ring of sweat glistens, obvious as pearls. You are a treat, she sighs, Treat Lovely.

Boob! he's thinking, boob!

Cupping his chin in her hand for a moment, turning up his face so he's peering into her eyes now, wide and pale as cabbage, Neville says, Tell me this one thing: Do you miss your mother very, very much?

He nods, twice, very, very, trying to ignore that sudden fist in his throat, taste of something fleshy and sorrowful, thick and profound as muscle, as an organ, another tongue, a permanent part of him, it seems. Like trying to consume his own heart; he will never be able to swallow it down.

I think of dying sometimes, she says, still clutching his face. Little Neville would always love me if I did, wouldn't he? If I was never here to do anything that would fuck things up, make him not? His memory of me would fade, I guess, but that gets replaced by whatever it is he might've hoped me to be. Good things, I'll bet, the best.

Fuck, she said, fuck! he thinks. His face where she's holding it burns, streaks, ribbons of red. And then he can't help himself, looking into her eyes he sees his own empty world, and etched into this, the vision of that breast. He just has to have it, lay his hand on the side of it the way the baby did, claiming this, if only for the moment, his. He reaches out, his hand shaking, and she guides him, now by the neck, the flat of her palm pressed warm and dry as a heating pad on his quivering skin, pulling his head, the side of his still-beardless face, down against her. His mouth closing over that nipple.

There, Neville says, stroking the back of his neck, losing her fingers in his hair that needs cutting, his father said, but he ignores his father; his mother liked long hair on boys. Are you in love with me, Treat Lovely? she whispers.

He shrugs, politely, burying his face further into the fleshy female warmth of her. It's OK, she says, Somebody's got to at some point.

There, she says it again. It'll be all right, she says. You'll see, it's all going to be all right.

IF LUCY RAN...

Where would you go?
The trick is to not get involved.

Not let yourself get attached. You've learned this about attachment: Jelly beans clump together when moist, seedpods bust apart, little bits clinging to other plants as if their lives depended on it, which they do, of course; in the fiercest depths of the ocean little swimming things wrap around coral and other matter so deep, not even scientists know for sure what color these are. If they're even a color. Maybe not. Maybe the world under is in grays and browns, colorless as the air over us.

And you've learned this: Your own skin is the wall that surrounds you, protects you, keeps you whole, contained, safe and apart.

But wouldn't it mean so much more if there was something else besides your breasts in their hands, just once in a while? Wouldn't there, couldn't there, be a possibility of something like love? They have to arrange you, they tell you, for the shoot. Spread you this way, that way, discover, uncover, the most appealing camera angles. You will be terrific, they assure you, their fingers inside the cinnamon-colored, satin, push-up bra. We need these pointed, what better way? Ice might work, but this is so much quicker. And nicer, too, isn't it? Can't you admit that? What harm is there, after all?

Where would you be if it wasn't for me? Couch surfing? Bed bingo? The two-minute breakfast?

When their hands slip down beneath the borrowed panties, the G-string, the bikini, a sheer-cinnamon thigh-high—yummy! the ad will proclaim, yummy undies, matches the bra (Naughty Angel!)—all reasoning's shoved aside. They could tell you doing this will create a certain look, the flush on the cheeks, wild yet sated, that forever-hungry-for-the-next expression in your eyes. The eyes say it all, they could tell you. The camera knows. It sees, records, makes permanent in an instant what a person cannot grasp beyond the moment. What is past the moment, after all, but another memory? It can put you, this one-time semblance of you, in a magazine, a catalog, a poster on how many walls? Beamed into a million households over the Internet, late-night television, a movie, perhaps? If you're really lucky. If you're good. The camera knows.

You know, too.

It's a way of getting by. A kind of an act of love, really, pretending who they are, what they say, is something like truth. Especially in the kiss that always eventually comes, as if this is some kind of obligation, a start, a finish, nothing needfully felt. You see yourself being kissed like watching a movie of yourself kissing, the opened mouth, their tongue then yours, a mirrored image, probing the roof of your mouth, their mouth. Without any real want, except maybe curiosity. For them it's a step, like first fastening the can opener into the can, the contents then spilled, consumed.

You watch, you, who the camera has immortalized for this moment. You, who can talk to the dead, read and become the lives you are reading, surf a new couch or bed every night. And not get swallowed up. Isn't this some sort of talent? A savior of sorts, you have rescued pregnant girls, babies, cats. You will yourself to not get attached.   No room for barnacles in this house! your mother once told you.   Your mother understood. You can't risk love for what must eventually, inevitably, be torn away.

Slip the mask down, slide it back up.   What does it matter? You are reborn again and again, into this old air.

ENDINGS

The wine had been souring her stomach it seemed ever since Cassandra fell, when every night Marybeth sat with a bottle, two bottles, whatever it took to get herself to the place where she wouldn't have to remember it: neck snapped clean, no look of alarm, no furrowed brow, little mouth pulled into an *O*; she looked like she was sleeping, her head with that tangle of curls turned toward one sure side. Now, when Marybeth seeks out the relief of more than a few anemic sips, half a glass tops these dragged-out, unbearably long evenings, her stomach rebels, forcing the burning red liquid back up her throat.

What sorts of endings are left?

One maybe like this: Marybeth finishes the garden and there are enough successful transplants to impart a sense of life, even if the seeded brown soil doesn't show it yet, looking empty and plain as plain old dirt. Bees in the newly planted clover, butterflies in the butterfly bush and milkweed, birds in the honey locusts and the papaw beyond the path. In the oak where it happened she imagines an owl, even occasionally hears it, its muffled cry. Huuuu Huuuu. This is trouble in Hawai'ian, the psychic told her, *huhū*. Where there's an owl there's death, even in the middle of St. Louis. Years from now, perhaps this garden will look in some small way like the prairie used to look, jumble of long grasses, ancient blooms, as if nobody but God had ever touched it.

Toby Manza appears where she kneels down, she knew he would, standing uncertainly behind the railroad ties that enclose the garden, the apartment-complex lawn marching in full and defiant and green. He diddles his sandaled toes in the grass, pushing at the shaved blades like so many annoyances.

The manager made his boy cut it, she tells him. Mow it down, the manager said, one inch, a military haircut. Why is she telling Toby this? Why does she bother telling him anything at all? Marybeth can hear the roar of cars from the highway, the squeal of the Metrolink, yet there's a sense of quiet in this garden, of grace. She peers up at Toby Manza without that familiar tightening in her chest, his long neck and head ringed by a late-afternoon sun. Remember Shady Tree this time of year? she asks him. Hot and slow, she thinks, the feeling of forever in those days. She doesn't expect him to answer. Rolls her eyes to make him understand the lack of impact his words would have on her now anyway, how unimportant they are, his words, his ideas, him she would have him believe.

Toby says, For chrissake, Marybeth, can't we just be friends?

Toby Manza, she tells him, Let's get this settled once and for all. We are not friends. You are still legally my husband. Remembers again the fat Canada goose sitting on the grave, black and cream colored, eyes glittering like hardened bits of metal caught up in those hollowed sockets; how it wouldn't move, just stared at her, those black, little eyes. How she didn't have the right to tell it to move, no claim to the name it sat upon. (And then the grandchild soaring down from the tree, arms for wings, bird boned and insignificant as feathers.) Inside that earth, a part of Marybeth and a part of Toby, too. And within this earth, the skin of this soil, the seeds she's planted, stirring inside their thin coatings, cracking upward.

I have to water the garden, she tells Toby.

Isn't that what rain is for? Come on, Marybeth, get up off that ground, will you? Toby Manza holds out his hands to her, and as he does she sees those other hands directly behind, the deep puncture wounds; she's certain it's those hands! His blood dripping steadily onto the garden, soil soaking it up, hungering for it, this sad and sudden grace. She sees the prairie returning, a sea of twisting, bending, waving grasses covering all of it, what lived wrong and what never lived, and what perhaps should never have lived.

Marybeth sees the deep-purple scabs on Toby Manza's own hands, brown spots like flung dirt, splatters of mud, fingers slippery-tight as the skin of newts, lines carved into his palms, map of his years lived in wrongness. She slides her own hand lightly across the scythe suddenly on the ground beside her, its blade newly sharpened by the manager's son. All determined gardeners need a scythe, she would have told him; in this ending that is what she would have said: Look to Ruth in the Bible.

Marybeth lets her husband help her to her feet, leaning heavily on his arm for only a moment. One possible closing, they merely walk side by side, zigzagging down the concrete path like any couple would.

In another they walk down the path, Toby Manza in front and Marybeth following, the scythe a silvery glint in her hands, his hands held out behind him. Is this the finish where Marybeth again witnesses blood feeding the earth, soil so greedily accepting? Toby Manza will always be more than he seems, larger than his own life, in hers.

It's in the last and, when she thinks about it, the dream of the near-perfect ending, that Marybeth takes Toby Manza's open hands, his fingers bloodless, chalky, as if they are fiercely cold, and she presses the berries into them chosen earlier for an arrangement of some sort—bird berries she's heard them called, though where is the bird mad enough to consume them? Red as a heart, as blood trying futilely to pump its way inside collapsed lungs, or immature lungs, uncertain as that one fragile and tremulous breath between life and death. Deadly nightshade.

And because it is Marybeth, because she is the gardener, because in the end he really does love her, doesn't he? like air, like breath, love is whimsical, not a palpable thing, nothing that closes up, shrivels up, shuts up or just withers away; nothing organic that must ultimately die. Toby Manza will accept her offering.

Fly away! she whispers to him, like he, too, could become some sort of bird, some mythological phoenix rising from the ashes of their own profane creation.

AND ANOTHER THING

Unusual relationships exist between butterflies and ants. Such relationships cover a range, from predation to symbiosis. For instance, the caterpillars of an Indo-Australian lycaenid live in the nest of the arboreal ant Oecophylla smaragdina *and devour its larvae. At emergence the adult is covered by a down of scales that are pulled off by the jaws of the pursuing ants. There are more specialized lycaenids that have larvae with glands that secrete a sugary substance. Even though the larvae of a certain Asiatic species eat up to 300 ant larvae each, the ants leave them in peace, appeased by their sugary secretions.*

It's as though something has cracked open inside her mother, Julia thinks, something wild and fluttery; if it had a color, this would be the boisterous yellow of rain slickers and yield signs, the Chicklets gum packages of her childhood. When was her mother this bright? Can madness be so sweet? She is mostly gone, Julia's mother, Not with the program, is how her father would have put it. My name is Carol, her mother shrills. But not such a wrenching in her voice these days, the heartbreaking awkwardness of one who for so many years wasn't even certain she should speak. This new voice is the lilting of a song.

Her mother's benign senility (is this senility?), a loquaciousness to it, a sociability never before seen in Carol. These voices, she says, radio voices she calls them, calling her at all hours—It'd be impolite not to answer them now, wouldn't it, Julia?

Carol has been reaching for Julia at times, holding out those grey sagging arms, as if Julia's a little girl again, like those arms are young and graceful again, full of a kind of promise; as if Julia had been the kind of little girl who might crawl into those arms and be comforted there, be not afraid there. Lately, once in a while, Julia becomes this little girl, laying her own head, its new crisps of gray and white, against her mother's flat, old breast, her mother's heart beating steadily underneath, remembering the things that were, that were not, that might have been. And thinking, this is OK. These are the things that no longer matter. And another thing, her mother whispers, then cannot say what this is.

They have moved to Chicago, another temporary position for Julia, at the Field Museum. That's OK, her mother told her, I know you're good enough to be permanent. Strangely, Carol seems to feel at home in Chicago, the alley behind their city apartment, a few scrubby trees cloying for the bits of sky in between the close-set buildings, the large greystones and brick city houses, empty rubbish bags and scraps of things caught in the trees' bony branches, pale, luminous, waving like kites or flags, something triumphant, or in surrender. There is the violent, frenetic pace and hum of the city around them, and Carol putters about the tiny plot of courtyard crabgrass that leads out to their dumpster, fingering carefully the caught bags and debris, as if these could take flight, as if they would leave her, boulevard moths, urban butterflies, familiar yet unique, fleeting, temporary.

It's like this in the city of Chicago: one side of the three-story greystone they live in, top floor, a tree-full boulevard, significant and agreeable and lined with stately turn-of-the-century homes turned into two-and-three-family rentals, the newer yet designed-to-fit-in, orange-brick apartment buildings, presentable as pumpkins. Go to the rear of any of these buildings, these grand houses, theirs for instance, and another world lives, a hidden world, much bigger, more inclusive, sucking breath behind the thin veneer of the other. An alley world of blowing refuse, stink of urine and strewn trash, home to the garbage scavengers; like rats, Julia thinks, visceral, vicarious, carnivorous, this underlife of the boulevard, surviving on the remains of the rest.

This is the world Carol calls home. Julia comes back from work and despite her admonishments, the numerous locked and double locked doors, porches, dead-bolted gates, there's her mother in the alley, chatting with one of these refuse pickers. Lives of others strewn about the alley from the plastic bags he's poked through, she's asking him if they prefer cans (they do, burn them down into a sheet of aluminum, each flattened piece for a price); would they consider bottles? even pickers get to choose. She's offered him snacks, an unopened bag of pretzels, a yellowy-green and a dark-red apple, and photos of her family; our family! thinks Julia.

His name is Darren, Carol tells her. I told him my name is Carol, Carol. Like the songs. He's a salvage man, that's what he said.

Julia thinks about calling Maggie, sending their mother back to Honolulu. I may have to send you away! Julia threatens. But Maggie is working religiously, she told Julia, on husband applicant number four. He's a minister, Maggie said, But as God is my witness, this man is no saint!

You could call it a senility of sorts, the geriatric doctor explained, his expensively coifed, silver-headed nod. Julia's in his Miracle Mile high-rise office, broad oak desk, tastefully subtle decor, her mother on the straight chair outside the door, staring blankly. That's a catchall term, he announced, Not so in vogue with the establishment these days. Depression might have played a role, but she seems content enough, doesn't she? We could medicate, but what's the point? I think, for the time being, we let her be.

I'm paying for his real estate! Julia thinks, the location of this office; why do I keep trying these doctors?

Let her be, let her be....

I don't want you out in that alley again, Mother! Julia says sharply, authoritatively, like speaking to a child. It's not safe. Who are those people? You don't know. They push shopping carts around. Poke through our garbage, stick their noses into other people's dirty business. Who can tell what they're really after? I have nothing against them, God knows there isn't anything permanent about my life either. But I don't want you out there when I'm not home, Mother. I need to trust I can keep you safe.

They're businessmen, Carol says, her filmy eyes, that dreamy, clouded look. Got a processing plant, Darren called it, those metal cans on the vacant lot where the building's boarded up, other side of the alley. You've seen the fires burning? They have routes, regular ways of doing things. They know when the garbage trucks come down each alley so they can get there first. They're productive, you see. They find things to sell. Different from your father, Julia. His things were to keep.

One smoggy, sultry July afternoon Julia comes home from the museum where she's lectured on the underground prairie, what might live under Chicago if Chicago weren't here: wolf spiders, various beetles, prairie crayfish in the little pockets of water underneath the long, gnarled roots of prairie grasses, ants, certainly ants. And she discovers the back porch door unbolted, her father's butterfly collection gone. The cabinet's glass doors hang open, unhinged, as if a stiff wind had swept through their third-floor flat.

Julia races down the three flights of wooden steps at the back of the greystone, into the ridiculous, little, grassy, closed-in area pretending to be some kind of a yard. The dead-bolted gate leading to their dumpster in the alley is also unlocked. Cluttered cooing noises of pigeons in the eaves near the cracked roof of the ancient garage, and other sounds, a crying, mewling like a baby, then the darting of some drab, little sparrow out of a spiky bush. And there's her mother, cross-legged and thick kneed in her rose knit pants, crunched down on the buckling alley pavement. She's surrounded by a scattering of balsa-wood cutouts and polystyrene, glass-headed insect pins, miniature labels and the more explicit cards that Julia's father kept so carefully under the insect boxes, all displayed like jewels in the glass-door cabinet. All in a tumult around her, strewn bits of this and that. And the numerous, the various, the rare or simply there-at-the-wrong-time, dead butterflies pinned to the polystyrene bottoms. Julia's mother is unpinning these, one by one, tossing them into the grey city air, as if they might fly free, as if they could go home.

Most have landed on the broken street, little stabs of outrageous color, some breaking apart like glass on the pebbly asphalt. One, a still-brightly patterned Angelwing butterfly, a Question Mark, is caught on a white plastic bag, hooked in the almost-dead bush beside the chain-link fence surrounding the dumpster. Julia has a memory of her father pointing to this butterfly, lifting it carefully with the tweezers so she could see the underside of its hind wing, the silver marking that looks like a question mark. See? he had said, not even a smile, They're questioning just what the hell we're all doing here. If there's a God, her father said, Here is his joke. Julia sucks in a clotted breath, Jesus! she whistles. The air is intolerable, unbreathable, smoky, summer city singe.

The ragged man is there, standing at a respectful distance behind the dumpster. Julia has called him this, *ragged man*, not wanting to use the name her mother calls him, his name. Carol said, He has a name. Julia's called him and the others *ragged*, *tattered*, and worse, sometimes just homeless, as if personhood can be named by a mortgage or rent. His name is Darren, Carol said.

Ageless or aged beyond the recognition of age, he is there, shopping cart piled high with cans and a few bottles, sheets of plastic, scraps of fabric, an old hose, cracks riveting its green surface the way lines crisscross a palm. He studies Carol, then Julia, then back to Carol, eyes black and long as beans, set in a face almost as dark, drawn out and blurry, like a mostly failed image, a negative of some former face. Shadows from the two sagging, blighted elms on the other side of the alley play across the back of a faded brick building, crossing, bending, weaving their thin kinds of light.

What the hell do you think you're doing, Mother? Julia pleads. As if there's a reasonable answer.

Fly! Carol commands the Question Mark, ignoring her daughter.

For God's sake, Mother, these are dead butterflies! They'll crumble to dust is what they'll do, some of them are almost as old as you. Julia knows the cruelty in those words, glances again at the ragged man. He's staring at her mother, ignoring Julia the same way she's ignored him. As if maybe it's Julia who's become invisible. Julia thinks how when lecturing at the museum she might project the image of a Question Mark on a screen; Highly migratory, she would tell her listeners, staging flights along the East Coast, spring and fall. It can't fly, Mother, Julia repeats. Been dead a long time, Father made sure of that.

Her mother's face seems to shrink for a moment, going blank in the way of the past, that careful, hiding kind of emptiness, like a mirror, reflecting only her fine-tuned features, nothing behind its thin glimmer of glass. The ragged man steps forward. His eyes glitter, a coal-like burn in his suddenly animated face. Very carefully, his grimy hand the size and color of a steak, he lifts the Question Mark out of the bush, placing it gently on top of his other hand. Fingers spread wide, surprisingly shapely fingers, Julia notices, long and significant on such a big hand, piano player's hands in someone else's life. The Question Mark's wings flare out the way it was pinned by Julia's father, forever caught, or so her father thought. The ragged man pokes at one wing, one second, precise as threading a needle, and the wing comes apart from the thorax, two imperfect halves on the whole of his hand.

Damn! mutters the man, not looking at Julia or her mother. Goddamn, he repeats.

Julia watches him, his almost mournful look, gazing at the butterfly parts, his hand still thrust out like an offering. She thinks about old butterflies, ragged, naturally aged, their tattered wings; butterfly warriors, she has called them.

Julia's mother shakes her head, lifting one limp shoulder then the other. Well, she sighs, shrugging, releasing her shoulders gently, arms settling back against her sides. As if that's that. And inches herself slowly up off the pavement. For a moment she's on all fours, pushing upwards with her hands; for a moment she looks like she, too, might fly, those arms bent at the elbows shaping themselves into wings, flabby yet delicate enough, rising with the grace and the certainty of a good song. Carol, her mother lilts, My name is Carol! Neither Julia nor Darren attempt to stop her.

OF GRACE AND LITHIUM

The DC-10 from St. Louis to Honolulu is only half full, and moments after its rumbly takeoff, shudder of giant white wings into the silvery air, the woman in the row behind Troy slides up to his row, the empty seat beside him. Hi, she smiles, You mind? She settles in, snapping her seat belt shut, arranging some crinkly kind of fabric skirt under her. Troy can't help but notice its length, short, her small, rounded knees pointing out.

Excuse me for being so forward, she says, I saw you in the terminal. This sounds like a cliché, but I think I know you.

He stares at her for just a moment. Green eyes, a pale, bleached quality to them like sea glass. The ocean, he thinks, am I remembering the ocean? surfacing again, easy as a dream. He notices the instances of gray here and there at her temples, her moon-shaped, eager face. They're about the same age, this woman and himself.

Right, Troy says, I recognize you. You live in the Grass Acres Apartments?

Did, she says, I did live there, my previous life. I know

you from there, too, now that you mention it. You took those girls in, didn't you? Weren't you that guy? The girl who had the baby and that odd, tall one? And cats, too. I thought that was nice. A really honest thing. A man takes in homeless girls and animals. I meant to get a cat myself, she says, arranging her carry-on under the seat in front of her, reaching down to tuck in its handle. As she does this, for just a moment, her breast grazes Troy's arm resting on the armrest between them. A sudden something is inside him, a current of it charging through him, something he can't quite identify. Though it seems like it should be familiar? A throbbing under his breastbone, hunched up like a hurt bird, a cringe, a loss.

I'm moving to Hawai'i, the woman says, St. Louis is history now. Hilo actually, I hope to find a place up Mauna Loa mountain. You know it's a volcano, don't you?

He nods, fixing his gaze ahead at nothing in particular. His face is red, the redness creeping down his neck, his chest; that surge of something now settling into a small hunger, emptiness in the pit of him.

If the mountain explodes, it explodes, she shrugs, That's the breaks. We all die one way or another. Though I doubt my fate is to be wiped out in a volcano. I'm more of the get-some-sort-of-disease-and-suffer-slowly type. Another volcano—I think it's maybe part of Kilauea or something, I've done some research—this one's been erupting for over a decade, building brand new land. Can you imagine? That's what I need. A place that's adding new land instead of gobbling up what's already there. I've got a job where I can go just about anywhere these days. Investing other people's money for them. A good time to have money to invest, though we'll see how long this lasts; nothing does, does it? She sighs, and then both of them are staring at the row of seats in front of them, the backs and tops of other people's heads, one pale and stubby as a tennis ball, another that would probably submit quite gratefully to the lathery wonders of a decent shampoo.

The most flattering part of a person is rarely the top of their head, Troy thinks, stealing a sidewards glance at this woman's head, her mostly brown hair clipped at the back into a tortoise-colored barrette, a leak of pale curls over her ears. He studies those shell-like ears poking through, then looks away again.

And the ocean, she says, I've decided I need it the way I need my own blood. I was born just a block away from the Atlantic, my first breath sea air blowing in through the screens. The Mississippi didn't do it for me. Sit beside the Mississippi and you're looking out at Illinois. I need my water huge and deep and wide enough where you can sit on any beach, stare out and see nothing else. It gives perspective, the reality of one's impact on the world. Not much, I'll tell you that, human beings are pretty overrated.

We call it the horizon, Troy grins.

Well I call it sanity. Her eyes meet his, then she slides her gaze down to her lap, before he can look away this time, her hands, slender fingers jabbing at the tray table. Nothing on her wedding finger, no rings at all.

You want to share some wine? she asks him. My treat. I hope you don't mind me sitting here. I'm celebrating the start of something. My own new life, she adds quickly, In Hawai'i. I'll have lived from one end of this country to the other, Boston to Hilo, St. Louis in between. You can't get a greater stretch and still be part of the U.S.A. She signals the flight attendant passing by with a cart stacked full of bottles and cans, asks for a Chardonnay, two glasses.

Troy smiles, thanks her, staring at the bottle on her tray. A greater stretch? Sounds like you're warming up to run a marathon or something.

She nods, Though maybe I've already run. Because here I am. Why are you going to Hawai'i?

He doesn't answer her immediately, it's not such an easy question as that. He glances at her again, that eager, nice-enough face. He thinks about Ada, whom he's left behind, and Lucy. Not Lucy Luck. His Lucy. If Lucy ran…, he thinks. He tries to picture her doing this, perhaps she's inherited his long legs. He sees her on Punalu'u Beach, where he believes she is still—no reason not to believe this—those good, long legs, long hair flung out like a pony's mane, something that floats into the air, or the sea, like a jelly-fish, a manta, a drifting, marvelous, luminous something. He really is remembering the sea again! He sees his Lucy there. She will be a swimmer, his Lucy. He can watch her and know her but she won't know him. And yet she's a part of him, isn't she? If she knows it or not, the very stuff that formed her, her nerves, her blood, those amazing legs, these are his, too.

I have a daughter, he tells the woman, She lives on O'ahu.

She's not sick or anything, is she? the woman asks anxiously. She frowns, then pours out the two glasses of Chardonnay, dividing the airplane-sized bottle exactly in half.   Just one thing, she says, Don't tell me anything unsettling about your life, OK? No impending disasters, not just yet, anyway. Your hobbies maybe, stuff like that. I had a husband and I loved him and he loved someone else so I left. End of story. Now I'm off to Hawai'i, push the reset, a new skin. You believe people can grow new skin, metamorphose that way? Like a caterpillar spins a cocoon, emerges a butterfly? She sips at the wine, peering into her glass a little skeptically, a little sadly, Troy thinks.

He looks into her glass, too, golden liquid like a warm, pale honey, but taste it and you just know it's tart. Nothing much the way it appears.

Right, Troy says, Well, I don't suppose my daughter is sick. He gazes out the window, mid-afternoon, high above the world, a smattering of gauzy clouds, the bright, vast hollowness of it all. Reaches into his jacket pocket, fingers the bottle of lithium. He thinks of Ada, his years spent loving her peeled away to a husk of something never fully uncovered, wanting only who he wanted her to be. His need, Troy's finally figured this out, was to make himself new in her. Make himself over again, a new beginning through her eyes. Those crippled, out-of-control years of his illness, finally conquered. Hunching down under his skin, he can still feel it there, the way lava inhabits the crust of the earth—but hardly bubbling, barely hot anymore, and not to erupt, if only he can hold it, contained, hidden, under control. Fingers the lithium possessively—it's his hand, isn't it? Opens the bottle. His same skin in the end.

Troy thinks of his daughter, his Lucy. She will have long hair, a tail in the wind, flying out free as she runs. She will have long legs and arms and a certain sweetness about her. She will understand algebra, read the classics, and soon perhaps, on her way to dental school, medical school, law school, whatever school she damn well feels like going to! She will have no need for lithium. She'll know love, his Lucy, smart enough to understand the tragedy of it, and to keep loving anyway. Because what else is there?

Troy stares out the jet's window, into a profound and limitless sky. He reaches for his wine and, turning back toward the woman, this time he looks straight into those sea-green eyes.

MIRACLES DON'T HAPPEN MUCH TO PEOPLE LIKE US

I

So easy it was almost pathetic. What sort of ignoramus leaves his keys in the ignition of his spanking new 2000 Corvette? Vette, excuse me, Vette he called it. Jubilee, he names the beaming black car; here's Toby Manza jabbing again—2000 is a Catholic Church Jubilee year and Marybeth had the not-too-good sense to tell him this, a celebration, a reckoning, reconfirming your promise to be a good Catholic.

Someone from Shady Tree might do it, leave the keys inside a car parked in an apartment parking lot. The most criminal thing happening there is when a bunch of teenagers go mailbox bashing or cow tipping. But a man born in New York? You'll not get the city out of that one, her father once remarked; Don't matter how many potluck suppers you schlep him to, city has him pocked permanent as acne.

Tell me you're not going back to that churchless place, Gomorrah in the corn? Toby had teased. Then Sandra, too weak for an argument, nonetheless declares no-way-in-hell was she going to Shady Tree, she'd rather just get it over with and die than shrivel up dry as an old bean in a no-place like that. She was staying in St. Louis with Daddy.

And where was Daddy these past years when he might have been something in his daughter's life, make her stop hanging with those motorcycle men so maybe she wouldn't have gotten the cursed sickness in the first place? Where was Daddy when her own daughter fell out of the oak? Was it Daddy rocked that little body till the medics dragged her away? Where was Daddy to give his granddaughter something like hope?

Toby said, What the hell, Marybeth, go back to that hole in the globe if you want, it's not my concern. Meet me at my place and we'll settle up, though what's there to settle? Sandra wants to stay in St. Louis. But when she got to his apartment he wasn't there. Jubilee was there, keys stuck in like an invitation, an offering, ready to roll.

Thou shalt not steal!

II

The first time the red-eyed Jesus appeared Marybeth was a child. Couldn't really be sure, maybe she's dreaming those eyes? Because there he was, larger than life in her room, glowing in the night whether she wanted him there or not.

Nonsense! her mother said, he'll protect you, keep you safe through the night.

Now I lay me down to sleep I pray the Lord my soul to keep if I should die before I wake I pray the Lord my soul to take. Because her mother made her pray it, and then her mother switches on the light behind that pig-sized, floor-model, glow-in-the-dark Jesus, arms stretching out from a plastic robe the color of cream gone bad, two black puncture wounds on the pinched open hands, eyes like two lamps beckoning, tiger eyes, lit-up, hungry things, mouth underneath, ravenous.

What if I don't want my soul taken?

It's a prayer, Mary Elizabeth, her mother said, That's how

we say it. And God doesn't just take a soul, it's not like a cookie or a slice of bread. When your time comes, and if you've been very, very good, your soul sprouts wings, flies up to him.

On the night the eyes burned red, two lumps of coal, miniature torches, dragon eyeballs, molten fireflies careening madly, Mary Elizabeth crunched her head underneath her covers, breathed in the musky scent of her sheets, scent of her mother's laundry detergent, the scent of some sort of normalcy and touched herself where she wasn't supposed to (a sin and nowhere to confess it!), rubbing hard like she's trying to erase it.

What color are Jesus' eyes? she asks the next morning, her mother's dimpled arms, elbows flapping and jerking like broken wings, vigorously rolling out a pie crust. Meat pie, shepherd's pie, nothing to look forward to, salivate over, the baking fragrance of something precious. We don't need sweet pies, her mother had said, Are we celebrating something? You think we're rich, just make desserts on a whim? Sounds of their farm erupting around them, cows mooing, roosters crowing, crows like fat, black darts circling, cawing, swooping down upon fields still damp, pearly beads of dew. Mary Elizabeth's twelve, on the verge of womanhood. Her mother told her this just last week, over bread dough then, grainy elbows, wattles of flesh on her upper arms.

You'll bleed from the inside, she informed her daughter, doesn't even look up from the dough. Dark red smear on your underpants is how you'll know. I put some Kotex and a sanitary belt in the upstairs closet. Loop the tails of the napkin through the belt buckles, tug down like you're snapping peas. Red is the color of a warning, Mary Elizabeth, her gray gaze lifting for just a moment, glittering like flint. Stay away from the boys, nothing but wreckage in their wake.

What color are Jesus' eyes? Mary Elizabeth repeats.

Her mother frowned, Why blue of course, what else?

III

The second time she saw red-eyed Jesus it's four years later, Mary Elizabeth sixteen and intent on getting that new kid to notice her, Toby Manza. Not so new, five years in Shady Tree, but he's from somewhere else! She gets these feelings when she looks at him, things she can't name, happening inside. A low rumbling in the pit of her like a warning, like wreckage, but already there's something breaking up in there and she's rubbing herself before sleep every night, like some sort of prayer.

One night they're riding the fields in Bug Tilton's dad's Chevy truck, Bug and his steady Mayanne Morris who's fast, Mary Elizabeth's mother announced, Mary Elizabeth and Toby Manza in the back, the bed.

Ha-ha-ha the bed! Bug shrieks, though who among them is completely sure yet what all to do on a bed? Things are done, of course, they know this much, irreparable things that excite you, that change you, make you ancient and new at the same time. They're muddin', which is mudding, which means driving late at night over the new spring fields after winter has released its stony grip, loamy soil softening, like excrement in places so you slick and skid and slop, tearing up those fields until the farmer who owns them blazes out in his bathrobe, shaking his fist, maybe even a shotgun. Toby Manza's sitting across from Mary Elizabeth, bump, bump, bumping about the bed of the truck, cold steel ridges underneath, stink of wet hay, manure, land flat and shining as a giant plate in the moonlight.

Though they've barely kissed, twice, not deep, no tongues—French kissing, Mayanne said authoritatively, You stick your tongue far as it gets down his throat the way the French do—even so, something curious is happening, something out of Mary Elizabeth's control. This buzzing like hundreds of locusts winging through her veins to that dark, secret center of her, that wet, hungry place, filled with the wild, the longing, the unspeakable (her future in all its grief, its guilt, its heartbreaking loneliness, but she can't know this yet) hum, humming. Slowly she inches apart her legs, two alabaster ribbons in the moonlight, middle-of-the-knee-length polyester skirt (their school takes a yardstick to suspicious legs, middle of the knee or you're sent home to change). His foot is there. Bump, bump, sneaker pushed off, foot's against her crotch, lightly at first like it's an accident; bump, bump goes the Tilton truck, rub, rub his toes under her skirt, other foot now, sliding up those satiny thighs, up between her legs. Then harder, and Marybeth pretending it isn't happening, that she doesn't even notice ten little sock-encased Toby-toes tapping out their rhythm in that place of nightly prayer, her head tossed back, dark red ponytail slung over the side of the pickup lolling like a tongue—red, the color of a warning! A hand clamps down over her mouth, hers? his? His? something begging to escape, a breath? a moan? her soul flying up to where he takes you?

Next weekend Bug gets the truck again, bucketing across Illinois through Gary, Indiana, to Lake Michigan, the Indiana Dunes. Dunes rising like false gods on this flat-as-a-sigh land, a half moon above them now.

And here is where the red-eyed Jesus appears, his second visit.

Guzzling a half gallon of vodka nabbed from Mayanne's parents and two six packs of Budweiser—Club Bud! Bug calls it—which Mary Elizabeth hasn't done before, not in this quantity anyway, head foggy, nose and mouth raw, don't you know anything could happen. And wouldn't it be OK if it did? This wreckage. Small steady waves pushing in against the sand, muffled hissing sound, pulling back. That deep, dank, lake-water smell.

Bug and Mayanne head back to the bushes, Mary Elizabeth and Toby still on the shore. And he undresses her, the first time any man except her doctor has seen Mary Elizabeth's nakedness. Tries to protest, doesn't she? her head a new weight that can barely shake itself, back and forth. Feels so exposed, grainy sand underneath, slick hands on her breasts, down between her legs.

It's OK, Toby whispers, Didn't I tell you it's about love?

If good souls fly up to heaven, where do the others go?

Head spinning, burn of the vodka, bubbles of beer in her throat, so at first Mary Elizabeth's only a little conscious of the water seeping, its darkness, cold clamminess at her toes now, her ankles, moving in as they lie on the sand; he's tugging her hand down between his legs, all the while inching them closer. She feels him, something strange and hard, knobby and fleshy yet somehow utterly familiar. Acid from her stomach snakes upwards; belches, moans, I'm going to be sick!

We could float in the water, skinny-dip, hold each other! Toby wheedles, desperate staccato this urgent new voice, his beery breath. He squeezes his own hand around hers, forcing hers to keep touching him, hot and prickly, like pulling on a pig's snout. Cold water's licking at her knees now. She shivers, his breath moist and warm, buzzing in her ear.

Toby! she's calling him, or she thought she did anyway. She thought she said it, didn't she say this? I don't know how to swim! But he's yanked her to her feet and he's hauling her out, his catch, his prize, his naked body a ghostly color of the moon quivering above them; almost silly this half moon, illuminating the little halves of his buttocks greenish like unripened pears. Was this happening? A dream? Water dark and yielding like moving through liquid butter, the greasy slow feel of it; and Toby pulsing his body against hers, cold press of the tiny, freshwater waves breaking like liquid sand, rush and hush of them, Toby whapping against her body now like he wants to move in, swallow her up. Shhhh, hush now.

Again she remembers Foxtail Pond, her father not looking at her and Mary calling to him, pleading, Daddyeee! He's staring into the harsh yellow sky, smell of the heat dry in her nostrils as down she went, the almost welcome terror and ease of it, profound silence into the darkening depths.

Toby's grabbing onto her but she slips anyway into what seemed a cavernous black mouth of lake water—though remembering later, it was probably at most five feet, not even high as her own height. Yet it's sucking her under, her mouth wide open letting it in, sandy bottom this time, soft and beckoning as a bed.

Until he appeared, red-eyed rays of heat, sizzle electric, zapping the cold water, shocking her, this burn, this ache, explosion in her lungs, this fierce need to be alive. Arms yanking her from above, dragging her up. Then she thought she felt it, was sure she felt it! the others below, thin trails of blood flowing out of his wounds into the dark water, lifting.

IV

Thoughts barely lucid, rattling about like pebbles, prickling the insides of her scalp. Roar of Jubilee's turbo-powered engine, pop down to third, ease into second, slip over to the dusty side of Route 55 where she's standing, hip thrust out, long arm like a spangle of spaghetti wrapped about a utility pole. Who else could it be?

Lucy Luck doesn't even look surprised. Cool car! she announces, tossing her backpack into the back, easy with the top down, doesn't bother opening the door, just catapults over it, into the passenger seat. Should be red not black, she proclaims, settling into the thick leather seat with a whoosh, a sigh; Red's the color of a sexy car.

Marybeth shakes her head, red's the color of wreckage, she thinks. Thank you so much for giving me a ride! Marybeth says.

I wasn't actually hitching but I'm glad you stopped, Lucy continues, barely a breath, stabs at the back of her hair grabbing it into a ponytail, releasing it onto her neck, into the breath of a hot breeze barely ruffling it.

Here's Lucy Luck! she cries, above the escalating rumble of the Vette as they shoot back out onto 55, hum of the sultry afternoon. I'm on the side of some godforsaken road in the middle of godforsaken nowhere waiting for the asshole photographer. Story of my life! she yells, Waiting for some asshole. I modeled for him, he was giving me a ride to Chicago. There's this modeling agency up there he's got connections with, he tells me, maybe he'll help me get some work. OK, I said, cool! What's in St. Louis for me anyway? It's not like I've got any kind of a home. So all of a sudden he swings off the highway, says he needs to drive into some little blink of a nearby town cause he used to live there, only he's got to be alone since it's real emotional and all. But he'll be right back, he assures me, half hour tops. Have yourself a cold pop while you wait! squeezes four quarters into my hand.

Big-hearted guy, right? A regular Father Theresa! Four quarters isn't even enough these days to buy yourself a bottle of river water. Pulls off over a bloody hour ago into the middle of nothing, not even the prairie bothers to grow. Lets me off at that gas station down the road a ways, but I got sick of the guys who worked there staring at me so I came out here. Staring at me! Should be the other way around; they all looked close and personal, if you get what I'm saying, like their fathers married their sisters and their mother did it with the family bulldog. Where'd you get the Vette, anyway? Stares hard at Marybeth; I never saw you with a car before, let alone a Corvette.

It's my...ex's, Marybeth says, I borrowed it. She eases into fifth, cruising speed, peering into the rearview to see where the traffic is, if there's any traffic, remembers the top's down so swivels a glance back over her shoulder, muggy wind in her face, heady scent of wildflowers growing at the sides of the road mingling into the heat and exhaust.

Geez that's some ex, letting you borrow a brand new Vette. With an ex like that, who needs a husband? You do him or something, give him weekly head?

For heaven's sake, Lucy, everything's not always about that.

Hmmm, she hums, Yeah right. Sex is currency, don't you know? Stable as gold, someone will always want it. And I'll bet you just borrowed it, borrowed a sports car, probably costs a hair under a hundred thousand or so, you think? We could nab ourselves a small town for what this baby's worth.

Marybeth shoots her a sidewards glance. Lucy's eyes narrow, pupils are little, black darts. What's really going down here, Marybeth?

He had two of them, Marybeth tells her, like this is some reason. Two fancy-ass cars, one pair of hands.

One pair of balls, Lucy growls.

Well, he sold the other. Marybeth shrugs, So maybe he doesn't know I borrowed it.

You lifted it! Didn't you? Wow, who would've thought. Maybe there really is another set of balls in the family, lady, big ones. My hat's off to you, or in my case my mask! Lucy grins, sliding her mask down for a second then shoving it back over the top of those wheat-colored bangs. Too hot! she snorts, Too hot for Marta. Hot day, hot babes, definitely a hot car.

I intend to return it, Marybeth tells her, clamping her jaw shut, chewing her teeth, tongue, popping open her mouth again; You figure me for some kind of thief? I needed a way back to Shady Tree. Not even Greyhound stops there anymore, wrote it right out of their route. That's how you know your place in the world doesn't matter a hoot to anybody else, when Greyhound won't even stop. How am I supposed to get back there then? Our daughter Sandra insisted on staying with him in St. Louis. I think she's going to be just fine, outlive us all, she's insisting again. He's got Sandra, I've got his car. Temporary trade.

You stole it, Lucy repeats, shaking her head, What a waste, herding this wild animal into some funky blink of a place called Shady Tree. You got a show car here, a muscle car. You should come up to Chicago with me where a fine vehicle like this would be appreciated.

Marybeth accelerates, 65, 70, 73, pops the cruise control in eight miles over the speed limit. Says, I heard they won't give you a ticket if you're under ten miles over, unless you're a teenager of course, or your skin's not their preferred color. Rag of her newly dyed hair flashing off the back of her neck, hot suck of summer wind. Hair red as his eyes, red-hot lava red—Burnt Sienna, the box announced. They fly past stretches of cornfields, leaves like dark-green glass glittering in the heat. And anyway, she thinks, is there anything more to lose?

Lucy shouts, I told you about the modeling thing, the Chicago plan? That's where the photographer was taking me.

But I didn't know for certain I was going until after that asshole dropped me off and he didn't come back. That's when I told myself, Lucy Luck, you're going there! I've had it with this kind of thing. I'm not headed up to be a model though, no way, I'm done with that funky business. I'm going to join the Venus's Butterflies, I've just decided it. If he hadn't been such an asshole I might have gone with him like we planned, ride up the Sears Tower elevator to the top, always wanted to do that, hang with him until he dumped me. For chrissake Lucy, I'm telling myself, there's nothing for you back in St. Louis.

Marybeth frowns, something suspicious about this one. Venus Butterflies, some kind of a club? Named for the planet or the goddess?

Lucy giggles, Would you believe a sex toy? The Venus Butterfly is something you strap on, like a garter belt. The straps are black lace and it's shaped like a butterfly. Fit it over the critical part, if you know what I'm saying. Gets you off. Got a battery pack and a remote so you can flip the switch, anytime, anyplace. Makes men obsolete. Like being kissed by wings.

Marybeth's cheeks are blazing. Oh for heaven's sake, Lucy! Get some sense here, this group's whole reason for existing is based on a sexual toy? Who makes these things up? How do they sleep at night, they think they're contributing something meaningful to the world?

Well geez, there's no harm in feeling good is there?

I wouldn't know anymore. Marybeth swivels her neck, staring at Lucy for just a second then back to the highway, black tarry pulse, heat of the afternoon. Are they homosexual or do they just hate men as a rule? Accelerates again, just enough over cruise to give Jubilee a nudge, a small kick. They rumble past farmhouses, more cornfields, bean fields, and the unplanted areas, unmowed grass burnt stiff as fingers. Land stretching far as the eyes can see, where sky meets flat and pale as a frosted donut, a horizon of corn and soybeans. Marybeth's tongue feels dry, gritty. Imagines a glass of wine, two glasses red as his blood, sliding coolly down her throat. Her chest aches.

For chrissake, Marybeth, I mean geez, who knows? Maybe they just nabbed the name. It's a good name, don't you think? Lucy tugs her hair back off her neck impatiently, releasing it to the hot breeze in floating webs. The idea being they don't need men. They're just women who want to live their lives in peace. A commune of sorts, grow their own food, buy things made only by women, from female-owned companies. I found out about them from this magazine, *In The Raw*. It's a back-to-nature zine. There's a photograph of a woman munching on raw garlic for varicose veins instead of male-created pills or shots or whatever. They do environmental things, too, like lying down in the middle of a foreclosed farm, holding hands and singing "Old MacDonald" to keep developers from ripping through, hammering out those butt-ugly track houses. For the greater good, they called it. I've had it with men. I've been trying to live my life through them since I left home and all it's done is keep me breathing, barely. Whatever they give, a place to stay, a measly ride up to Chicago for chrissake, they take that back. They treat us like plastic plates, eat off you, throw you out. Well guess what guys, flesh might be biodegradable but plastic hangs around forever.

What about kids? Marybeth asks, for the sake of argument. If those butterfly women want babies they'll need men, even artificial insemination is served with male sperm.

Lucy rolls her eyes. Yeah, well, what's perfect?

Marybeth nods, I'll tell you what, you can pray.

Oh, please! You telling me about God here? A theological question for you: so how come your granddaughter died?

God didn't cause that, I did, she answers flatly, her hands wrapped around the steering wheel suddenly sweating. You wouldn't understand.

So what about cloning? Maybe that's what all the fuss is about, makes not only men obsolete but God, too, when you think about it.

Marybeth glares, this girl beside her in Toby Manza's Corvette, her hollowed-out cheeks, chin sharp as a fist, two pole-straight legs like tree trunks stuck up on the dash, those untied combat boots, tight black shorts, shaggy golden leg hairs lit up in the late afternoon sun. I caused Cassandra's death, Marybeth tells her again—something in her needs to hear these words take shape in this car, hear them find some truth.

Lucy throws up those skinny arms, grins. Oh and me without my Saturday night special! Should I be scared? Quaking in my boots? You don't look the murdering type.

My baby daughter and granddaughter wouldn't have been born and they wouldn't have died but for me, Marybeth announces, pursing her lips, flat black stretch of road like an exclamation mark.

Whoa lady, for someone who's supposedly a God-freak you're kind of stealing the thunder here, aren't you? Lucy flips down her mask, adjusts it. Maybe it's not too hot for Marta after all.

Marybeth aims her eyes on the road, straight ahead, straight as a fence, a wall, highway to hell. I'm not saying I forced that child up into that tree or even that I could change the nature of her, born to climb and whatever else comes from that. But she's my flesh and blood, wouldn't have been born at all if I didn't give birth to Sandra. There are things you don't know about, things people do that cause their own damn tragedies, create the habit of these. One daughter didn't breathe, one gets AIDS, and then Cassandra. I thought I wouldn't have to bear that guilt, what a fool I was for thinking it, Marybeth mutters; Though what would you know, seems to me a person behind a mask's got to be blinder than most.

Maybe Marta's an angel, Lucy shrugs, You never know. I've talked to her! she whispers suddenly, leaning in close. Marybeth can feel the sizzle of warm breath on her arm through the mouth-hole of the mask. Hand stretching tighter around the steering wheel, fingers the color of bone.

I told you I can talk to dead people, didn't I? Lucy says. So, I'm telling you I've spoken with your granddaughter.

Marybeth swivels her head, whip of wind through her hair, stinging her eyes where tears suddenly burn. Shoves Lucy away. Shut up! Marybeth hisses.

Miracles don't happen much to people like us. That's what Cassandra said. Said it's what you used to say. Am I right? Did I get it? I am right, aren't I! Tugging the mask back up, a joyless grin. You're wrong though, were you expecting a miracle from heaven, is that the kind you're looking for? I'm the type that needs hands-on reassurance. It wouldn't take a lot, after all I talk to dead people. All one of them would have to say is, Hey, he's real! Did coffee with him the other day. Something like that. He was supposed to be part human, huh? A man wouldn't just stand there and take it, we're talking crucifixion for chrissake, nails in the extremities! That Ada, calls herself a psychic, she was an agoraphobic. Her son disappears and she just shuts down, never sets foot outside her apartment. Well, she's out now and it's because of Cassandra falling from that tree. Maybe that was the miracle.

That was my granddaughter! Whistles it out between her teeth, jaw clenched; Marybeth can feel the little muscle popping and twitching near her mouth.

Yeah? Lucy says, reaching out a long scraggly hand, nails the peeling purple of the insides of a plum. She taps Marybeth's wrist. I'll tell you something else. You know who Cassandra was? We're talking Greek mythology, I read you know. She lightly strokes Marybeth's frigid arm, skin so cold at her touch Marybeth can't imagine ever feeling warm again despite the smoky heat of the late afternoon roiling the road in front.

Cassandra was the prophetess of doom. Doomed to speak the truth, and no one to believe her.

V

The early evening wind, sudden fierce snag of it whirling through Lucy's hair and before she can grab it the Marta mask is torn from the top of her head, drifting off into an inky sky, a kite, a bird, something that flies away. Just like that it's gone. She doesn't mention this to Marybeth, driving hard behind that wheel, eyes burning into the shimmer of spinning blacktop.

Marybeth is not someone to tell this kind of thing to, not at the moment anyway. Tension rooted in every part of her, veins throbbing at her neck, stabbing out like gnarled roots, fingers white as soap gripping the wheel. She's angry, Lucy gets that, but at what? What difference can any of it make now? The kid's been dead since February and that's the truth of it. Skin, bones, a little girl's neck breaks like a pencil; aren't we human, after all? Lucy sees the exit to Shady Tree, how many miles to Shady Tree printed on the sign. Marybeth wails past without even slowing down.

Lucy closes her eyes, head pressed back against the warm, supple leather—the smell of wanting love, she thinks, that's what these kinds of cars are—what you buy instead of love. Tries to grieve for Marta, drifting somewhere, maybe caught in the branches of some farmer's tree, on a rooftop or a barn; maybe carried off by a hawk, an eagle, farther than Lucy has been.

There is this memory, a couple days before discovering Marta for the first time. Lucy in a shimmery-red cocktail dress, the woman at Goodwill where she bought it called this dress, from the sixties when the skirts got shorter and shorter. Bony knees poking out like two knobby messengers, two pale promises. It's a strapless number, the woman calls it, held up by Lucy's own chest. God's gifts, someone in the streets called her breasts, You got to share, he said.

There's somebody out there had a good time in that number, the woman said wistfully, a mole like a map at the end of her chin. Missouri, this mole was shaped like *misery*. Dressed to kill, the woman said.

Lucy wore that dress on her eighteenth birthday, her freedom birthday. No one on the streets knew it was her birthday. No one she knew, knew her birthday anymore, except her mother and her sister whom Lucy hadn't seen for almost two years. Would they remember it was her birthday today?

She was waiting for a bus to go somewhere, looking like she had somewhere to go, all dressed up, those nice, long legs, feet burning, throbbing, matching heels the mole-woman dug out of the Goodwill shoe bin—one size too small, ten dollars for the set. The night before Lucy had lifted a ten from a guy's wallet, it had come to that; but he'd have wanted to get her a birthday gift, wouldn't he? shouldn't he? if he knew? She schlepped around with the box the woman stuck the dress in, now empty and wrapped in some discarded wrapping paper fluttering at the top of a dumpster. Lucy didn't even have to dig for it, teddy bear print, a child's gift. This was Lucy's present to herself, pressed against her, waiting for that bus like she was going to someone else's party, bearing a gift for someone else. As if she knew the sorts of people who had birthday parties, as if she was the sort of person who had these kinds of friends, someone to invite her to their party. A regular kind of life where the box Lucy held would not be empty, and Lucy could dress up, look sharp, smell sweet, be deserving of love. This is no good way to deserve love! her mother once said. Lucy and her sister, shivering in a snowstorm had managed to pop open a basement window and crawl headfirst into the home their mother had locked them out of. No good way to deserve love.

VI

Night now, a moonless dark, millions of stars sparking the sky. Marybeth swerves the Vette off 55, an unmarked road leading to some farm, Lucy guesses, pitch-black emptiness of so many miles in between whatever the hell was out there. Slides onto the rutted dirt shoulder at the edge of the road near, what? a cornfield? planted too recently to be very high, no dry tassel sounds in the wind when the engine shuts off, just the hollow night. Marybeth stumbles out of the car, slamming the door, and Lucy knows she's crying though she can't exactly hear her, something about the hunch of her shoulders in the darkness. Heads into the field with Lucy bolting out of the car, running to catch up with her.

You passed Shady Tree, you know, a while back? Lucy calls out, coughing, sucks in a stabbing breath. I thought you wanted to go there. We can turn around, OK by me, or maybe you could come to Chicago with me?

Lucy hears her sobbing now, gravely and low. Oh geez, Marybeth. Look, I'm sorry for what I said about Cassandra, if that's what set you off. Please, will you just stop a minute? I'm out of breath. I can't keep following you, I feel like these things, these plants are grabbing me, trying to trap my ankles or something.

Marybeth hesitates, turning back toward the lanky shadow in the darkness. The smell of the night thick and moist, a rich-dirt smell. Move in between the rows, you some kind of a fool? she mutters, You're not trampling the growth, are you? A farmer depends on these. He's not some slick yuppie-type trading slips of paper. This is real. You can sink your teeth into this. Don't you know a cornfield when you're in one?

Lucy shrugs, Maybe I've never been outside St. Louis. Or maybe I have, but it wasn't to some stupid cornfield, that's for sure. She steps toward Marybeth, who steps back a little. Lucy reaches her hand out. It hangs between them in the velvety darkness. You want me to tell you about it, Marybeth? If you come back to the car I will. I've never told anybody. I'll tell you if we can go back to the car.

Marybeth sighs, Have you no shame? Why in the Lord's sweet name should I give a damn? What I wouldn't do for a gallon of burgundy about now, you make me want to drink.

Can't we please go back? We can get some. Drive to the nearest town, pick a bottle up, or go to some bar maybe. This is creeping me out. The stars are too close. They look like they could swoop down and bite us. What this place needs is some neon. Listen! What the hell's that? A coyote or something, but there's so many of them. God this is creeping me out!

Marybeth has stopped crying completely, even stifling a small laugh. You really haven't been beyond the arch much, have you, Lucy? Where's all that toughness now, that attitude? It's the prairie calling, for heaven's sake.

Geez, what the hell? Calling who?

They hear it again, a distant howl and the echoing howls, a high-pitched screech then a chattering like a ring around them, dominoes of sound set into the night. Lucy lunges toward Marybeth, grabbing her hand. Jesus H. Christ! she squeals.

You shouldn't say his name like that, Marybeth snarls. That Jesus calling? I don't think so! It's the prairie, I told you, the cries of the vanishing prairie. Malls, Bob's Big Boy, Tasty Creme, miles of so-called elite housing developments color of the soil they stripped. Yuppie-Hiltons I call these, three-car garages, one ugly sprawl of a house looks the same as the next. Who's going to pay for what this land's become? That's what the crying is about, who's going to pay?

For chrissake, sounds like zombies or something and they're really pissed. I'm going back to the Vette. Please, Marybeth! I'm sorry for the things I said about Cassandra, honestly I am, and miracles and Jesus and all of it. I don't know, who knows? We're not supposed to know, are we? You want to go up to Chicago with me? We don't have to be Venus's Butterflies.

Marybeth laughs a hard laugh. You're a piece of work, Lucy, one of a kind. Oh for pity's sake, come on back to the car then.

They walk under pinpricks of stars, black cushion of sky, a humid breeze rustling the young plants like tissue; no trees, nothing to alter its path. I feel right out here, Marybeth says, That's the thing, like I can breathe a decent breath. I should've never left. How many places we get in this world to feel right in? Maybe I really was born with an ear of corn behind my ear like my father used to say. Farm kids, he said, you can take them off the farm but you can't take the corn out of them.

Not me, Lucy sighs. I've always wanted to go to the top of the Sears building in Chicago, see the world from that height. Imagine being that high and you don't have to climb some mountain to do it. Not so many mountains in St. Louis, huh?

I'll bet Toby Manza's Corvette a man built that Sears tower. If you're a Venus's Butterfly, would you be able to go up in it? If a man built it, if a man invented the elevator you ride in? Seems to me if you don't want a man in your life, why you just don't have him in your life! Whose choice is this, anyway? Why would you need some club telling you it's OK not to?

They climb back into the car, cricket sounds then the howling starts up again. Christ, Lucy shivers, Can you fire this thing up or what? At least pop the top back on! I hate the prairie, she announces, I've just decided that.

Marybeth fingers the keys in the ignition, hollow jingling sound, the sound of what she's left behind—Toby Manza, the keys to his car, his apartment, his job, even his security box at the bank—his life without her. I like the open sky, Marybeth states flatly, The sky on top. Look, she says, maybe I could drive you to Chicago, but I don't think I'm up for any Venus's Butterflies. I'm more in the caterpillar stage of things myself. Come to think of it, I don't know if I'm ready for Chicago. Cities make you behave a certain way to survive them, that keep-your-eyes-on-your-feet kind of hurriedness. I'm a slow person, stare-at-the-sky approach. I'm not so sure I was any good in St. Louis and she's a toddler compared to Chicago. Besides, I don't own a cell phone. They got them growing out of their ears in Chicago, I saw it on a TV show.

It's not like it's a prerequisite, Lucy says, Own a cell phone or don't, Chicago will be there just the same. But here's an idea, let's drive to the beach!

The lakefront? Been there, almost drowned. I don't swim, you know.

I bet before today you never stole a car, either. Let's go to the beach, Lucy says, What do you think? I'm talking ocean here, the real thing, the Atlantic! We just roll onto route 90 and cruise east, the whole damn way. I've seen it on a map. 90 all the way into Massachusetts, then we could shoot up 95 to Maine. I saw that, too. I have a memory or a dream, something about Maine. That's what I meant when I said I may have been out of St. Louis. You want to hear? I'll tell you if you start this baby up and get us the hell out of this corn! Besides, won't your ex-husband send the police out looking for you? They could be crawling down 55 as we speak. They won't think to look in Maine.

Tell me your story first, Marybeth says, I'll warm up the engine. I don't like heading out without any definite direction. The East Coast seems like another world to me. I'm not the head-out type. Anyhow, I doubt Toby will call the police. He's pulled that before. He'd be embarrassed to again. Comes from a heritage that knows how to control their women, or that's what he told me anyway. Marybeth laughs, Besides I left a note, said I'd return it when I'm done.

OK, but you need to at least promise you'll rev the engine a few times so I don't have to hear that goddamn howling.

Why do you insist on swearing? Damn's OK, you don't put the God in front.

That dog-darn howling, Lucy says. Oh, geez! stretching those long, milky arms into the night, So listen. My mother always told us she didn't know who our father was. Could be any of ten or so men out there, she'd say, And they're all losers, every stinking one of them. So I have this memory where they're fighting, I'm maybe four, my sister's a baby. My mother says I dreamed it, but after this is when she begins getting strange.

I think it's my father she's fighting with because I remember him leaving. So here's the thing, I think he took me with him! For a while, not long enough to have a really clear memory of it, you see, I mean I was just a little kid. My mother had this boyfriend from Maine. There's a picture she has, her and this guy and other people, too, at some barbecue; she claims she doesn't remember any of them. But she's never ripped it up, thrown it out or burnt it like she's done with all the rest of our photos. Rock Harbor, Maine, is scribbled on the back. In the memory I have, the man is the same one in the picture, the one holding her hand, that possessive way people hold hands where you just know they believe this is it, the one that lasts.

I remember a really long car ride, I'd sleep, wake up, he'd feed me something, I'd sleep again, wake up and we'd still be in the car. Then he's taking me to some place like a breakwater, gray rocks sticking out into a harbor of some sort, water the color of ice. There was this smell, it had to be the ocean, what else could it be? This salty, tangy kind of a smell. Never been able to find it in the world since. I poured a container of salt into a puddle once, can you believe it? Just to see if I could reproduce it. Anyhow, so my dad and I—who else?—we're walking and this seagull dive-bombs into the rocks right in front of us. It's still for a few seconds, gets up and kind of staggers about, makes a few attempts to take off, aborted-like flights, then off he goes wheeling into the air, crying like his heart is broken.

We're just standing there, the two of us, watching the whole thing. I think my father held my hand. I can almost remember the touch of that, his hand fitting over mine like a mitt. I don't remember him saying much, but I'm sure this is real. How would you dream in such detail?

I suppose he took me back to St. Louis after that and I never saw him again. I get to wondering though, sometimes, if it's his voice I hear late at night. Maybe it's him and not those dead people after all; maybe he talks to me in my head using different voices. He wouldn't want me to feel alone, that's the reason I'll bet. Any dad of mine wouldn't want me to be alone. So that's what I meant when I said maybe I've been beyond the arch. No cornfields though, nothing howling in the night but my own self, sometimes. You ever wake up, the sound of someone's crying and turns out it's you?

VII

Marybeth stares at the girl, her sharp profile shining in the dashboard lights. She revs the engine a little, Lucy had asked her to do this. Reaches out, runs her fingers down a feathery lock of Lucy's hair. The hair is grainy, but soft, too, like a tassel of corn. Marybeth says, OK, since we're doing true confessions. You ready for this? Because here's mine. Sometimes, just sometimes, I like to believe she didn't really die.

Lucy jerks forward a little, turns and gazes at Marybeth. What? Who you talking about?

The first one, daughter number one. I know, I know what you're thinking, it's crazy. Toby would've had me committed if he knew, but I just wonder sometimes, not all the time mind you, but every once in a while, if she really was dead. She was perfectly formed, this perfect tiny body, all that separated her from life was breath. What did we know? We were kids ourselves. You didn't grow up so fast, those days. We were playing in adult bodies but were kids. Maybe when Mr. Tucker finds her and calls the police, maybe they discover the smallest little pulse pumping under her skin. She would've been so cold, but how would we know? You hear about children drowning or frozen out in the snow, and the cold keeps them, like a freezer, preserves them until they're warm and can breathe again. So maybe they take her to the hospital, but they keep it quiet! Pretend to the press she's dead. Even dig a false grave to prove it.

Jesus Christ, excuse me, but why the hell would they do that? Lucy asks. That's really off the wall, Marybeth, and I thought I was crazy for what I told you!

Marybeth shakes her head, I don't know. Maybe they wanted to protect her, the way they talked about her parents—they didn't know who we were but you would've thought we were demons from hell the way folks talked. Maybe someone who worked for the county wanted to take her home. That's what I'd most like to think. Someone who couldn't have children, who would love her, who didn't live in Shady Tree but not too far away, takes her home and raises her. She'd be older now, older than Sandra. You've heard about people who lose a family member in, say, a boating accident, how they don't find a trace of them, how they never give up? You never know, these people think, he—the family member—could've been rescued, living out his life someplace like Samoa, with amnesia. I wonder what she'd look like, who she'd favor, me or Toby Manza. Sandra is her father from the get-go, except for her eyes. She's got my eyes.

Lucy shakes her head. Hell's bells, you take the prize lady.

Marybeth shrugs, Yeah, well, like I said, most of the time I don't buy it. Just sometimes I like to believe it; like a dream, you know, gives me a little hope. Know what? I think I might remember this road! Marybeth peers out the car's front windshield into the soupy dark. Son of a gun! We're not all that far from Shady Tree, after all. This road runs east, it's on the map. We drove to the lake on this road the night I almost drowned. Second time I almost drowned, but that's another story. I'll just bet you can connect to the highway from it; if it's the road I'm thinking of, cuts across the bloody state.

Heading east? What am I hearing here, Marybeth?

Marybeth backs out the Corvette, maneuvering it in the opposite direction, flat rip of darkness stretching ahead. My father always told me I should learn how to swim.

Lucy grins, How fast can this thing go? I'll bet it could scare the howl right out of those prairie zombies! Two days tops and we could be wiggling our toes in that cold, salty water, the smell of it, nothing like it in the world. Geez, that's what I need, put my feet into the Atlantic, squiggle my toes. There's a type of butterfly that lives out its life in about the time it would take us to get there, I remember reading this somewhere. What it would take us to cruise out 90, dunk our bodies in the sea, a butterfly's lived its whole life span.

You're not going on about those sex toys again, are you Lucy?

Lucy leans in close. Marybeth feels the silky slide of wheat-colored hair on her wrist, her own hand wrapped tightly around the steering wheel. Marybeth, she says softly, almost a whisper, You ever wonder if it's all some sort of a dream? Like maybe we're not really here at all and what we think of as a life span is just a goddamn good night's sleep? Do you think about things like that? You turn over, blink open your eyes and everything is different. Like maybe the millennium happened in your sleep, and suddenly you're a whole lot older, worn out as if you lived a lifetime but you can't recall it, nothing to grab onto. Oh geez, that's a scary thought. In the end nothing to hold onto. I'll bet that's how those butterflies feel, no sooner than their wings pop out of the cocoon they're taking off, eating, drinking, screwing, dying.

Marybeth slams her foot down hard on the accelerator, the Vette growls then purrs into its sudden speed. Move over, Miz Luck, I need some elbow room here.

Are we running away? Lucy shouts over the roar of the accelerating engine.

Between the cottony clouds, dark feathers, pale wings, Marybeth sees him begin to take shape. Thou shalt not steal— you cannot hide! The Corvette lunges forward, an untamed beast, arms beckoning long and fierce as a tree, an oak tree! giant and brittle, bending toward them but not touching, not reaching, simply ahead. His eyes, not red after all, not blue, the color of stars, luminous.

My mom called it a Jesus hole, Lucy yells, pointing up through the blackened windshield at the circle clouds make, stars burning like lit-up match heads. We'd sit outside, before she got strange, some rented porch or another, and we'd stare at the sky, my little sister on her lap. My sister didn't give up on her, that's the crazy thing. Not me, not Lucy Luck, just me, myself and I. One of us is gone now, poor Marta. Maybe she soared up there into that Jesus hole in the evening wind, you think? Lucy sighs, at least Marybeth thought she heard this, a good, clean exhale of breath over the engine's ragging.

Want to know how I found Marta? She looked like she was made out of ceramic, didn't she? Like some Elizabethan mask or something. But she was just plastic, painted to look more than she is. I saw her in an antique shop window in the loop, about four years ago. I peered inside that glass, it was like looking at the negative image of myself through a mirror. Eye holes black and empty, somehow I just knew she needed my eyes to see. Only three dollars and fifty cents, the guy said when I went inside. Clearance sale, he said, he was cleaning out the stuff nobody seemed to want. Well honestly, I'll tell you what, I didn't even have that much money, not even three bucks to my name. So when he was busy helping someone else I lifted Marta from that window, and I walked out of that store. She didn't even have enough worth to the guy to have one of those electronic tags on her, you know, that sound the alarm. But I mean geez, can you steal your own self?

Marybeth, one fist balled around the steering wheel, grabs Lucy's hand with her other hand. Lucy's fingers are strangely cold and Marybeth feels bad about this. She squeezes them, feeling the blood, the sudden warmth beat through. Inside

Marybeth the pulse of the engine's roaring. I suppose we're both thieves after all, she thinks, Lazarus moving out of death, struggling to be free.

Toby Manza's Corvette rockets forward like some terrorized stallion, bulleting down the empty farm road, plummeting over ruts and bumps in the pavement as if these are little stones, granite annoyances, smallest of bothers. Dark-horse racing, satiny black Jubilee, hooves pounding the worn land until they seem to lift off, front legs, back legs, now light as skin cells, translucent scales, these fine, new wings, metallic butterfly swooping up toward the starry sky. No guilt, no regrets, just the touch of another's flesh, and Marybeth's foot solid against the accelerator.

J AIMEE WRISTON COLBERT is also the author of *Climbing the God Tree* (winner of the Willa Cather Award in Fiction) and *Sex, Salvation, and the Automobile* (winner of the Zephyr Prize in Fiction). Her work has appeared in such journals as *TriQuarterly*, *New Letters*, and *Prairie Schooner*. Originally from Hawai'i, Colbert now teaches at SUNY-Binghamton University.